KU-605-366

BRING THEM HOME

D.S. BUTLER

THOMAS & MERCER

This is a work of fiction. Names, characters, organizations, places, events, and incidents are either products of the author's imagination or are used fictitiously. Any resemblance to actual persons, living or dead, or actual events is purely coincidental.

Text copyright © 2018 by D. S. Butler
All rights reserved.

No part of this book may be reproduced, or stored in a retrieval system, or transmitted in any form or by any means, electronic, mechanical, photocopying, recording, or otherwise, without express written permission of the publisher.

Published by Thomas & Mercer, Seattle

www.apub.com

Amazon, the Amazon logo, and Thomas & Mercer are trademarks of Amazon.com, Inc., or its affiliates.

ISBN-13: 9781503904934
ISBN-10: 1503904938

Cover design by Emma Graves

Printed in the United States of America

BRING THEM HOME

BRING
THEM
HOME

ALSO BY
D. S. BUTLER

Lost Child

DS Jack Mackinnon Crime Series:

Deadly Obsession
Deadly Motive
Deadly Revenge
Deadly Justice
Deadly Ritual
Deadly Payback
Deadly Game

East End Series:

East End Trouble
East End Diamond
East End Retribution

Harper Grant Mystery Series:

A Witchy Business
A Witchy Mystery
A Witchy Christmas
A Witchy Valentine
Harper Grant and the Poisoned Pumpkin Pie

PROLOGUE

'I'm not sure about this,' Sian Gibson muttered to her friend as they crept along the school corridor. There was no one else around as the other children had gone back to the classroom.

Emily turned around and pressed a finger against her lips. 'Shhh. Do you want someone to hear? Mrs Morrison will go mental if she catches us.'

Sian wished someone would hear them. She wanted to get caught before they left the school grounds. Her mother would be furious if she found out she'd skived off.

It was different for Emily. She was always in trouble and didn't seem to care. In fact, the entire Dean family were trouble, according to Sian's mother.

Emily looped her arm through Sian's and pulled her along. As they made their way past the line of colourful coats hanging from hooks on the wall, Emily grinned. She passed Sian her yellow coat before putting on her red anorak. Sian's coat was only a month old, but Emily had the same anorak as last year. The cuffs were ragged, and there was a small hole by her right elbow.

She usually turned the sleeves up carefully so the other children wouldn't notice the frayed hems, but today she was too excited to care.

The girls were mounting a daring escape and leaving school a full five minutes before the bell signalling the end of the school day.

Ahead of them, the door to the playground was open. Nothing stood in their way. Sian felt her stomach tighten. She couldn't back out now. Emily would think she was a baby.

As they left the school corridor and stepped out into the cold October afternoon, Sian shivered. She looked back over her shoulder towards the classroom windows. Their classmates would be sitting cross-legged on the floor listening to the teacher reading another chapter of *The Magician's Nephew*. Sian wished she was back there in the warm with them.

Emily tugged her arm. 'What's the matter with you? Don't you want to see the ponies?'

'I didn't say that. I just don't see why we have to leave school early. We'll be in so much trouble if Mrs Morrison finds out. What if she calls my mum?'

'She won't find out if you get a move on. Hurry up.'

Sian's mother said Emily was a bossy little madam and she didn't like her spending time with the 'Dean girl'. Sian had begged to be allowed to go to Emily's for tea and had been surprised when her mother had finally relented. She'd be having kittens if she knew they were creeping out of school early.

It was only five minutes, though. Surely that couldn't get them into much trouble. Emily had insisted they leave school before the bell rang because she said she didn't want any of the other children finding out about the ponies.

Emily was horse-mad at the moment. All she'd talked about for the past six months was ponies and horses. Her parents had told her they weren't wasting money on horse-riding lessons, but Emily walked to the stables every Friday afternoon and watched Sian's weekly lesson with her Welsh cob Florence.

Emily watched those lessons with such longing it made Sian feel guilty. Now, Emily was about to have her own riding lesson. She was glad for her friend but didn't understand why they had to keep it secret.

Sian loved horses. There was something comforting about the smell of the stables, and stroking the soft muzzles of the gentle ponies was the best feeling in the world, so she didn't know why she was feeling so nervous.

It was probably because she was afraid of being caught. Emily was right. She was a baby. She hated getting into trouble.

It was silly really. If anyone should be panicking about getting caught, it was Emily. After all, Sian would probably be given a stern telling off and not allowed to watch TV for a week, but if Emily's mother found out, she'd tell Emily's dad. Sian was terrified of Emily's dad. He was a huge man with a temper. But his shouting and threats didn't stop Emily getting into trouble. She didn't seem to care.

Sian followed her friend, crossing the path and heading towards the fence that ran along the side of the playground.

The girls climbed over the wooden fence but Sian stumbled, landing on her hands and knees on top of a pile of soggy brown leaves.

Emily rolled her eyes but held out a hand to help her up.

Sian took a last longing look at the warm lights of the classroom glinting between the trees. Finally, she brushed her clothes free of leaves and bracken and followed her friend into the woods.

She'd been excited about going to Emily's for tea. Sian's mother always picked her up from the front gates, but Emily was allowed to go home on her own even though she was only ten. She used a shortcut along the side of the playground and the wood which led out on to Longwater Lane. But today they weren't going straight to Emily's house. Today they were meeting Emily's new friend, who was going to take them to see some ponies and let Emily ride one.

At the thought of the ponies, Sian perked up a bit and walked a little faster. She shoved her hands deep in her pockets as the cold, damp

October air made her shiver. It wasn't raining, but drips of moisture fell from the branches above them, landing on their hair and coats.

'Where's your friend meeting us?' Sian asked, no longer whispering now there was no one around to hear them.

'Just through here,' Emily said, pointing deeper into the woods. She grinned at Sian. Her eyes were sparkling and she bounced with each step like a puppy.

Suddenly she turned to Sian, the excitement on her face replaced by fear. 'What if I can't do it? What if I fall off? Or the pony doesn't like me?'

Sian shook her head. 'Of course the pony will like you, and you won't fall off. Somebody will hold the reins for you if it's your first lesson.'

Emily nodded but didn't look convinced.

Sian reached out to squeeze her friend's hand, then both girls jumped when they heard leaves rustle in front of them.

The afternoon was dark and gloomy, making it hard to see. A prickling sensation ran along Sian's spine as a tall, thin figure loomed in front of them.

At first, nobody spoke and then Sian stammered, 'Is this your friend?'

Emily finally found her voice. 'Yes, the one with the ponies.' Emily's voice was louder than usual.

Sian wished Emily's friend would step away from the trees so she could see them properly, but in the next moment, she wished they'd just go away. For some reason, she felt an overwhelming need to run back to the classroom.

'I told you not to tell anyone.' The voice was gruff and angry.

Sian's hands tightened into fists in her pockets to stop them from shaking. She shuffled back a few steps. Sian wanted to return to school, but she was scared for her friend. She shot a glance at Emily and saw she was frowning.

'I'm sorry,' Emily said. 'It's just that Sian really likes horses too, and she always lets me come to her lessons.'

Sian waited for the figure to reply, but for the longest time all she could hear was ragged breathing.

'Fine. This way,' the figure said finally, before turning around and heading deeper into the woods away from the school and Longwater Lane. Sian had never gone in this direction before.

'Is this the way to the stables?' Emily asked. Her voice wasn't as loud now.

The figure walking in front of them said nothing.

CHAPTER ONE

DS Karen Hart collected the evidence files from her desk with a sigh. The case was going nowhere and, much as it pained her, she was going to have to clear it from her active cases. Mary Clarke, a domestic abuse victim, was now refusing to give evidence against her husband. For the past few days, Karen had been trying to persuade her to move to a women's refuge in Lincoln. It had all been for nothing. An hour earlier, Mary – purple bruises still on her arms and neck – had slammed the door in Karen's face after threatening to have her charged with harassment.

'What's up, boss?' DC Rick Cooper asked, nodding at the files in Karen's arms.

'I'm taking the Mary Clarke paperwork to be filed. The case is finished.'

'Not enough evidence for the CPS to press charges?'

'Not if Mary keeps insisting she fell down the stairs.' Karen clutched the blue cardboard folder. 'There's not much we can do unless she decides to accept our help.'

Rick frowned and leaned against the desk. 'Let's just hope we get a chance to help her before her husband finishes her off.'

Karen shuddered.

'Sorry, boss. That was an insensitive thing to say.'

Karen shook her head. She knew Rick was right: Mary's life was in danger, and it was frustrating and infuriating to watch the situation unfold.

DC Sophie Jones looked up sharply from where she was sitting at her desk in the open-plan office. 'Surely there's something else we can do, Sarge. We can't just give up.'

Sophie was a new member of the team and had only recently achieved the rank of detective constable. She was a hard worker, but idealistic. Karen thought she'd eventually make a good officer, though she'd only worked with Sophie for two months. The young woman was a stickler for rules and punctuality, and Karen imagined she must have been the class swot when she was at school.

With her curly brown hair, pink cheeks and angelic expression, Sophie was a stark contrast to Rick. If she looked like an angel, he resembled a mischievous imp.

Rick was a good-looking man and he knew it. He had tanned skin, evidence of his Italian ancestry on his father's side, and wore his dark hair slicked back. His cocky smile was quick to surface, and he always wore a little too much aftershave. That aside, Karen was glad he was a member of the team. He worked hard and she trusted him.

'No one's giving up,' Rick said to Sophie. 'But we can't prosecute if Mary doesn't want us to.'

'But that's ridiculous,' Sophie said, getting to her feet and walking around the desk. 'There has to be a way we can make Mary Clarke see sense.'

Rick glanced at Karen and rolled his eyes as if to say, 'See what I have to deal with?'

'In an ideal situation, we'd push ahead with the charges, Sophie,' Karen explained. 'But from experience, I know it's not going to stick.'

Sophie was about to open her mouth to protest again when DI Scott Morgan entered the office area with Superintendent Michelle Murray and the three officers looked up expectantly.

Superintendent Murray didn't often visit the CID offices. She had a large office on the top floor of Nettleham police headquarters, and only occasionally came down to the lower floors to attend key briefings. Today she looked concerned, her dark eyes even more intense than usual.

Beside her stood DI Scott Morgan, as immaculate as always. He'd been the leader of Team Three for just over a month, and Karen hadn't yet worked out what made him tick. Her last DI had been an open book. But Scott Morgan didn't give much away.

Superintendent Murray spoke first. 'We've had a report of two missing girls, both ten years old, from Moore Lane Primary School in Heighington.'

Karen dumped the files on her desk and checked her watch. It was only just after four p.m. 'How long have they been gone?'

'They were seen just before three o'clock when the class finished rehearsing for the school play. Their teacher noticed they were missing at three fifteen.'

That was unusual. Children tended to disappear on their way to and from school rather than during the school day.

Karen shifted her attention to DI Morgan. Unlike the superintendent, who looked tense, his face was impassive.

'Is there any reason to suspect foul play?' Rick Cooper asked.

DI Morgan replied, 'Not yet. A uniformed unit is already on the scene, conducting a preliminary search of the woods beside the school and the surrounding streets, but it's possible the girls decided to leave early of their own accord and will turn up at home wondering what all the fuss was about.'

'Let's hope so,' Superintendent Murray said in her soft Scottish accent. Karen had never heard her raise her voice. She didn't need to. Everyone at Nettleham HQ knew Superintendent Murray's gentle tone was deceptive, and woe betide anyone who assumed she was a soft touch.

'It's Heighington again, boss,' Rick muttered, looking at Karen.

She gave a curt nod, understanding what Rick was getting at. She turned her attention back to the superintendent, who was issuing instructions to DI Morgan.

'You and DS Hart should get to the school straightaway. I'm sure DC Cooper and DC Jones can set up the incident room in your absence. Keep me updated.'

Superintendent Murray turned and walked away, and Karen reached for her coat.

◆ ◆ ◆

When they were in the fleet car with DI Morgan at the wheel, Karen asked, 'What do we know about the girls so far?'

'Two girls. Both ten years old. Sian Gibson and Emily Dean. The head teacher of the primary school is Jackie Lyons. She's the one who reported the girls missing. The girls' teacher is Roz Morrison, and she says that although Emily Dean is a difficult child, it's unlike her to sneak off during the school day, and it's very out of character for Sian.'

Karen nodded. 'And we haven't spoken to the parents yet?'

'Not yet,' DI Morgan said. He put his foot down as they pulled away from a junction. 'But they've been informed.'

Karen was about to suggest that she talked to the parents of the two girls while DI Morgan spoke to the teachers, but before she could, DI Morgan asked her about Rick's comment.

The car came to a stop in front of traffic lights, and Karen turned to look at DI Morgan. She hadn't realised he'd picked up on it as he'd been talking to the superintendent at the time.

Less than eighteen months ago, Karen had been seconded to DI Freeman's team after a young woman had disappeared from Heighington. Heighington was only a small village and normally very safe and Karen couldn't help thinking it was a pretty big coincidence to have a similar case in such a short period. Hopefully this one was a false alarm and the girls would turn up safe and well. It still ate away at Karen that they hadn't been able to track down Amy Fisher, the nineteen-year-old who'd disappeared without a trace. Even though Karen had only been on the periphery of the case, it still stung that they hadn't been able to get a result.

'Did you hear about the Amy Fisher case?'

DI Morgan nodded. 'The nineteen-year-old who went missing from a village in Lincolnshire over a year ago? Yes, if I recall correctly, there were plenty of suspects but she wasn't found.'

Karen was impressed. DI Morgan had been based in the Thames Valley when Amy Fisher went missing. Then again, she should have guessed he would recall some details of the case. In the short time she'd known him, she'd noticed he liked to accumulate knowledge.

'Amy lived in Heighington,' Karen said quietly.

DI Morgan considered that information for a moment before replying, 'It's unlikely to be related to our missing girls. Emily and Sian are ten. Amy Fisher was nineteen. If the incidents were related and we were dealing with a predator targeting young girls, we'd expect them to be in a similar age range.'

Karen knew he was right but his reply irritated her. It sounded like something straight out of a textbook.

Nettleham was north-east of Lincoln, and they needed to cross the River Witham to get to Heighington. Travelling on the congested A15 was not ideal but, fortunately, the route wasn't as busy as usual, and they reached Canwick Hill within ten minutes.

Karen's mobile beeped. It was a message from her sister on the family group chat they'd set up with their parents. She'd check in with them later. After muting the app, she slid the phone back in her pocket.

As DI Morgan turned left on to Heighington Road, he asked, 'Do you have any local knowledge of the area or know anything about the girls' families?'

Karen lived just two miles away from Moore Lane Primary School in the neighbouring village of Branston. She'd moved there with her family ten years ago. Branston was full of happy memories. After her husband and daughter had died in a car accident, Karen hadn't wanted to leave the area. If she did, she felt she'd be leaving a part of them behind.

'I know the head teacher, Jackie Lyons, is well respected and active in the community. I'm not familiar with Sian Gibson's family, but I think Emily Dean could be the daughter of one of the Dean boys.'

DI Morgan frowned but didn't take his eyes off the road as they sped past the open fields. 'The Dean boys?'

'The Dean family are known to the local force. They're forever getting into trouble, petty crime mostly.'

'Go on.'

'It goes back to Matthew Dean, their father. I guess he's about sixty now and does a few jobs here and there. If you ask him, he'll tell you he labours on local farms, but I suspect most of his income comes from criminal activities. He's been prosecuted multiple times, and he's been inside twice for long stretches. Once for actual bodily harm, and once for stealing farm machinery. He's got two sons and the youngest, Dennis, is as bad as his father. I can't say for certain, but I'm pretty sure Dennis has a daughter called Emily.'

DI Morgan nodded slowly. 'We'll have to find out if they're involved in any active feuds. In my experience, criminal families like that don't tend to get on well together, and if someone holds a grudge against the Deans . . .'

Karen looked at him. 'The Deans are a pain in the neck, but even so, it's hard to imagine anyone targeting two children to get back at them.'

Karen leaned forward in her seat, willing DI Morgan to travel faster along the straight road. She knew uniform were already on the scene and had started the search, but in a case like this every second counted.

'I have heard rumours that Dennis's wife kicked him out a few months ago,' Karen said.

'If that's true, and Dennis Dean feels he's being denied contact with his daughter, it's possible he made a grab for Emily.'

Karen exhaled heavily. If Emily was, in fact, a member of the notorious Dean family, things could escalate quickly. The fact that another child was involved made her feel uneasy.

As they turned off Heighington Road and entered Moore Lane, Karen swore under her breath. The lane was packed with parked cars, but DI Morgan took it all in his stride and parked a distance away from the school.

Irritated by the precision of his parallel parking, Karen yanked the door open as soon as the car was stationary.

They walked quickly towards the small school. Groups of parents stood close to the entrance, many of them holding their children's hands, reluctant to let go after they'd heard about the two missing girls. They were hanging around, anxious for any news, but Karen wished they'd go home. Unless they had information to pass on, they were just getting in the way.

In a crowd like this it would be easy to miss something important. Karen scanned the gathering, looking for anything suspicious, but all she saw were the concerned faces of parents and the wide-eyed, confused expressions of the youngsters, who didn't really understand what was going on.

A young mum, wearing a navy-blue jacket and tight jeans, pushed her way towards them. 'Are you the police? What's going on? Have you found the little girls yet?' She tossed her long brown hair.

'We don't have any news at present,' Karen said and walked around the woman, heading quickly to the double doors at the entrance to the school.

Before they managed to get inside, Karen felt a tug on her sleeve. She swallowed a sharp retort, and DI Morgan slowly and deliberately leaned over and removed the man's hand from Karen's forearm.

'I understand that you're extremely concerned, sir, but we need to get inside and do our job.'

The man swallowed and ran a hand through his light brown hair. 'Of course, sorry. It's just I think I've got some information for you.'

Karen had already turned away and had one hand on the door ready to enter the school, but his words stopped her dead.

'What information?' DI Morgan asked.

'Well, actually it's not me. It's Danny, my son.'

DI Morgan and Karen looked down at the young lad standing beside his father. He had brown hair and big, expressive brown eyes, and he looked absolutely terrified.

'Do you have something to tell us, Danny?' Karen asked.

The boy's lower lip trembled, then he looked up at Karen and replied, 'I saw them climb over the fence in the playground. I saw them leave.'

CHAPTER TWO

DI Morgan went to check on the progress of the search, leaving Karen to speak to Danny Saunders and his father, Matthew. The head teacher, Jackie Lyons, had escorted them to an empty classroom and left them to talk.

Karen sat gingerly on one of the tiny chairs and tried to cram her knees under the low desk. She began by telling Danny he wasn't in trouble and explaining that anything he could tell her might help get the girls home safe. But Danny wasn't concentrating. His wide eyes were looking around the classroom. Various posters decorated the walls, along with a brightly coloured chart which listed the pupils' names.

'Are you okay, Danny?'

Danny nodded absently but didn't take his eyes off the chart. Karen followed his gaze but nothing looked unusual. It was just a list of pupils, some with a red sticker beside their name, others with gold stars.

'Concentrate, please, Danny,' his father said sternly. 'You need to answer the policewoman's questions.'

Danny nodded meekly and turned back to Karen. 'Sorry.'

'How old are you, Danny?'

'He's eight,' Mr Saunders answered for his son.

'I'd really like Danny to answer these questions, please, sir,' Karen said.

'Of course, sorry,' he said and held his hands up. He looked even more uncomfortable than Karen with his large frame perched on one of the child-sized chairs.

Karen leaned forward so she was eye-level with Danny. 'Can you tell me exactly what you saw, please, Danny?'

'I already told you. I saw them. I saw them leave.'

'Was anybody else with them?'

Danny shrugged and broke eye contact.

'And what time did they leave?'

Danny shrugged again. 'I don't know. I saw them when I was on my way back from the toilet. It was nearly home time, I think.'

'Did you tell a teacher you'd seen them leave?' Danny's father asked.

Karen wished he'd stay quiet and leave the questions to her, but she couldn't judge him too harshly. She was sure he really did want to help them find the two girls, but he was concerned about his son. Still, she must have communicated her displeasure silently because he looked at Karen and muttered, 'Sorry, sorry. Carry on.'

'I didn't tell the teacher,' Danny admitted, keeping his eyes fixed on the desk. 'I thought maybe they were allowed to leave early or maybe they had a dentist appointment like I did last week.'

'Did you see where Sian and Emily went after they left the school, Danny?'

Danny blinked a couple of times and then replied, 'I don't know.'

Mr Saunders opened his mouth to prompt the boy, but before he could, Karen shot him a look.

'It's very important you remember, Danny. You're not in any trouble. You understand that, don't you?'

The little boy looked at Karen as though he were deciding whether to trust her. 'I . . . I saw them go outside and followed them.'

'You did what?' The question exploded from Danny's father's mouth as he twisted in the small seat, his knees crashing against the desk. 'You know you're not allowed to leave school.'

Karen pushed on, ignoring Mr Saunders's outburst. 'It's okay, Danny. You're being really helpful. Now, tell me what you saw when you followed them.'

Danny's cheeks were flushed as he looked down at the desk. 'I don't want to.'

'I don't care what you want, young man. You need to tell us exactly what happened right now.' Danny's father was fuming, and despite her irritation, Karen could understand why. A million thoughts must be running through his head right now, while he imagined how it would feel if Danny had been the one to go missing.

◆ ◆ ◆

Outside, DI Morgan was walking along the edge of the playground, picturing the two young girls climbing over the fence. What had been behind their decision to leave school early?

DI Morgan sighed. If he knew that, then he suspected he'd be a lot closer to finding Emily and Sian.

He'd spoken to the officer in charge of the search and been impressed by the clear-headed and strategic way in which they'd operated so far. He'd given permission for the officer to draft in extra uniformed officers to start on the house-to-house enquiries.

The stretch of woodland beside the school was narrow. This area of Lincolnshire was known for wide-open fields, not woodland. That should work in their favour. Whichever direction the girls took, if they were on foot then they'd have had to walk across open fields, which would greatly increase the likelihood of them being spotted. If they were lucky, a member of the public would spot the girls and report the sighting to the police.

Unless, of course, they weren't on foot. If they'd been taken and put into a vehicle, they could be some distance away by now. Tracking them wouldn't be easy.

He took one last look at the fence and the woodland beyond. The time of year didn't help the search. The floor was a carpet of brown and orange, and a gust of wind shook the branches of the trees, sending yet more leaves dancing in the air. DI Morgan turned and began to walk back to the school.

Ideally, he'd have liked to talk to the parents in their own homes, but the head teacher had already informed both mothers, and as was only natural, they'd each wanted to come straight to the school.

He wondered if Karen had managed to get any more information out of Danny Saunders. In the short time he'd known her, DI Morgan had been impressed by the detective sergeant. She had a knack for talking to people and getting them to open up. DI Morgan knew his talents lay in other areas. Friendliness and warmth weren't top of the list. He'd been called distant and cold by his ex-partner, and he thought she could have a point.

Sometimes, DI Morgan hated the suspicion with which he viewed the world. He'd like to believe it was a side effect of becoming a police officer, but he'd always had a level of cynicism and mistrust even before he'd joined the police. And there was something about Mr Saunders that made DI Morgan uneasy. The man seemed eager to help – too eager.

DI Morgan took a deep breath and walked back into the school building. Ahead of him lay a task he dreaded. He'd have to talk to the parents of the missing girls.

◆ ◆ ◆

'Danny's being really helpful, Mr Saunders,' Karen said.

Mr Saunders looked torn between wanting to hug his son and read him the riot act. Finally he settled for putting a hand on the boy's shoulder. 'It's all right. I'm not angry. Tell us what you saw.'

Danny began to speak in a shaky voice. 'I wanted to know where they were going. So I followed them into the playground and saw them climb over the fence. They were talking for a while and then they walked off into the woods. I followed them, but I hid. I didn't want them to see me.'

'But why . . .?' Mr Saunders began to ask and then abruptly shut his mouth when he remembered he was supposed to be keeping quiet.

Karen nodded and waited for the boy to continue.

'I couldn't hear what they were saying, but I think Emily was angry with Sian because she fell over.'

'Who fell over, Danny? Sian or Emily?'

'Sian. She tripped when she climbed over the fence. Then they walked into the woods. I think they were meeting someone.'

Karen felt a prickle of apprehension run down her spine.

'Jesus,' Mr Saunders muttered.

'Who did they meet, Danny? Did you see anyone else in the woods?' Karen asked softly.

Danny bit his lower lip and blinked several times. 'I'm not sure.'

'Was another child with them? Or a grown-up?'

Danny thought for a moment and swallowed hard. 'I couldn't see very well.'

'That's okay. Just try to explain what you saw.'

'They were looking at something, but I couldn't see anything except shadows.' Danny's face crumpled.

'Well done, Danny. You've been very helpful,' Karen said, wondering if the little boy had seen someone else in the woods. That would certainly increase the likelihood that the girls had been taken rather than wandering off on their own.

She asked the boy a few more questions and then looked up as DI Morgan walked into the classroom.

Karen smiled at Danny. 'That's all for now. You did very well.' She looked at Mr Saunders. 'I have your contact details. If we need anything else, we'll be in touch. Thank you.'

Mr Saunders stood, lifting his son up and giving him a huge hug before carrying him out into the corridor.

As they followed them out of the classroom, Karen quickly told DI Morgan what Danny had seen, before calling the station so DC Cooper could coordinate delivering the information to every officer involved in the search.

When she hung up, she turned to DI Morgan and said, 'Rick has set up the incident room, and he's getting background on both girls' families.'

'Good.' Before DI Morgan could say anything else, they heard heels clicking on the floor, echoing along the corridor.

They turned in the direction of the noise. It sounded like someone running towards them. A tall, blonde woman came into view, closely followed by Jackie Lyons, who appeared out of breath.

Horror and anguish contorted the blonde woman's face. 'Have you found Sian?'

Her desperate question meant she needed no introduction, but the head teacher presented her anyway.

'DI Morgan, DS Hart, this is Leanne Gibson. Sian's mother.'

CHAPTER THREE

Leanne Gibson skidded to a halt in front of them. 'Have you found her yet?' she asked breathlessly.

Under normal circumstances, Leanne Gibson would be considered a very attractive woman, but with worry etched on her face and distress contorting her features, she looked haggard. Karen's heart went out to her.

DI Morgan introduced himself and Karen.

'Let's go in here,' he said, indicating the empty classroom. 'We can tell you what we know and ask you some questions about Sian.'

Leanne nodded and her eyes filled with tears. 'I can't believe this is happening. I knew I shouldn't have let her go home with Emily Dean. Why did I change my mind? What was I thinking?'

'It's not your fault,' Karen said as she opened the door to the classroom.

Leanne had just walked ahead of them when they heard more footsteps.

'Ah, this is Emily's mother, Jenny Dean,' the head teacher said, walking towards the tall, dark-haired woman.

Jenny Dean made a stark contrast to Leanne Gibson. Jenny wore dark skinny jeans tucked into black high-heeled boots and a red top that was so tight it fitted her like a second skin. Her dark hair fell in messy waves to her shoulders, and although she was heavily made up, most of the kohl had smudged beneath her eyes.

DI Morgan shot Karen a questioning look and she nodded. Karen recognised Jenny from her time in uniform. Emily *was* Dennis Dean's daughter. It would make liaising with the family difficult because the Deans held such resentment towards the police.

'He's taken her, hasn't he?' Jenny snapped, shrugging off the head teacher's attempt to put a comforting hand on her shoulder.

'Do you mean you think Dennis has taken the girls?' Jackie asked, tucking her hair behind her ears and taking a step back from Jenny.

Karen felt like taking a step back from Jenny too. The woman was filled with raw, unstable emotion. Her gut told her the sensible option would be to separate the two mothers and question them individually. She turned to DI Morgan and suggested she talk to Jenny in another classroom. DI Morgan nodded his assent, but before Karen could lead Jenny away, Leanne walked back out of the room.

'Why didn't you pick them up from school?' she demanded, raising her voice. 'They're only ten. I can't believe you'd just leave them to make their own way home.'

'It's not far,' Jenny said defensively. 'Besides, I'm sure they're fine. My good-for-nothing ex has probably taken them for a pizza or something. He just wants to put the fear of God into me. That's him all over.'

Leanne's face crumpled. She was desperately trying not to cry. 'Do you really think he'd do that?'

The anger in her voice had dropped and she almost sounded hopeful, as though she wanted to believe that was what had happened because that meant she'd get her daughter back safely. She shook her head. 'Why would he have taken Sian too?'

'I take it you've spoken to Emily's father?' DI Morgan asked Jenny.

Jenny hesitated and then bit down on her lower lip. 'No, not yet. He's not answering his phone, but that's probably all part of his plan to wind me up.'

'What sort of parents would use their daughter to get back at each other?' Leanne asked, her voice trembling.

'Oh, spare me the hoity-toity act,' Jenny snapped.

Before it could escalate into a full-blown argument, DI Morgan intervened. 'If you'll come in here, please, Mrs Gibson.'

He led Leanne into the classroom and nodded, signalling Karen to take Jenny to another room.

'Mrs Lyons, is there another classroom we could use so I can talk to Jenny in private?' Karen asked.

'Of course, although you're welcome to use my office if you'd like? The chairs are probably a bit more comfortable.'

Karen nodded gratefully. 'Thank you.'

As the head teacher led them to her office, Karen shot a sideways glance at Jenny. She was picking nervously at the stretchy material of her top, the words leaving her mouth in a jumble as she spoke. Karen guessed she didn't want to stop talking because, if she did, then she'd be forced to consider the possibility that her husband hadn't taken Emily and Sian, and what that might mean.

'It's gotta be him. It's exactly the sorta thing Dennis would do. He's angry with me, and he uses Emily as a way to get back at me. Last week, he arrived to pick Emily up, and I could smell alcohol on his breath, so of course I didn't let him take her. I mean, what sort of mum would leave their child in the care of a drunk man?' She narrowed her eyes and glared at Karen. 'And I know what you're thinking, looking down your nose at me like that. But I only live two minutes away. And Emily loves walking home on her own. I'd never have let her do that if I didn't think she was safe. We live in Heighington. It's hardly the same as living in the middle of Lincoln.'

Her words were prickly, driven by worry and guilt. Karen said nothing, waiting for her to say everything she needed to get off her chest.

They entered the office, and the head teacher left them. Karen sat down on one of the comfortable chairs and scooted around to face Jenny. She didn't want to sit across from her with the desk a barrier between them. Trust was crucial in a situation like this.

'We have officers trying to track down Dennis,' Karen said. 'If he has taken the girls, then we'll know soon enough.'

She nodded for Jenny to sit down in the chair opposite hers.

Jenny sat and swallowed hard, rapidly blinking back tears. 'You don't believe Dennis took them, do you? You think someone else has taken them. You think they've been abducted by a . . .' She broke off, unable to complete the sentence.

In a matter of seconds, Jenny's mood had changed. The defensive, angry woman had dissolved into a trembling mother gripped by fear.

'We're keeping an open mind, Jenny,' Karen said, keeping her voice soft. 'We can't afford to discount any possibilities at this stage. We just want to get the girls back as quickly as possible. Now, can you tell me why you think Dennis may have taken Emily and why he would have taken Sian as well?'

Jenny bit on a fingernail. 'Like I said, he was angry with me for not letting him see Emily last weekend when he'd been drinking. But I don't know why he would've taken Sian too.'

'If he did take the girls, where would he have taken them? Would he take them out for something to eat or to the cinema?'

'I suppose he could have done, though last week he said he was broke and couldn't give me any money. I was furious cos they were about to cut off our TV and internet. I told him just because he's walked out on us doesn't mean he can ignore his responsibilities, and I'd take him to court if I had to. That caused another argument.'

The cheerful ring of a mobile phone sounded from the depths of Jenny's oversized red bag, and she delved inside before pulling out an iPhone. Karen noticed it was a newer model than her own.

Jenny's eyes widened as she looked at the screen. 'It's him. It's Dennis.'

CHAPTER FOUR

Back in the classroom, Scott Morgan was attempting to calm down Leanne Gibson.

'He's on his way,' Leanne said, responding to DI Morgan's question about her husband's whereabouts. 'He was working in Nottingham today, but he's driving back now.' She turned her head and looked out of the window. 'Shouldn't we be out there searching? I mean, we're not doing much good just sitting in here, waiting.'

'Our officers are carrying out a thorough search, Mrs Gibson. I know it's difficult but I need to ask you some questions. Have you noticed anything strange about Sian's behaviour recently? Anything out of the ordinary?'

Leanne Gibson frowned. 'Like what?'

'Has Sian mentioned any new friends? Is she allowed access to the internet?'

Leanne's face paled. 'Oh God, you think she's been groomed by someone, don't you?'

'We just need to get a fuller picture of Sian's life, Mrs Gibson.'

Leanne clutched her hands together and took a deep breath. 'She's got a Facebook account, but she's not supposed to use it without telling me what she's looking at. I approve all her friend requests. It's on the iPad at home. Apart from the iPad . . . she doesn't have any access to the internet. She isn't allowed a phone. I try to limit the time she spends on the iPad too. Otherwise, she'd always be on YouTube watching videos. You know what kids are like these days.' Leanne shook her head and studied her hands. 'Sian's a good girl. She knows she's not supposed to talk to strangers. She wouldn't just go off with someone she doesn't know. I've told her a million times that she's not to go anywhere without telling me first.' Leanne looked up. 'Do you think it's possible Dennis Dean has taken them? It's awful, but I almost wish he has. It's better than thinking some stranger has abducted them.'

'We're just trying to gather all the facts. We don't even know if the girls have been taken. They could have wandered off on their own.'

Leanne nodded but she didn't look convinced.

She clenched and unclenched her fists as DI Morgan ran through his questions. Each one made the anguish on her face worse, and he wished he didn't have to put her through it, but he had no choice. They needed answers.

After a few more questions, tears were trickling down Leanne's cheeks. At that point, Karen knocked and stuck her head around the door. 'Sorry to disturb you, sir. But I'd like a word, please.'

Karen gave him a meaningful look, and Leanne turned around in her seat to stare at Karen, watching her with a mixture of hope and dread in her eyes.

'I'm sorry. I won't be a moment,' DI Morgan said, excusing himself and going out into the corridor to talk to Karen.

'Development?' He knew Karen wouldn't have interrupted his interview with Leanne if it wasn't important.

'Jenny's just received a call from Emily's father, Dennis. He says he doesn't have the girls and he only just got her message. He sounds distraught, sir. I really don't think he's taken them.'

DI Morgan sighed. 'There goes our working theory. If Emily's father doesn't have them, it's looking like the girls either wandered off on their own, or were taken by a stranger.'

Karen nodded. 'I agree.'

'Has anything come up from the searches so far?'

Karen shook her head. 'I haven't heard anything, but I haven't checked in since I started talking to Jenny.'

'We're going to need to talk to Dennis Dean as soon as possible.'

'He's on his way here. Jenny told him she was at the school.'

'Fine. We can speak to him here.' He began to turn away and then changed his mind and turned back. 'Tell me, Karen, did you notice anything odd about Mr Saunders?'

Karen frowned. 'Danny's father? No, he seemed upset. But I guessed that was because he was imagining how he'd feel if it were his son who was missing. Why? Did you get an odd vibe from him?'

DI Morgan paused and then said, 'It doesn't matter. Let me know when Dennis arrives.'

At well over six feet tall, Dennis Dean was a big man. His broad shoulders and muscular arms, thanks to his job as a labourer, made him a very intimidating presence. He'd had plenty of run-ins with the police in the past so Karen hadn't expected him to be cooperative.

She'd been right. It took DI Morgan a good ten minutes to calm him down after he arrived at the school. Dennis interspersed answers to their questions with insults. He was angry, rude and altogether unpleasant to deal with, but Karen couldn't shake the feeling he was telling the truth when he told them he had nothing to do with his daughter's disappearance.

'Can you think of anyone who might want to target your family in this way?' DI Morgan asked.

The question was like a red rag to a bull. 'Are you trying to blame this on me? Typical bloody police. Why aren't you out there looking for them, instead of in here asking me stupid questions?'

'We have lots of officers looking for Emily and Sian, Mr Dean,' Karen said, keeping her voice calm. 'We need to ask these questions. Do you have any idea who could have taken them? Someone who holds a grudge against you, maybe? Or has anything happened recently that may have made Emily want to run away?'

The arrogant, furious expression on Dennis Dean's face melted away and was replaced by a look of pure fear. 'I don't think so. Emily can be a hot-headed little thing, but she wouldn't worry her mum and me like this.'

'Has she ever run away before?'

Dennis shook his head. 'Not recently. I remember once, when she was five, she packed up her dollies and made herself a jam sandwich. Said she was going to live with the Little Mermaid. She was crazy about that film.' He broke off and ran a hand through his tousled black hair. Then he fixed his bright blue eyes on Karen. 'It's not like her at all. You have to find her. Someone's taken her. I know they have.'

As DI Morgan pressed on with the questions, pushing sensitive subjects, which earned him sharp, unhelpful replies, Karen tried to weigh up the evidence they had so far.

It was starting to look like this could be a genuine abduction.

Sian's father, Thomas Gibson, had arrived at the school in a panic, and they hadn't managed to get much useful information out of him. Jenny Dean's mother, Louise Jennings, had also arrived at the school to comfort her daughter and take her home. A liaison officer had been assigned to each family, and Karen hoped the officers would get more information from the parents when they were back in familiar surroundings. It wasn't that they didn't want to help. The shock of the situation made it hard to think straight and process information normally.

Both sets of parents seemed reluctant to leave the school, probably because it was the last place the girls were seen. But it was important to get them home. Once word got out, which it was bound to soon as every parent with a child at the school knew about it, the press would be swarming all over the village.

'I don't know what sort of man you think I am, Inspector,' Dennis said through gritted teeth, 'but nobody I know would take a grudge out on an innocent child.'

'So you've had no bust-ups recently? You can't think of anyone you've annoyed or had a disagreement with?'

Dennis screwed up his face and looked like he was going to launch into another tirade, but then he suddenly stopped and said, 'Maybe there is something.'

Karen tensed.

'We let Odd George live on a plot of land at the back of Dad's place. It's just a bit of scrubland, full of weeds, but recently Dad's got it in his head to get planning permission and build a bungalow there, so he told Odd George to leave.'

'Odd George?' DI Morgan asked and raised an eyebrow.

Karen spoke up. 'George Barrows. He's lived in Heighington all his life and does odd jobs here and there. He used to live with his mother until she passed away ten years ago, and he couldn't afford the private rent. I always thought George was a good friend of your father, Dean.'

Dean shrugged. 'That's as may be, but they seem to have fallen out. Just yesterday George turned up, hammering on the door, three sheets to the wind. He said he's getting legal advice for unlawful eviction and promised we'd regret double-crossing him.'

Karen nodded. She didn't know George Barrows well, but she couldn't imagine him abducting two young children. Still, they couldn't discount it out of hand without speaking to the man first.

'We'll check it out,' DI Morgan promised.

Dennis had refused to let a family liaison officer come to his father's house, which was where he'd been living since Jenny had chucked him out, so they made sure they had all his contact details before he left.

'You don't think he's going to do anything stupid, do you, sir?' Karen asked, watching the hulking figure of Dennis Dean lumber down the corridor and out of sight.

'Probably,' DI Morgan said drily and then turned to Karen. 'I think we should locate George Barrows as soon as possible. I'd like a word with him.'

CHAPTER FIVE

The children's teacher, Roz Morrison, was still too distraught to string more than a couple of sentences together. She was taking the girls' disappearance hard and blamed herself.

When Karen told her Dennis Dean had denied taking Emily and Sian, she grew even more agitated.

'If only I'd noticed they'd gone missing earlier.' Her hands fluttered up to press against her forehead and she sighed. 'But in the rush after the rehearsal, I didn't notice they weren't with the others.' She dropped her arms so they hung limply at her sides. 'The children were in high spirits and a little boisterous, which was why I asked them to sit in the reading area so we could continue *The Magician's Nephew*. I wanted to calm them down, but if they'd been in their normal places, I'd have noticed earlier.'

'Come on, Roz. It's not your fault. They'd only been missing a few minutes when you raised the alarm,' Jackie Lyons said.

The head teacher seemed a sensible woman and Karen was glad she'd kept her calm.

Karen was pretty sure they weren't going to get much more out of Roz. She hadn't seen the girls leave and had alerted the head teacher as soon as she'd noticed Emily and Sian were missing. When she'd calmed down a little, it would be worth talking to her again to get some background on both of the girls. It would be interesting to find out if the teacher was aware of any family trouble. They'd already had a few hints that Emily Dean's home life wasn't a particularly happy one.

Roz Morrison clasped her hands together and mumbled, 'I'd like to help in the search, if that's okay?'

'I think that would be fine,' Karen said. 'We've set up a coordination point at the back of Longwater Lane and search parties are being organised from there. It's important you search in one of the organised groups and listen to what the officer in charge tells you.'

Roz nodded obediently and reached for her coat.

Karen could understand the woman's need to take part in the search. She needed to feel like she was doing something to track down the children.

'There are already some photographers and journalists at the front gate. You may want to leave via the playground, Roz,' Jackie Lyons said, her voice fading at the end of the sentence as she remembered that was the way the girls had left the school.

Roz bowed her head as she buttoned up her coat and then walked slowly out of the room.

'Thanks for your help, Mrs Lyons,' Karen said, turning to the head teacher. 'We'll probably need to talk to you again soon.'

'Of course.' Jackie hesitated. She put her hand over her mouth and then lowered it before saying, 'There's something I want to tell you. It might not be important, but it just struck me as a little odd.'

Karen nodded encouragingly, and then waited for the woman to continue.

'Well, when Leanne Gibson arrived, she was distraught as you'd expect. I told her where to find you and followed her. That's when I saw her run into Matthew Saunders.'

'Danny's father?'

'Yes, that's right,' Jackie said. 'At that point, she couldn't have known Danny had seen the girls leave school. But her reaction to Matthew Saunders seemed very strange to me.'

'In what way?' DI Morgan asked.

'Danny's mother is a GP at the Heighington practice. She works long hours so Matthew is the parent who picks Danny up and drops him off at school. He's quite friendly . . .' The head teacher leaned a little closer to Karen. 'I don't like to gossip, but he's quite popular among the mothers at the school gates.' She raised her eyebrows meaningfully.

'And is he friendly with Leanne?'

Jackie nodded. 'Very much so. They're always teasing each other and laughing and joking at the school gates. That's why her reaction today seemed so strange. When she saw him in the corridor, she just stopped abruptly and snapped, "What are you doing here?"'

Karen frowned. 'And what did he say to that?'

Jackie shrugged. 'Nothing. Nothing at all. He looked very surprised at her outburst, and then he watched her hurry past. Leanne didn't give him much of a chance to answer. She took off again, running towards you.' The head teacher shot them an apologetic look. 'I'm sorry. There's probably nothing in it. Leanne was just overwrought.'

'You did the right thing by telling us,' DI Morgan said. 'In cases like this, you never know what could be important. Any odd behaviour could be relevant. If you come across any other information, don't be afraid to let us know.'

Jackie looked somewhat reassured. 'Right, I will.' She took a deep breath and glanced beyond Karen to the window. 'Let's hope the girls are home before dark.'

Karen shivered. There wasn't much chance of that now. The sky was already tinged with red and the sun was dipping close to the horizon. The sun set early at this time of year.

They thanked Jackie for her assistance and made their way to the main entrance. The forensics team would soon be here, and although there was little point in scouring the classrooms for trace evidence, the officers would need access to the playground area. Jackie had told them she didn't mind staying at the school for however long they needed. She wouldn't feel right going home to her warm, comfortable house when she knew the two girls were still out there somewhere, cold and alone.

DI Morgan and Karen walked straight past the small group of journalists gathered by the school gates. It wouldn't be long before the national press were here. Superintendent Murray was organising a statement, and it would be up to her and the other members of the gold command to decide whether to set up a child alert. It was a difficult decision.

On the surface, it seemed like the logical thing to do. Alerting the general public through social media meant people would be vigilant and on the lookout, but every time a child alert was issued, the response from the general public was overwhelming. The manpower it took to sift through all the responses was astronomical. No call or tip could be overlooked, just in case, and right now, they wanted the phone lines free so any genuine sightings would get reported immediately.

Karen was glad the decision wasn't hers to make.

'No comment,' she muttered as they made their way past the photographers' flashing cameras.

DI Morgan stared stonily ahead as he marched towards the car.

The image of Thomas Gibson, looking crumpled, dishevelled and bewildered as he arrived to collect his wife was fixed in Karen's mind. Hopefully, the families would have some peace before the press worked out where they lived.

'We should pay George Barrows a visit first,' DI Morgan said as they approached the car. 'Would you mind driving? I want to call in and see how Rick's managing with collating all the information.'

'No problem. After we've spoken to George Barrows, I thought it might be worth paying Nigel Palmer a visit,' Karen said as she took the keys and slipped into the driver's seat.

Before Karen had a chance to explain further, DI Morgan said, 'Nigel Palmer? He was one of the suspects in the Amy Fisher case, wasn't he?'

Karen tried to hide her shock. It wasn't easy to get much past DI Morgan. He hadn't even been in Lincolnshire at the time of Amy Fisher's disappearance, but he'd obviously made it his business to familiarise himself with the case.

'Yes, that's right. He owns farmland bordering Moore Lane Primary School. It's possible the girls walked through the small copse and on to his land. He's got various outbuildings too. It can't hurt to have a word with him.'

DI Morgan fastened his seatbelt. 'Maybe so. I wouldn't rule anything out at this stage, but I think it's more important to bring everyone up to date with a briefing at the station after we talk to George Barrows.'

Karen tried to suppress the annoyance she felt, but she wasn't fast enough. She saw from DI Morgan's sober expression that he'd picked up on her irritation.

'Right,' he said as Karen indicated and pulled away from the kerb, 'why do you think it's important to visit Nigel Palmer before the briefing? From what I know of him, he's an old man, and the missing girls are much younger than Amy Fisher. What makes you think paying him a visit would be a better use of police resources than attending the first case briefing?'

'He's got a lot of outbuildings,' Karen stubbornly repeated. 'There are ditches on his land too. Emily and Sian may have been playing and . . .' Karen trailed off and then let out a long breath. She was losing this argument. How did she explain she wanted to talk to him because she'd always felt there was something not quite right about the Palmer

36

family? That wouldn't go down well with her new boss. He didn't seem like a man to base his judgement calls on feelings.

She shot a quick sideways glance at DI Morgan. 'It wouldn't take long. We could ask him and his family to keep an eye out for the girls.'

'DC Cooper has already made a point of calling the landowners in the area and asking people to be alert and on the lookout for two young girls,' DI Morgan said reasonably. 'He requested people check barns and outbuildings and search any location where two young children could hide.'

For some reason, his practical and logical approach aggravated Karen, but it wasn't DI Morgan's fault. She was really annoyed with herself and the fact she couldn't explain her hunch.

Even without any evidence, she knew Nigel Palmer was a nasty piece of work. Her senses were screaming out a warning. It was too much of a coincidence for two more girls to go missing not long after Amy Fisher had vanished. Karen hadn't known DI Morgan for long, but she already understood he wouldn't be swayed by talk of gut instinct. He was a man who liked to deal with facts.

Karen tried a more logical direction for her next argument. 'There's no evidence against him, sir. But I think the man's hiding something. When we were looking into Amy Fisher's disappearance, several people in the village had stories to tell about how badly he treats his own kids.'

DI Morgan nodded as they headed along Station Road. 'I'm not saying that Nigel Palmer is a good man, but we need to prioritise, DS Hart. If it would make you feel better, we can have uniform pay him a visit sooner rather than later.'

'It's not a question of making me feel better, sir.' Karen's hands gripped the steering wheel tightly as she fought the urge to snap at her boss.

The worst thing was, DI Morgan wasn't wrong. He made a good, valid point, and Karen was letting the emotion of the case get the better of her.

She sensed him watching her, but she kept her head still, her eyes fixed on the road.

'This is where Dennis Dean lives,' Karen said, slowing the car.

She parked at the end of the cracked driveway and looked up at the narrow, semi-detached house. 'His father owns the property, but he's moved in with Jolene Parkinson, who lives a few doors down.'

They walked towards the house, stepping over the weeds growing through the cracks in the concrete.

DI Morgan pointed to the path that led along the side of the house. 'Does that lead out on to open fields?'

'No, there's just a bit of scrubland and the new housing estate further back. Beyond that, it's farmland.'

'Who does the farmland belong to? Not Nigel Palmer?'

Karen shook her head. 'No, the fields are part of Morrisons' farm. But George has his caravan on the small bit of scrubland at the back of the house. The Council have had a few complaints, but most people around here feel sorry for him.'

They knocked on the front door and waited for a while, but there was no answer. As the side gate was unlocked, they made their way to the back of the house, walking along the crumbling path.

'I wonder when they last cut the grass,' DI Morgan said as the back garden came into view.

It wasn't just the grass that was too long. The whole garden was overgrown. An old washing machine covered in patches of rust was dumped next to the neighbours' green wire fence. Although it was now almost dark, grey-tinged vests and underpants hung limply on the washing line.

They ducked under the line, and once they had rounded the ramshackle garden shed, they could see that the fence at the back of the garden had been taken down to allow access to the caravan.

George Barrows's home was small and not exactly top of the range. Karen doubted it could be towed away in one piece. The white paint was cracked and peeling, and the entire caravan leaned to one side. A dirty net curtain which sagged in the middle was pulled across a steamed-up window.

DI Morgan turned to Karen. 'Ready?' he asked, raising his fist to bang on the door.

Karen nodded and held her breath. Her previous encounters with George Barrows had not been pleasant, and she wasn't looking forward to this one.

CHAPTER SIX

The caravan lurched and squealed in protest as they heard movement from inside. The door squeaked on its hinges as it opened, and George Barrows, known locally as Odd George, peered out, looking suspiciously at DI Morgan.

When his gaze fell on Karen, he relaxed a little bit and rolled his eyes. 'Oh, it's you. What am I supposed to have done this time?'

His nicotine-stained fingers scratched his grey stubble.

'Put a shirt on, George,' Karen said, nodding at his baggy vest. 'We want to talk to you, and we're not going to do it in there.' She pointed at the cramped, dark interior of the caravan.

George hesitated as though he were considering refusing just to make their life difficult, but in the end he shrugged and went back inside to grab his top.

'There's no sign of Dennis,' Karen said softly so George wouldn't overhear.

DI Morgan understood her meaning straightaway. 'If he really thought George was involved, I'd expect Dennis Dean to be here trying to shake the truth out of the man.'

'Exactly.'

They stood back as George climbed down the steps of his caravan and shut the door behind him. He pulled a packet of cigarettes out of his grubby trousers and lit one.

'Go on then, what's all this about?' he asked.

'We want to talk to you about two little girls, George. Sian Gibson and Emily Dean went missing from school a few hours ago.'

The look of shock on George's face was either genuine, or he was a brilliant actor. Knowing George as she did, Karen guessed the former.

'Jesus, Dennis's little girl? Has his father heard about this?' George rubbed his stubbly chin and looked towards the house.

'Do you know anything about it, George? Because if you do, you'd better tell us now before you get into any more trouble.'

The shock vanished from George's face and was replaced by an expression of absolute fury. He gestured wildly, waving his hand holding the lit cigarette close to Karen's face. 'What are you suggesting?'

'Stop waving that cigarette around,' DI Morgan snapped.

George froze. The calm, gently spoken detective inspector sounded furious, and even a little frightening.

George took a step back. 'Well, you can't just come here and suggest I'd know something about that. I'd never hurt a little girl.'

'Maybe you didn't intend to hurt them, maybe you just wanted to hide them away somewhere to teach Emily's dad a lesson,' Karen suggested.

George frowned, his forehead puckering. 'But why would I do that? I get on well with Dennis. His dad's been ever so good to me and—' George broke off and then a grin spread over his face. 'Very cunning.' He chuckled to himself. 'Oh yes, very cunning.'

'If you continue to muck around when two little girls are missing, I'm going to be very tempted to forget about police protocol.' DI Morgan almost growled the words.

George's face fell, and he quickly said, 'You don't understand. I don't mean to laugh, but well – can't you see?' He turned to Karen. 'He's playing you. Look, I'm no grass and I don't wanna get Dennis in no trouble. But if what you say is true and his little girl is missing, then this could be important.'

'Spit it out, George,' Karen said.

'You know as well as I do that Dennis has no time for the police. If he thinks his little girl's in danger, then he's gonna go after whoever he thinks has taken her. He's not gonna be honest with you, is he?'

George was only saying exactly what they already suspected, but short of assigning a unit to track Dennis, there wasn't much they could do. Persuading a career criminal to trust them was no easy task.

'All right, so where is Dennis?' DI Morgan asked. 'Why did he mention your name?'

'Probably to keep you busy and out of his way,' George replied with a smug smile.

'He wants us occupied so he can go after the person he really thinks has taken Emily,' Karen said.

George nodded confidently. 'Got it in one, PC Hart.'

Karen didn't bother to correct him. He'd known her as a uniformed PC for a long time and old habits died hard.

'I'm sure Dennis believes he's doing the right thing, George. But he isn't. If you waste any more time, there's a real chance we won't get these girls back. If you're really concerned about Emily and Sian, tell us what you know.'

George rubbed his hand over his chin again. 'I don't tell tales on my friends, love. You'd better try someone else.'

'You wouldn't be telling tales, George. You'd be helping to find two little girls. Dennis is out of his mind with worry. He's not thinking straight. Tell me this: if something happens to those girls in the next couple of hours, and you could have told us something to help find them, but you didn't – how are you going to feel?'

George's expression clouded over. He took a deep drag on his cigarette and blew the smoke up into the sky, which was now dark.

Karen felt like snatching the cigarette out of his hand, throwing it on to the floor and stamping on it. But instead, she waited, hoping that her words got through to him. He was a troublemaker, a drinker and a petty criminal, but she had to believe there was some decency in him somewhere.

Eventually, George sighed. 'All right. I don't know for sure, but my guess is he's gone to speak to Lewis Marks.'

'Lewis Marks?' DI Morgan repeated the name and shot a look at Karen. She nodded, indicating she knew who Lewis Marks was. 'Why would he want to speak to him?'

'Well, Lewis was in the pub the other night mouthing off about how Dennis and his father had ripped him off and how he was gonna make sure they paid.'

'So you think Lewis may have taken the girls to teach Dennis a lesson?' Karen asked.

George shrugged. 'I didn't say that. But I think that's probably the way Dennis's mind is working.'

'You'd better be telling us the truth, George,' Karen said, pointing at him, and then she turned up the collar of her coat and began to walk back along the garden path.

George laughed. 'Why would I lie to you? When have I ever lied to the police?'

'More times than I can count,' Karen said, shivering as she trudged behind DI Morgan, trying not to trip in the darkness.

'I take it you know where this Lewis Marks lives?' DI Morgan asked when they got back to the car.

Karen nodded. 'I do, sir, and it's not far.'

In less than two minutes, they had travelled around the back of the housing estate and pulled up outside Lewis Marks's house. It was a pleasant new-build detached home in a small cul-de-sac.

Karen groaned as she turned off the engine. 'It looks like Odd George was right, sir. That's Dennis Dean's van.'

DI Morgan looked stonily at the old Ford Transit. 'We'd better get inside.'

CHAPTER SEVEN

Before they reached the uPVC front door, it was yanked open by a pale-faced woman with shoulder-length red hair, carrying a baby on her hip. She snapped at them, 'You took your time!'

Karen frowned. Although she'd had dealings with Lewis Marks on multiple occasions, she'd never seen this woman before.

'Is Lewis Marks at home?' DI Morgan asked.

The woman slapped a hand against her forehead. 'Of course he is. Why do you think I called you? He's about to get seven shades of you know what kicked out of him by Dennis Dean.'

As if on cue, they heard shouting.

The woman flapped her free hand, signalling for them to hurry up. 'They're in the garden. Lewis was out there having a smoke, and Dennis turned up all sweetness and light and told me he wanted a quick word. I'd have never let him in if I'd known.'

DI Morgan led the way inside, and Karen followed. French doors led from the kitchen on to the garden patio. The security light was on, and Karen's stomach twisted when she spotted Dennis Dean brandishing a large hammer.

A few feet away, Lewis stood with his hands in the air. They couldn't hear what he was saying, but his mouth was constantly moving, talking

nineteen to the dozen, trying to extricate himself from his current pre-
dicament, as he backed away from Dennis.

'What's your name?' Karen asked the woman as the baby started
to cry.

'Laura.' She didn't turn to look at Karen but kept her gaze locked
on the drama unfolding in the garden.

'You should take the baby upstairs, Laura.'

She hesitated, then did as Karen advised.

Lewis was a kid. All mouth and no trousers was how Karen's mother
would have described him. He liked to play the hard man, but all he
did was sell a few knock-off goods here and there. What on earth was he
thinking? Getting on the wrong side of the Deans was a serious mistake.

DI Morgan marched towards the doors and yanked them open.
'What are you doing here, Dennis? I thought you were taking part in
the search for Emily.'

Dennis Dean swung around towards them, holding the heavy hammer above his head. The security light gave his face an eerie glow.

'I'm getting the truth from this lowlife,' Dennis said, jerking his
head towards Lewis.

'Oh, thank God you're here,' Lewis said, inching closer to DI
Morgan. 'He's gone and lost his mind. I have no idea what he's talking
about. He's an absolute nutter.'

That was clearly the wrong thing to say. Dennis growled and raised
the hammer higher, causing Lewis to flinch and whimper with fear.

'Put the hammer down, Dennis,' DI Morgan said.

'I can't. It's the only language someone like him understands,'
Dennis said as he took a step closer to Lewis.

'Just put the hammer down, Dennis. Or we'll have to arrest you,'
Karen said. 'How can you help look for Emily if you're locked up?'

Dennis's body tensed, and for a horrifying moment Karen thought
he might be preparing to fling the hammer towards her instead. But

he didn't. His shoulders slumped and he dropped the hammer on the floor. It landed on the grass with a dull thud.

Lewis scrambled around them, desperate to get back inside the house safely.

'Not so fast,' DI Morgan said. 'We've got some questions for you.'

Lewis turned to them. His round baby face crumpled, and his lower lip quivered. His fine fair hair was smothered in hair gel, making it stick up at odd angles. Karen wasn't exactly up on the latest hairstyles, but she was pretty sure Lewis's look went out in the early nineties.

'We heard you were making allegations in your local pub a few nights ago,' DI Morgan said, fixing him with a stern look. 'You claimed that Dennis's father had ripped you off and you were going to teach the Dean family a lesson.'

'No, I would never. I didn't. I . . .'

Karen held up a hand. 'Save it for someone who believes your lies, Lewis. We have two little girls missing from Heighington and we intend to find them. If you know anything about it, you'd better come clean sharpish.'

Lewis frowned and looked genuinely confused. 'Two little girls?'

'My Emily,' Dennis roared, taking a few menacing steps towards Lewis. 'She's gone missing from school, and you were full of all the big man talk about how you were gonna pay my dad and me back.'

Lewis shook his head rapidly and stepped away from Dennis until he was pressed against the wall of the house. 'No, look, I just had a few drinks. I got a bit mouthy. I didn't mean it, and God knows I'd never touch your daughter. Jesus, you can't think I'd be involved in something like that.' Lewis turned to DI Morgan. 'I promise. I don't know anything about it.'

Karen was inclined to believe him, and she thought they were wasting their time. They needed to get to the briefing room so they could organise a plan of action. The search would continue late into the night despite the limited visibility, but it was looking more and more likely that the girls had been taken. If they'd been injured or lost, the officers and PCSOs carrying out the comprehensive search of the area should have found them by now.

Plus, she was itching to go and pay Nigel Palmer a visit, just in case the old farmer had something to do with Sian and Emily's disappearance. If she looked Nigel Palmer in the eye and studied his body language, she was sure she'd be able to tell if he'd had anything to do with the missing girls.

Dennis put his head in his hands. He believed Lewis, and now that his suspicion and fury had dissipated, there wasn't much left holding him together.

'Come on, Dennis. Let's get you home,' Karen said.

She put her hand on the big man's shoulder and steered him towards the doors, surprised at the ease with which he let her lead him through the house and out front towards the cars.

'I don't know what to do,' he murmured.

'Leave it to us. I promise you we'll do everything possible to get Emily back.'

Dennis shook his head. 'What can you do? It's been hours. If she's been nabbed by one of them child snatchers, she could be anywhere by now.' He raked a hand through his hair. 'I can drive myself home,' he said and moved towards his van.

'Oh no you can't. I can smell the alcohol on your breath,' Karen said. 'Get in the car and we'll take you home.'

'I only had one,' Dennis said, attempting to stare Karen down.

'We could do a breathalyser test, but we really don't have time, so just get in the car.'

Dennis gave Karen a rebellious look but did as she asked.

'When a child is abducted, the person responsible is often someone they know and trust,' DI Morgan said as he opened the passenger door. 'Most of the time it's someone known to the family. I'm not saying that's the case here, but if you've noticed anyone acting a bit differently recently, Dennis, you need to tell us. You can't try to sort this out on your own.'

Dennis sat in the rear passenger seat, staring ahead glumly at the headrest in front of him.

Karen got in the driver's seat while DI Morgan called into the station for an update. Dennis perked up a little, listening to the one-way conversation. But when it became clear there was no fresh news, he stared despondently out of the window.

She pulled up outside Dennis's house, this time not bothering to pull into the driveway. 'We'll keep you updated, Dennis. It might be best if you stay at home tonight in case Emily tries to get in touch.'

Dennis said nothing as he climbed out of the car, which lifted with a squeak when free of his bulk. He slammed the door before stomping up towards the house.

'Back to the station, sir?' Karen asked, glancing at DI Morgan as she prepared to pull away from the kerb.

'You don't have to keep calling me sir, you know. I don't mind you calling me Scott.'

Karen shrugged. 'Sorry, it's a habit. I suppose the new recruits find it easier to be on first-name terms, but if it's all the same with you, I prefer to stick to calling you sir.'

'Fair enough. If you're really keen on speaking to Nigel Palmer, then I could drop you there now. But I'd need to take the car. Superintendent Murray will expect me to lead the briefing.'

'That would be great, sir,' Karen said.

'All right. Let's go straight there, and then I'll drive back to Nettleham. You'll have to make your own way back to HQ.'

Karen nodded. 'Not a problem.'

Karen drove along Station Road up to the junction and then took a right. A mile or so out of the village, she turned right again into a narrow country lane lined by fields on each side.

After they passed an old windmill that had been damaged by fire years ago, Karen said, 'That's the Palmer farm.'

A huge barn dominated the smaller redbrick farmhouse. Both buildings were set well back from the road and surrounded by open farmland. There were lights on in the house, lending it a warm and cosy feel. But Karen couldn't help shivering as she thought of the residents inside.

'I imagine it's quite picturesque in the daylight,' DI Morgan said, taking in the dark, flat landscape.

Karen nodded as she turned off on to the bumpy, single-track private road. 'If you like that sort of thing. The place always seemed a bit barren and stark to me.'

DI Morgan put a hand on the dashboard as the car dipped into a pothole and bounced back out again. 'Do the entire family live here?'

Karen pulled to a stop outside the farmhouse and paused a moment, watching the bats as they swooped to catch insects attracted by the car's headlights. The weather had turned cold, and she was surprised the bats were still active. She guessed they must roost in the barn.

'Nigel Palmer lives here with his daughter and son. His wife left him years ago. His son, Jasper, supervises most of the farm work these days, and the daughter – I've forgotten her name – looks after the home and takes care of her father. They're an odd family,' Karen said.

'Odd how?'

'I think Jasper and his sister have always been scared of their father, and even though they're in their early forties now, they still tiptoe around him. Jasper takes after his father. He's short-tempered and has a mean streak. The daughter's a quiet, mousy thing, always seems scared of saying the wrong thing and getting into trouble.'

DI Morgan nodded. 'Okay. Well, find out if they've seen anything, and if they know either of the girls. Keep it casual.' He glanced at the dashboard clock. 'I'd better get a move on. The briefing's in thirty minutes, and Superintendent Murray's not going to accept any excuses for my absence.'

'I won't need long,' Karen said, sure that after a few minutes with Nigel Palmer, she'd be able to tell if he knew anything about the girls' disappearance.

They got out of the car. Karen stared at the farmhouse as DI Morgan walked around to the driver's side.

He followed her gaze and looked towards the glowing lights of the house. 'Are you comfortable going in there on your own?'

Karen turned to him. 'Absolutely. I think it's worth taking the time to talk to him.'

DI Morgan glanced at his watch. 'I could come in with you if you'd prefer.'

Karen shook her head. 'No, sir. There's no need. You've got more important things to be getting on with back at the station, but I appreciate you giving me the time to do this.'

'Do you want me to arrange a ride back to the station for you?'

'No need. I have a friend who'll give me a lift.'

DI Morgan hesitated, and Karen was almost sure he was going to change his mind and insist she return to the station with him. Then he nodded and slipped into the driver's seat. 'See you back at the station.'

As he made a three-point turn, the car's tyres crunching over gravel, Karen squared her shoulders and walked towards the farmhouse.

CHAPTER EIGHT

Nigel Palmer's daughter opened the front door. She was a good six inches taller than Karen with a pale, thin, pinched face, and when she recognised Karen her features tightened.

She shot a look over her shoulder and then turned back. 'I thought all this was over.'

As soon as she spoke, Karen remembered her name. Cathy. Cathy Palmer, the poor, put-upon farmer's daughter.

'Evening, Cathy. You don't mind if I come in, do you?'

Without waiting for an answer, Karen slid past Cathy and stepped into the hall. Striding forward, she crossed the flagstone floor of the hallway that led to the huge farmhouse kitchen.

Beside a large open fireplace, sitting in a wooden rocking chair with a blanket over his knees was Nigel Palmer. A clear plastic loop of tubing ran beneath his nose and was linked to an upright oxygen canister behind the chair.

'I don't think it's a good idea to have that canister so near to an open fire, Mr Palmer,' Karen said.

The old man turned his wizened face towards Karen. Like his daughter, he was tall. Though he sat hunched in the chair, Karen had seen him standing before and knew he was at least six foot four. He was very, very thin. Nigel Palmer had emphysema, and it appeared his condition had worsened since the last time she'd seen him.

Nigel sneered at her. 'Spare me your fake concern, officer.' He leaned forward in his chair. 'Shut the door, Cathy, you stupid girl! You're letting in the cold.'

'It is shut, Dad,' Cathy said, stepping forward and then standing beside the large table in the centre of the kitchen. She clasped her hands together in front of her. 'Can I get you a drink? A cup of tea?' she asked, in an effort to be hospitable.

'She won't be staying long enough for that,' Nigel Palmer said. 'What is it you want?'

Karen took a step back away from the crackling fire. It was stiflingly warm inside the kitchen. 'Two girls went missing from Moore Lane Primary School this afternoon. As you know, the school backs on to your land and—'

'No, it doesn't. Our land ends before the wood.'

'Well, your land is very close to the school, and we believe the children could have walked across your fields, perhaps sheltering or playing in one of your outbuildings.'

Nigel Palmer's face took on a nasty smile. 'You mean, you think I'm involved.' He cackled with laughter. 'You just can't let it go, can you. You blamed me for Amy's disappearance, and now you're trying to pin another crime on me as well. Honestly, how the hell do you expect me to have done anything in this state?' He gestured at the oxygen tank behind him.

'How awful,' Cathy said. 'Those poor girls. It's so cold tonight. Do you think they wandered off and got lost or . . .'

'We don't know. That's why we need you to check any outbuildings or ditches. There's a full-scale search going on across the village and surrounding countryside. It'll go on into the night, but it's not easy in the dark.'

'Typical police. Stating the obvious,' Nigel Palmer wheezed as he turned away and stared into the fire, watching the flickering flames.

'Is your brother about?' Karen asked Cathy.

'No, he's been cutting back hedges over in the far fields today. He'll have left the tractor in the top barn and headed for a drink after work, I would guess.'

'What do you want him for anyway?' Nigel Palmer said, stifling a cough. 'Jasper's got nowt to do with it. He's been working all day.'

Karen shrugged. 'If he's been working in the fields, he might have seen something.'

'I'm sure if he had, then he'd have been in touch with the police, the good, law-abiding boy that he is.' Nigel Palmer broke off into a coughing fit, and Karen wondered if it was genuine or whether he was laying it on thick for her benefit. It wasn't unheard of for suspects to go to extreme lengths to avoid questioning. When Karen had been in uniform, a man had faked a fit to try and stop them searching his car. They'd had to call out paramedics to get him checked out before the search. His tactics only delayed the outcome, though. They'd discovered thirty individual wraps of heroin and crack in a plastic bag in his glove box.

'You've not heard anything from Amy then?' Karen asked. It was an empty question, one meant to prod and needle the old man to see if he had any conscience. The truth was, Karen had long given up hope that Amy Fisher was still alive.

Amy Fisher had been renting one of the outbuildings on Palmers' farm at the time of her disappearance. She'd used it as a studio, printing materials with vivid colours that she then used to make scarves and bags. There'd been a huge search of the farm after she went missing, and the lack of evidence tying Nigel Palmer to the teenager's disappearance did nothing to persuade Karen he was innocent. The farm was the last place Amy was seen alive.

She was convinced he lay at the centre of the mystery, and Karen wouldn't let it go. She couldn't.

Cathy spoke up nervously. 'No, we haven't heard anything from Amy.'

Karen bit down on the inside of her cheek and wondered if Cathy was as helpless as she appeared. It was uncharitable of her, but she couldn't understand why anyone would choose to stay here with this evil man. Had she never wanted to do anything with her life? She cooked and cleaned and looked after her father only to be shouted at and belittled. Had years of emotional abuse ground her down and turned Cathy into a timid woman afraid of her own shadow?

'It's strange Amy didn't keep in touch, Cathy. She'd been quite close to you, hadn't she?'

Cathy shot an anxious glance at her father and then lowered her gaze to the floor. 'We chatted now and again, but we weren't that close.'

'I can see your father's in no position to search the outbuildings himself. If you're prepared to give me the keys, I can organise some uniforms to go over the buildings with a fine-tooth comb. We need to make sure the little girls aren't trapped somewhere,' Karen said, directing her gaze at the farmer's daughter.

'Over my dead body. You're not getting anywhere near my buildings without a warrant. The state you left my place in last time was a disgrace,' the old man shouted.

Karen looked at him coldly. 'You sound like a man with something to hide, Mr Palmer.'

Nigel Palmer wiped the spittle away from the side of his mouth and gave a pathetic little cough. 'No, love. I'm just a man who's been screwed over by the police on more than one occasion.'

'We can get a warrant, but it'll look bad for you. No one else has asked for one. Everyone wants to cooperate and see the girls home safely.'

Nigel Palmer narrowed his eyes. 'Fine. You can have access to the outbuildings. I don't see why I should let your lot trample through my home again, touching everything with their sticky fingers. But suit yourself – you police usually do.'

'I'll call Jasper,' Cathy said as she walked back over to the kitchen counter, where a cheap mobile phone was charging. 'He'll want to help. I'm sure he can ask some of the lads at the pub to give him a hand searching too.'

Karen nodded. 'Thanks. I'd appreciate it. As you can imagine, the parents are very worried.'

'How old are they?' Nigel Palmer asked.

Karen had been on her way out of the kitchen and turned back to face him.

'Ten years old. Far too young to be out on their own on a night like this.'

Nigel Palmer shuddered, and his eyes darted around the room as he frowned.

'What is it?' Karen asked. If she didn't know better, she would have said Nigel Palmer looked afraid.

'Nothing. I just wanted to know how old they were, and while you're here, tell us what they look like and what they're wearing. Jasper will want to know that sort of thing if he's out looking for them.'

Karen stared at him for a long time before answering. Was Nigel Palmer hiding something?

CHAPTER NINE

Cathy saw Karen out. Her face creased in confusion when she saw the empty driveway. 'Didn't you drive here?'

Karen pulled her mobile out of her coat pocket. 'I had a colleague drop me off.'

'Are you walking back? Do you need a lift?'

Karen shook her head and held up her phone. 'Thanks, but I'm going to get a friend to pick me up.'

Cathy nodded and was about to close the door when Karen called, 'Keep an eye out for those girls, Cathy. Please.'

Cathy lifted her head, and her eyes met Karen's. 'Of course.'

The lights from the farmhouse were dim but illuminated the access road just enough to make out the potholes. Karen pulled up the address book on her phone. Scrolling through the contacts, she paused at the name Amethyst. Karen had nearly backed out of the first session when she'd learned the counsellor's name. She'd suspected the office would be adorned with crystals and smell of incense and the therapy itself would be new-age mumbo jumbo, but the office had been decorated in shades of beige and white, and Amethyst had been very focused on evidence-based techniques.

Karen hadn't seen her since they'd finished cognitive behavioural therapy. The therapy had helped her take a step back before making decisions. It had given her the tools to separate her thoughts and actions from her feelings. After talking to Nigel Palmer, Karen thought she could use a top-up session. It had been a long time since she'd felt herself sinking back into that single-minded approach. It was too late now but maybe she'd call in the morning.

Karen started walking towards the main road as she dialled Christine's number.

Christine was her neighbour. A sixty-year-old widow who had never had children, she'd been over the moon when Karen, Josh and Tilly moved in next door. Josh had joked about it, and they'd giggled about their overenthusiastic and slightly nosey neighbour. But they'd grown close to Christine, trusting her to mind Tilly when they went out. Immediately after the accident, Christine had been an angel, cleaning, cooking and taking care of the house. When Karen could barely put one foot in front of the other, Christine was there by her side, quietly encouraging her to return to day-to-day life. Even now, if she needed something, the first person she would call on was Christine. And it worked both ways. Two months ago, Christine had had a cancer scare, and it had been Karen whom she'd asked to accompany her to the hospital for appointments.

Christine answered on the fourth ring. 'Hello.'

'Christine, it's me. I'm sorry to interrupt your evening, but I could really use a favour.'

'Name it,' Christine said.

'Could you pick me up and take me to the station at Nettleham?'

'Where are you?'

'The Palmers' farm.'

Christine huffed under her breath. 'What are you doing there?'

'Did you hear about the little girls that went missing?' Karen asked.

Although it had only been a few hours since Sian Gibson and Emily Dean had disappeared, Christine had her finger on the pulse of village life. She was a member of the WI and very active in the community. There wasn't much that went on in Branston without Christine knowing about it – although this was Heighington and not far away, it was possible the news hadn't yet reached the local gossip network.

'No. What happened?'

'Two girls went missing from Moore Lane Primary School. Nigel Palmer's land backs on to the school, so I wanted a word with him.'

'That's terrible. How old are the children?'

'Only ten.'

Christine took a sharp intake of breath. 'Hold tight. I'll be there in five minutes.'

Karen hung up and used her mobile as a torch as she walked down the narrow private lane, avoiding the dips filled with freezing water. The night was getting rapidly colder, and Karen's breath formed small clouds in front of her.

As good as her word, Christine was there just as Karen made it to the main road. She slipped into the passenger seat and was immediately bombarded with questions that she did her best to answer, although at this stage of the investigation she didn't have much information.

'I should get back to Nettleham before the briefing wraps up,' Karen said, checking the time on her phone screen as they headed towards Lincoln.

'I hope you find them tonight,' Christine said. 'Poor little mites must be freezing. That's if they're still outside,' she added ominously.

Karen nodded. 'Most children are taken by someone they know, usually a family member.'

Christine gave her a sideways glance as they came to a stop at the traffic lights on Canwick Hill. 'But you don't think that's the case this time?'

Karen exhaled deeply, puffed out her cheeks and shook her head. 'I don't know. But I've got a bad feeling.'

Christine shivered as she pulled away from the lights. 'You suspect Nigel Palmer again.' It wasn't a question.

Karen took a deep breath and phrased her response carefully. Christine was a good friend but there were some aspects of the investigation she couldn't talk about. 'The circumstances are very different to Amy Fisher's disappearance.'

Christine's hands tightened on the wheel. She'd been close to Amy's parents, befriending them soon after they'd moved to the area when Amy was tiny. 'I know you can't talk about the case.'

'I haven't given up on Amy, you know. It must seem like that because the investigation has been scaled back, but she hasn't been forgotten.'

'I know.'

'Have you spoken to Janine and Bill recently?' Amy's parents had moved back to Scotland a few months ago. Janine had been convinced Nigel Palmer was behind her daughter's disappearance.

A month before they left the village, the police were called to remove Janine from the Palmer farm. She'd been drinking and had hammered on the front door, demanding answers and refusing to leave until she got them. Nigel Palmer had threatened to press charges.

'I've not spoken to them since they moved. I've called a couple of times, but they don't return my calls. They don't speak to anyone from the village any more.'

'That's not healthy.'

Christine gave a sad smile. 'They're just trying to deal with their grief the best they can and talking to me brings back painful memories, I suppose.'

Karen nodded. 'Understandable. There's nothing healthy about losing a child. They need to do whatever they can to get through each day, I guess.'

'It's hard for them to move on without knowing what really happened to Amy.'

Karen stared down at her hands for a moment before turning to Christine. 'I need to be careful with this case.'

'What do you mean?'

'I keep looking for a link to what happened eighteen months ago. I should be able to separate this case from what happened to Amy, but I can't. I keep thinking there's a pattern there, a reason behind it all, but I can't see it. I feel so helpless, like I did after Josh and Tilly.'

'You wanted to make sense of the accident, and no one could blame you for that. Sometimes terrible things happen for no reason.'

'When I was talking to Nigel Palmer, I could feel myself wanting to push harder. I wasn't cool and calm, I was furious. I'm worried I'll lose perspective again.'

'Losing Josh and Tilly was different. You wouldn't be working this case if your boss didn't think you could handle it.'

Karen looked out of the passenger window. Christine was right. She had spent months trying to analyse the crash that killed Josh and Tilly. She'd convinced herself it wasn't an accident, even going so far as to accuse her colleagues in traffic of a cover-up, despite having no evidence to back up that theory. Things had spiralled quickly. It was only thanks to her DI at the time that she'd got the help she needed to recognise her feelings while understanding she didn't need to act on them.

There was another reason Karen had asked her friend to pick her up, rather than asking someone from the station for a lift or waiting for a taxi. Christine knew people. She'd lived in Branston all her life, and had close friends in Heighington and Washingborough.

'I thought maybe you could put the word out to see if anyone knows or has seen anything.'

Christine nodded. 'Sure.'

By the time they got to Nettleham, Karen was feeling a little better. Her time spent in Nigel Palmer's company had put her on edge and left her with a faint nausea. But seeing Christine had restored her. When they reached police HQ, Christine dropped Karen as close to the entrance as she could.

'Thanks very much, Christine. I owe you one,' Karen said as she climbed out of the car.

'Don't be ridiculous. You don't owe me anything. I just hope you find those girls.'

'Me too.' Karen shut the car door, waved her friend off and hurried into the station.

◆ ◆ ◆

The briefing room was packed, and the session looked to be almost over. Karen grabbed one of the last remaining seats next to Rick.

DI Morgan stood near the front talking to Superintendent Murray.

'How are things progressing?' Karen asked.

Rick had a look of grim determination on his face. 'We've spent the last few hours combing through the background on each family. There's a couple of anomalies that DI Morgan wants us to investigate further. But nothing that's going to crack the case, unfortunately. We've phoned around most of the businesses and farms in the area and asked people to keep an eye out for the girls. The big news is, the super's put out a child alert.'

Karen raised an eyebrow.

Rick nodded. 'Exactly. We're getting some help from other forces to monitor the calls. Apparently, they've already been pretty overwhelming, and the hotline's only been running for an hour.'

'I'll bet,' Karen said and then settled back into her chair as Superintendent Murray called everyone to attention and said a few words to end the briefing.

When it was all was over, Superintendent Murray asked DI Morgan and Karen to come to her office.

DI Morgan shut the door behind them, and Superintendent Murray sank into her chair. She rarely appeared ruffled, but today she looked very stressed. 'In the last hour, we've had numerous responses to the Missing Child Alert. Are you happy with the allocation of officers? I know we get vast amounts of information from the general public after an alert.'

'About one hundred possible sightings so far,' DI Morgan said, not sounding terribly excited about any of them. 'Other reported sightings can be ruled out due to location and descriptions. But I think the floodgates are going to open as the alert spreads across social media.'

Superintendent Murray pinched the bridge of her nose with a thumb and forefinger. 'Let's hope one or more of the responses turns out to be helpful.'

'So far, the team's coping with the number of calls, which is good. Whether or not we're going to be able to follow up on every one in a timely fashion is another matter,' DI Morgan said.

'If needed, we can bring in more staff to cover. But I need you two to focus on the girls' families. I don't need to remind you that stranger abductions are very rare. It's very likely that they've been taken by someone they know and trust. That means our focus is best directed at the families and any information they can give us. We know the Deans have a history of mixing with criminals, and the girls could have potentially been targeted because of that. But I also want you to keep looking into Sian Gibson's family. Her father owns a software development company. DC Cooper told us his business has seen remarkable growth over a short period of time. That type of expansion doesn't usually happen without putting a few noses out of joint on the way.'

Karen nodded. 'Yes, ma'am.'

There was a knock at the door. Superintendent Murray barked, 'Enter' and DC Sophie Jones poked her head in the room.

'Sorry to interrupt, ma'am, but we've found something.'

'Well, don't just stand there,' her boss said, leaning forward. 'Come in. What did you find?'

'A glove belonging to one of the girls.'

'Where was this glove found?' DI Morgan asked.

'In a hedgerow close to the school, just past the boundary of the wood, bordering on Nigel Palmer's farmland.'

'Who found it?' Karen asked, expecting Sophie to say a member of the public out for a jog or walking their dog.

'Jasper Palmer. He was out looking for the girls on his land, following DS Hart's request.'

'You spoke to Jasper Palmer?' Superintendent Murray asked, turning to Karen.

Karen shook her head. 'No, not directly. I stopped by the Palmer farm just now to ask them to keep a lookout for the girls and to check their outbuildings. Their land borders the edge of the school,' she explained.

'I'm aware of that,' Superintendent Murray said, without taking her eyes from Karen. 'Why did you visit the Palmer farm in person? All the farms and landowners in the area have already been contacted by DC Cooper, haven't they?'

Karen shifted uncomfortably. She knew the superintendent wanted to know if she'd received a tip-off or whether she had any evidence to suggest Palmer's involvement. But she had neither of these. Just a feeling, and that wouldn't stand up to the superintendent's scrutiny.

'We were passing, ma'am. I dropped Karen off, so she could have a word with them, and I came back here to organise the briefing,' DI Morgan said.

'Are we sure the glove belongs to one of the girls?' Karen asked. A glove found in a hedgerow could have been there for a long time. There was no reason to suspect it had to belong to Sian or Emily.

Sophie nodded. 'Yes, I should have explained. It has Sian's name tag inside. Apparently, her mother tags everything because she's always losing her belongings.'

Karen's interest intensified. 'I'd like to talk to Jasper about this finding, ma'am.'

The request was met with a stony silence from the superintendent.

'I think it's better if I talk to Jasper Palmer, ma'am,' DI Morgan said. 'And DS Hart could go and visit the Gibson family.'

Karen had the distinct impression they wanted to keep her away from the Palmers. 'I really think it's better if I talk to Jasper. I know the family, and I'm sure I'd be able to get more out of him.'

DI Morgan did not look amused. Karen couldn't blame him. She was going directly against his wishes in front of the superintendent. Not exactly a wise move if she wanted to win over her boss.

'I agree with DI Morgan,' the superintendent said. 'You might be a little too close to the Palmers to be objective, Karen.'

'I can assure you I keep an open mind when doing my job.' As soon as she said the words, Karen knew she had gone too far. You didn't snap at the superintendent and get away with it.

There was an awkward silence, and Sophie stared at her in surprise. It made Karen feel like a naughty schoolgirl.

She sighed. 'But if you think it's best, I'll go and speak to the Gibson family while DI Morgan talks to Jasper Palmer.'

Superintendent Murray gave a tight smile. 'Good. That's settled then.'

'A question, Sophie,' DI Morgan said. 'Have the Gibsons been told Sian's glove has been recovered?'

Sophie shook her head. 'Not yet, sir. Because it was labelled, we didn't need them to identify it, and we didn't want to upset them.'

DI Morgan thought for a moment. 'I think they'll be grateful if we're honest with them. I think we should tell them. Plus, we need to know if Sian was wearing that glove today.'

'Yes, do that. Then we need to tell the search team where the glove was found so we can coordinate in a tighter area. It's possible Sian lost the glove before today, in which case we don't want to focus too much on it yet.' The superintendent nodded to indicate they were dismissed.

As they filed out of the office, she called Karen back. 'Just a moment, Karen.'

She waited until DI Morgan had left and shut the door. When they were alone, Karen braced herself for a dressing-down. She'd deserve it too. She shouldn't have lost her temper.

'Right, do you want to tell me what all that was about?' Superintendent Murray asked.

'What?' Karen asked, putting on her best innocent expression.

The superintendent sat back in her chair and scrutinised Karen. 'You seem very reluctant to visit the Gibsons. I know your daughter was younger than Emily and Sian when you lost her, but this case must be especially hard for you. Are you finding it difficult to deal with the parents?' The superintendent gave Karen a sympathetic smile.

Karen swallowed the lump in her throat. If she'd lived, Tilly would have been ten now. The same age as Emily and Sian. She felt her irritation melt away. She'd expected a few cutting remarks, not concern.

'No, ma'am. It's not that. To be honest, it's the history with the Palmer family. As you know, I was working on the Amy Fisher case, and Nigel Palmer—'

Superintendent Murray finished Karen's sentence. '—Nigel Palmer was a major suspect in the enquiry.'

Karen nodded. 'With two cases concerning youngsters going missing in such a short time and such a small area . . .'

'True, but the disappearance of a nineteen-year-old woman wouldn't necessarily be related to the disappearance of two ten-year-old girls. Besides, an individual who targets children is unlikely to be the same predator who targeted a young woman.'

Karen bowed her head. 'That's exactly what DI Morgan said.'

Superintendent Murray pushed some papers out of the way then leaned her forearms on her desk, studying Karen. 'How are you getting on with DI Morgan? Is he fitting in well?'

'He's very thorough, ma'am.'

Superintendent Murray tried and failed to suppress a smile. 'You say that like it's a bad thing, Karen.'

'Not at all. He works hard and bases his decisions on logic.'

'So there are no problems in the team?'

'None at all, ma'am.'

'That's good to hear. Now, you'd better get to the Gibsons' house and try to uncover something that helps us work out what has happened to these two little girls.'

CHAPTER TEN

Leanne Gibson's heart was fluttering in her chest. From the moment she'd heard her daughter was missing, she'd experienced an almost constant surge of adrenaline. It made her feel light-headed, dry-mouthed and shaky. She was on high alert, and every noise made her jump.

She wiped a cloth over the kitchen counter, finding a small comfort in the familiar domestic task. As she moved the cloth back and forth over the same spot, she stared out at the dark garden and the fields beyond.

Was Sian out there, scared and alone, or had someone stolen her away? She didn't want to imagine either option, but the scenarios ran through her mind whether she liked it or not.

She felt like she was living in a nightmare. How could this be happening to her daughter? It wasn't fair.

She was a good mother. She'd hardly let Sian out of her sight since the day she was born. She didn't even like members of her own family babysitting. Why had she relented and allowed Sian to visit Emily Dean's house for tea? She imagined police officers and locals out there in the darkness, still searching. They wouldn't give up just because the sun had set, would they? She'd have to ask the family liaison officer because she couldn't let that happen. If they stopped looking for Sian, then Leanne would go out and search the woods and fields herself.

Thomas had persuaded her to stay at home, away from the search. He said there was still a chance that Sian would come home of her own accord, but Leanne was starting to think that was very unlikely. Sian was a good girl, and she wouldn't make them worry unnecessarily. She'd had it drummed into her from an early age not to talk to strangers. She wasn't even allowed to visit the corner shop on her own.

Thomas had gone to join the search party, and deep down, Leanne was glad he wasn't in the house. His presence made her feel so guilty.

It was ridiculously selfish to think of anything other than Sian at a time like this. In the grand scheme of things, did it even matter any more?

When the police officers had spoken to her at the school, one of them had looked at her in a way that made her feel exposed. The police officer's blue eyes had a steely glint, and she'd had to turn her head while she answered his questions. If she looked into his eyes, she was sure he'd discover what she was hiding.

She'd confess everything if she thought it would help bring Sian back home. But her secret couldn't have anything to do with why Sian was missing.

Could it?

◆ ◆ ◆

DC Sophie Jones was waiting for Karen when she arrived back in the main office area. Sophie jumped up from her desk and dashed over. 'I hope you don't mind me saying so, Sarge, but I thought the super treated you very unfairly.'

Karen raised an eyebrow.

Sophie continued, 'Everyone knows the history you had with the Palmer family on the Amy Fisher case. It made sense that you should be the one to question Jasper Palmer about the glove.'

'The superintendent thought otherwise, Sophie.' Karen's tone was clipped, and she tried to hide her irritation. She was annoyed at her own unprofessionalism. It was very unlike her and didn't set a good example. She'd been wrong to show her frustration at being told not to question Jasper. She believed in the line of command and challenging the superintendent's authority was out of order. 'The superintendent didn't make the decision out of malice, Sophie. She decided on the best course of action, and we have to go along with that.'

Sophie's eyes widened, and she folded her arms over her chest. 'Well, if it were me, I'd be spitting feathers. This finding could crack the case wide open. I mean, you hear about criminals taking trophies from the scene of the crime. Maybe Jasper Palmer took the glove as some kind of keepsake.'

'If he did, it's more likely he'd have kept it to himself, don't you think?'

Sophie thought for a moment. 'True, but maybe this is his way of getting involved in the case. I read about that too. Criminal deviants integrate themselves into the search or aftermath of a crime. They get a sick kick out of being involved in the investigation.'

'You've certainly spent a lot of time reading,' Karen said.

Sophie's face fell. 'Is that a bad thing?'

'Of course not. But DI Morgan did make a good point. Nigel Palmer was our number one suspect after Amy Fisher disappeared, but if he's abducted two ten-year-olds, it would mean his MO has changed dramatically, which is unlikely.'

'MO: his modus operandi,' Sophie stated, looking pleased with herself.

'Yes. Now, are you ready?'

Sophie did a double take. 'Ready? For what?'

'I thought you might like to come with me and talk to the Gibsons. It would be a good learning experience. It won't be easy, but I'm sure you're up to it.'

Sophie nodded eagerly. 'Absolutely. I'll just grab my jacket.'

As Karen picked up her raincoat that she'd flung over the back of her chair earlier, she watched Sophie eagerly grabbing her bag and mobile phone, while struggling to put on her coat at the same time. She certainly had enthusiasm for the job. Karen would have to say something to her on the way to the Gibsons' house. She couldn't have Sophie turning up full of beans, grinning. It wasn't appropriate.

Before they left the station, Karen had a quick word with DI Morgan. She'd still much rather she was going to question Jasper Palmer, but she ignored the nagging feeling gnawing at her and focused on the Gibsons instead.

'Should I mention anything about Leanne's run-in with Matthew Saunders earlier?' Karen asked.

DI Morgan thought for a moment before replying. 'No, I don't think so. We should be able to talk to him before it gets too late.' He glanced at his watch. 'Focus on finding out as much about Sian as you can. Get the names of people who visit the house regularly or see Sian frequently. And go over the things she's allowed to access on the internet. Try to find out if she could have used a computer, smartphone or tablet without her parents' knowledge.'

Karen nodded. 'Will do. I'll see you back here later. Good luck with Jasper.'

DI Morgan looked up, and a smile tugged the corner of his lips. 'From what you've said, it sounds like I'm going to need all the luck I can get.'

◆ ◆ ◆

The Gibsons lived in a new-build, three-bed detached house on Beech Road. It wasn't far from the village centre and was one of the latest wave of new houses to be tagged on to Heighington.

Karen looked enviously at the small neat patch of grass. There were no trees around the new development, and the street looked pristine. Leaves had smothered Karen's garden in the last week, and she couldn't even see the grass beneath the brown and orange carpet. It would take a few back-breaking hours with a rake to clear the ground. Maybe she'd get to it at the weekend if they'd found the girls by then.

'Now, remember what I told you,' Karen said, turning to Sophie. 'Be polite and sympathetic and leave the questioning to me.'

Sophie nodded. 'Absolutely, Sarge. My lips are sealed.' She made a zipping motion over her mouth.

They walked side by side up the driveway. The downstairs lights were on, and a pair of child-sized wellingtons nestled beside two adult pairs near the front door. Karen swallowed hard. A soft rain had begun to fall. She hoped the girls had found some kind of shelter.

If they were still alive.

The front door opened before they reached it. Thomas Gibson stood silhouetted in the doorway.

'Is there any news?' he asked, his voice tinged with desperation.

'I'm afraid we haven't found them yet, Mr Gibson, but there is something we'd like to discuss with you.'

He nodded rapidly and opened the door wide so they could go in.

They stepped into a pleasantly decorated, narrow hallway, painted in shades of grey and duck-egg blue, with bright white woodwork.

Thomas led the way through the kitchen into a large conservatory that had been added on to the back of the house. As they walked past the family-size chrome fridge covered with colourful childish drawings, Karen bit down on her lower lip.

Everywhere they looked there were signs of Sian. There were various photographs displayed on the windowsills and a children's word game on the kitchen counter.

The family liaison officer, Nicky Stinnett, sat beside Leanne at a glass-topped table. Karen was full of admiration for anyone who could support people going through such a traumatic event. Family liaison officers needed to be sympathetic and kind without absorbing the feelings of sadness that surrounded them. Being around grief-stricken families all day wasn't an easy job.

Leanne Gibson's hands gripped a coffee mug tightly, her hair hanging limply around her face. Only a few hours had passed since Karen had last seen her, but she looked like a different woman. The stress and panic had taken hold. She stared at Karen and Sophie with bloodshot eyes.

Karen saw a flicker of hope pass across Leanne's features and hated having to tell her they had not yet located Sian and Emily. The bitter disappointment on her face was painful to watch. She began to shake. Thomas stepped closer to his wife, putting a hand on her shoulder. 'Please, sit down. What do you need to talk to us about?'

Sophie took the seat beside Leanne, and Karen slid in opposite her. Thomas remained standing rigidly behind his wife.

'We've found an item of clothing we believe belonged to Sian, and we wanted you to confirm it's hers.'

Leanne jolted, her hands jerking the coffee cup, spilling the contents over the glass table.

'I'll get something to clear that up,' Nicky murmured and walked past Karen into the kitchen.

'It's a glove,' Karen clarified quickly, knowing that the parents would fear the worst. 'Sian could have lost it at any time. It doesn't necessarily mean anything bad has happened to her.'

Leanne made a sound, a cross between a bark of laughter and a sob. 'Something bad *has* happened to her! She's been abducted!'

Karen focused on Leanne. 'I've got a photograph here of the glove. If you could identify it as Sian's, and tell us if you know whether she lost it before today?'

Karen pulled up the image on her smartphone and showed it to the Gibsons. 'It has her name tag inside.'

Thomas's eyes filled with tears, and Leanne's lower lip wobbled before she put her hands over her face.

Thomas managed to nod and then cleared his throat. 'Yes, that is Sian's. I don't know when she lost it . . .' He looked towards his wife.

'She had it this morning when she went to school,' Leanne whispered.

Karen leaned forward, trying to make eye contact with Leanne. 'Okay, that's good. We now know we're searching in the right location. We're still out there looking for her. It looks like Sian and Emily left the school together.'

Karen didn't want to give the couple false hope. They all wanted to believe the girls had wandered off on some misguided adventure, but it was looking more and more likely that they had been abducted. Preparing for the worst was a terrible expression, but false hope could be more devastating.

Nicky had made everyone fresh coffee and carried it through to the conservatory on a tray.

'If you're up to it, we'd like to ask you a few questions about Sian's home life,' Karen said.

'I've already told you. She's a happy little girl, and we don't have any problems at home,' Leanne said.

'I know,' Karen said gently. 'The information I'm looking for is regarding the other people in Sian's life. I'd like to know things like who Sian sees regularly. Is she involved in extracurricular activities? Do you have friends who regularly visit the house or babysit? I need to know everything you can tell me.'

Thomas reached for his wife's hand and squeezed.

'Of course, we'll do anything we can to help.'

The questioning was hard. The last thing Karen wanted was to make things even harder than they already were. With each new line of enquiry, however, she could see she was grinding them down further, making them doubt friends and family and every detail of their lives.

'We hardly ever go out and leave Sian,' Leanne said. 'We've only been out without her about three times this year, haven't we, Thomas?'

'That's right,' Thomas said. 'I mean, we're not the partying type. I work long hours and most of the time we're happy watching films together and getting a takeaway.'

Karen glanced across at Sophie, who was doing very well so far, staying quiet but taking it all in.

'On the occasions you did go out, who looked after Sian?' Karen asked.

Leanne blinked. 'My mother. Except . . .' She broke off and looked at her husband.

Thomas rapidly shook his head. 'Don't be ridiculous.'

But Leanne was having none of it. She turned back to Karen.

'The last time we went out was in September for my birthday. My mum had come down with tonsillitis so she couldn't look after Sian. We'd booked the new Thai restaurant in Lincoln, but we could have cancelled. We *were* going to cancel.'

'Who looked after Sian for you on that occasion?' Karen looked at Leanne then Thomas, who had paled considerably.

'Thomas's brother, Nick. He lives in the village.'

'Had he ever looked after Sian before?'

Leanne's eyes widened, and Karen guessed her mind was running through horrendous possibilities of what could have happened.

'No, that was the first time.'

'Did Sian mention anything when you got home? Was she upset?' Sophie asked, unable to hold her tongue any longer.

Leanne nodded. 'Yes. Yes, she was upset.'

'Wait a minute,' Thomas said, raising his voice. 'Sian was upset because Nick had stopped her playing with the iPad. He went to read her a story and found she was still playing games. She knows she's not allowed to play with it unsupervised, so Nick took it away. That's why Sian wasn't happy. He didn't hurt her or anything.'

'That's what Nick told us. We weren't there. We don't really know what happened,' Leanne said and wrenched her hand away from her husband's.

'We'll have a word with Nick. It's probably like your husband has said.' Karen was eager to reassure Leanne, so she didn't start a witch-hunt with no proof.

'Are you going to speak to him now?' Leanne said, planting her palms flat on the table and starting to stand. 'Shall I phone him? I could get him to come here.'

Karen shook her head. 'There's no need for that. I think it's best if we talk to him separately.'

Leanne looked so traumatised. Karen rested her forearms on the table and leaned closer. 'I can't begin to understand how difficult this is for you. We have to ask all these questions. But that doesn't mean your family and friends are guilty of anything.'

Leanne nodded, but she didn't look convinced.

When they got outside, a few feet away from the Gibsons' house, Sophie turned to Karen and asked, 'How did I do, Sarge?'

'You did well.'

'I know I was supposed to keep quiet, but the question left my mouth before I could stop it.'

'It's fine. It was a sensible question, and I'd have asked it myself. It's always a good idea to think before you speak, though. You need to weigh up how the parents will react to certain information.'

'Yes, I understand what you mean,' Sophie said. 'Leanne has latched on to the idea that her brother-in-law upset Sian.'

Karen opened the car door. 'Exactly. For all we know, it's exactly how Thomas Gibson described. Her uncle took the iPad away, and she became upset. We still need to talk to him, though.'

As they got into the car, Karen checked the time. 'In fact, I doubt DI Morgan will have finished questioning Jasper yet, so I think we've got time to go and pay Nick Gibson a visit now.'

'Excellent,' Sophie said, grinning as she buckled up.

CHAPTER ELEVEN

'It's spooky out here, boss,' DC Rick Cooper said, leaning forward in the passenger seat and squinting at the dark farmhouse.

DI Morgan pulled on the handbrake and looked at Rick in surprise. 'Is it?'

He thought it was quite pleasant. The Palmer farmhouse was certainly isolated: surrounded by fields, accessible only by a country track and a good mile from any other house. But then DI Morgan had always relished solitude.

He had to admit he'd experienced a feeling of unease earlier when he'd dropped Karen off to talk to Nigel Palmer. He wasn't the superstitious type and would never describe an inanimate object like a house as eerie. But the tension had been coming off Karen in waves, and he'd been concerned. She was obviously deeply invested in the Amy Fisher case, which was perfectly understandable. No police officer liked an unsolved case hanging over them, but somehow, with Karen and the Palmers, it seemed a little too personal – which was why he'd offered to go into the farmhouse with her.

It was also the reason why he wanted to talk to Jasper himself. He wanted to see what it was about this family that Karen didn't trust. Although he hadn't liked the way events had unfolded in the superintendent's office. He'd intended to have a quiet word with Karen to explain. Instead, the impromptu meeting had seen her reprimanded, which was unfortunate. He liked Karen. She was a hard worker. But DI Morgan knew better than anyone that emotion could be the enemy when you were investigating a case.

'There were bats here earlier,' he said and enjoyed the look of terror on Rick's face. Who would have guessed the cocky detective constable was scared of the dark and a few flying mammals?

'Come on. It's just a farmhouse,' DI Morgan said and opened the car door.

Rick followed him, his eyes darting left and right as they walked towards the farmhouse.

DI Morgan shook his head. 'Pull yourself together,' he said and then knocked on the front door.

The door was opened by a tall woman with fair hair and large blue eyes. She stared at DI Morgan without saying anything and then her gaze shifted to Rick.

'DI Morgan and DC Rick Cooper. We'd like to talk to Jasper.' DI Morgan showed his warrant card.

The woman nodded and stepped back. 'Come in,' she said in a quiet voice.

They stepped inside the farmhouse, and the woman led them along a narrow, dark hallway. DI Morgan asked for her name.

'I'm Cathy,' she said, sending a shy glance at Rick, who treated her to one of his confident grins.

Rick was a good-looking lad, but there was a time and a place for flirting and it wasn't during interviews. DI Morgan delivered a chastising look, and the grin slid off Rick's face.

Cathy led them into an enormous farmhouse kitchen. A great table stood to one side. Above it, copper pots and pans hung from the rafters. A huge open fire piled high with logs was pouring out heat, and DI Morgan removed his coat.

Sitting beside the fire was an old man. He was extremely thin and clearly not well. His grey hair was combed to the side in an ineffective attempt to cover a large bald patch. He had bushy grey eyebrows which shot up when he saw DI Morgan and Rick.

'Two visits from the coppers in one day. What have we done to deserve this?' He spluttered the last few words.

Karen had mentioned Nigel Palmer's emphysema. She'd also said she didn't believe it was that bad, and he probably laid it on thick for their benefit. DI Morgan guessed that was wishful thinking. Karen wanted to believe this man was strong and capable enough to abduct a healthy nineteen-year-old woman and two ten-year-old girls. But DI Morgan couldn't see it. This man was genuinely sick. Even his skin had a grey tinge.

'We're here to see your son, Mr Palmer,' Rick said.

Rick looked more comfortable now he was inside. DI Morgan thought it was quite a cheery kitchen, although it wasn't exactly modern. There was a large Aga in one corner, and the work surfaces were all scrubbed pine. A large butler's sink sat under the window. There was certainly nothing sinister about the inside of the farmhouse.

The old man nodded. 'What are you standing there for, girl? Call your brother.'

Cathy scurried off out of the kitchen and into the hallway. They heard her footsteps as she climbed the stairs.

'You've heard about the young girls going missing?' Rick Cooper asked as he walked around the farmhouse kitchen, looking up at the shimmering copper pots.

'Would you stop pacing around. You're making me feel giddy,' Nigel Palmer snapped.

Rick did as he was asked and came to a stop opposite the old man, close to the fire. 'Any idea where they could be?'

'I don't know why you're asking me. What would I know about it?'

'Maybe you heard something?' Rick suggested.

'Like what? I'm stuck in this chair all day, every day. And believe it or not, I don't have people beating my door down, eager to listen to my sparkling conversation.'

'You do surprise me,' DI Morgan said drily, earning him a glare from the old man.

'You lot are all the same. I had that woman police officer here earlier. Asking questions, making snide suggestions. I've had enough. It's harassment. That's what it is.'

DI Morgan and Rick turned when they heard heavy footsteps on the stairs. A moment later, Jasper Palmer walked into the kitchen.

He was an imposing presence. Very tall, very thin, with a classically handsome face, short, fiery red hair and bright blue eyes.

His mouth curled up at one corner with a smirk. 'I see my dad has been keeping you entertained.'

'That's enough of your cheek, Jasper,' the old man said and then coughed. 'Tell them what they want to know so they can get out of my house.'

Jasper smiled and shrugged. 'As hospitable as ever, Dad.' He held out his hand and gestured to the table. 'Want to sit down?'

DI Morgan thanked him, and he and Rick sat on one side of the table, with Jasper on the other. There was no sign of Cathy. She hadn't returned after calling for her brother.

'Where exactly did you find the glove, Mr Palmer?' DI Morgan asked.

'In the far field. Not far from Station Road. I told Inspector Bertram this already.' Jasper fixed him with a bored look.

Inspector Bertram was leading the search and had already filled them in. But when he was questioning someone like Jasper Palmer, DI Morgan liked to ask the same questions in a slightly different way and see if the answers were consistent. It was easy to be consistent when telling the truth. When people lied, their story often changed.

DI Morgan leaned forward, elbows on the table. 'Were you searching alone?'

Jasper smothered a yawn. 'Sorry, late night last night and I had to be up early this morning cutting back the hedges.'

'Early!' Nigel Palmer's voice came from behind them. 'You call seven a.m. early? In my day, I was up working those fields by five every morning come rain or shine.'

Jasper rolled his eyes and turned his attention back to DI Morgan. 'But no, to answer your question, I wasn't alone. I had three men with me. We heard about the little girls going missing, and when Cathy told me you thought they might have walked across our land, we decided to go and check all the fields and outbuildings, just to make sure they weren't hurt or stuck somewhere.'

'Could you give us the names of the men who were searching with you, please, Mr Palmer?' Rick asked, holding his notepad and pencil in front of him. It was all for show as they already had the names.

Jasper narrowed his eyes and paused for effect. He enjoyed the attention. 'Tony Briggs, Brian Patterson and Lionel Mallard.' The names rolled off his tongue innocently enough, and DI Morgan assumed he was telling the truth.

'You haven't seen anyone hanging around the village recently?'

'Hanging around?' Jasper responded.

'Yes, anyone who looked out of place or seemed suspicious.'

'I don't go into the village much,' Jasper said. 'I visit the pub most nights for an hour or two, and then I come straight home.'

He rested his chin on his hand and smirked. His bright blue eyes sparkled as though the questions amused him. He was playing a part rather than answering the questions earnestly. There was nothing wrong with his responses. He was saying all the right things under the circumstances, but DI Morgan couldn't shake the feeling that Jasper was taunting them.

'You won't have any objections, of course, if we continue to search that area.' As if on cue, they heard the whirring blades of a low-flying helicopter.

Jasper shrugged. 'We've got nothing to hide. If the girls are on our land, then of course we want you to find them. Isn't that right, Dad?' Jasper jerked his chin in the direction of his father, who merely grunted in reply.

After they'd asked Jasper a few more questions and endured a few extra mean-spirited comments from Nigel Palmer, DI Morgan and Rick left the farmhouse.

'What did you make of them, boss?' Rick asked as they trudged towards the car.

DI Morgan turned and looked over his shoulder at the farmhouse. He thought he caught a movement in the upstairs window, but as he stood there staring up, the windows were dark and empty. Perhaps it had been Cathy Palmer passing by, watching them as they left. The thought made DI Morgan shiver. It was unlike him to be so fanciful.

'I knew it,' Rick said with a broad grin. 'This place creeps you out as well.'

'It doesn't creep me out, Rick, as you so eloquently put it.' He didn't add that it wasn't the place that creeped him out but rather the people that were in it.

CHAPTER TWELVE

While DI Morgan and Rick were talking to the Palmers at the farm-house, Sophie and Karen had arrived at Nick Gibson's flat.

He lived above the hairdresser's in Heighington. It was a tiny one-bedroom place, and as soon as he let them in the door, Karen guessed he lived alone.

It wasn't just that the place was messy, with used cups and plates left out on the coffee table in the living room – his niece was missing, and household chores were probably low on his list of priorities – but that it was kitted out as a bachelor pad. Despite the limited space, a large bar complete with optics and a variety of spirits had been set up in front of the window, a jukebox with flashing lights and an old-fashioned arcade machine jammed in beside it. A massive widescreen TV with a satellite box beneath it took centre stage, an old, black leather recliner in the middle of the room facing the screen. The other two chairs were hardback pine and looked as though they were once part of a set. They didn't look comfortable. Despite the bar and jukebox, it wasn't a room that welcomed visitors, and Karen suspected Nick Gibson spent a lot of time alone.

'Can I get you tea or coffee?' Nick asked.

Sophie had called into the station for a quick background check on the drive over. They knew already that Nick Gibson was thirty-two and worked at the potato factory in Branston. He looked older, mainly due to his receding hairline and the fact that his forehead was creased in a frown.

'No, thank you,' Karen said. 'We're fine. We just popped by to ask you a couple of questions if that's okay?'

Nick nodded. 'About Sian, you mean? I just came in to get warm. I've been out searching. We're doing it in shifts,' he said.

'Yes, about Sian.' Karen studied him carefully.

Nick perched on the arm of his recliner and gestured for Sophie and Karen to sit on the hardback chairs. They did so.

'When did you hear the girls were missing?' Sophie asked, surprising Karen by starting off the questions.

She sat back, deciding to give Sophie a chance to lead, although prepared to change the direction of the questioning if needed.

'Soon after they'd noticed the girls were gone from school. My brother called me on his way back from work. He knew it was going to take him a while to get back and he wanted me to make sure Leanne was all right. I can't believe it. You don't expect something like this to happen in a place like Heighington.'

'No,' Sophie said. 'Are you close to Sian?'

He shrugged. 'She's my niece. I see her quite regularly. I go around to Thomas and Leanne's for a Sunday roast now and again. She's a good kid.' He broke off and then ran a shaky hand through his thin hair.

'Leanne told us you looked after Sian about a month ago,' Sophie said.

Karen winced. It wasn't the most tactful approach. She'd gone in for the kill a little early.

'Yes,' Nick said slowly, blinking a couple of times. 'What's that got to do with anything?'

'Apparently Sian was quite upset when her parents got home?'

Nick stared at Sophie. 'I don't like where this is going. What the hell are you suggesting?' He growled the words through gritted teeth.

'We're not suggesting anything, Mr Gibson,' Karen said, attempting to rescue the situation. 'We're trying to get a picture of Sian's life by talking to the people who are close to her. We're following up on anything that's upset or concerned her recently. Perhaps she confided in you about something?'

Nick's clouded expression cleared. 'Oh, I see. I thought you meant she was . . . you know, upset because I'd done something to her.' He pulled a face as though disgusted at the thought. 'Yes, she was quite annoyed with me, but she'd been naughty. I let her stay up and watch television, and then she promised me she'd clean her teeth and go to bed as soon as the programme had finished. Then when I went up to check on her and read a bedtime story, I found she was looking at the iPad under the covers. I told her off. There's nothing wrong with that.'

'Of course not,' Karen said. 'There wasn't anything else bothering her?'

Nick shook his head.

'Do you remember what she was looking at on the iPad when you took it away from her?' Karen asked.

Nick frowned, and his face paled. 'Do you think it's someone online?'

'We don't know at this stage. We're looking at every angle.'

Nick tilted his head up and looked at the ceiling. He pursed his lips together and then shook his head in frustration. 'I'm sorry. I can't remember. I don't think I even looked at it. I just took it away and turned it off.'

'You didn't see her looking at Facebook or Snapchat?'

'No, sorry.'

Karen had managed to put Nick at ease. He was answering more confidently now and she had to admit she believed he was responding truthfully, although she did wonder why his initial reaction had been so defensive.

'Thank you for your time, Mr Gibson. We'll be in touch.'

◆ ◆ ◆

By the time the detectives arrived back at Nettleham HQ and exchanged information, it was getting late.

Sitting in DI Morgan's office, Karen looked at her watch and bit down on her lower lip. 'Do you still want to go and talk to Matthew Saunders tonight?'

'Yes,' DI Morgan said, reaching for the phone on his desk. 'I'll call ahead and tell him to expect us. I'm keen to find out why Leanne Gibson reacted so strangely to him at the school when, from what Jackie Lyons said, they were usually friendly.'

Karen stood up, preparing to go and grab her coat and bag. 'I agree. We should talk to him as soon as possible. I don't think we'll get a straight answer from Leanne.'

Before they headed out, DI Morgan asked Sophie to look into Nick Gibson's background. If there was any dirt to be found, he wanted her to find it. He'd asked Rick to speak to the search team coordinator and provide an update to the family liaison officers for both the Deans and Gibsons, to bring them up to speed.

As yet, the search had yielded nothing more promising than Sian's glove, and now that it was dark, hopes were fading. But while there was still a chance the girls could be out there, hurt or injured, they weren't ready to call off the search.

DI Morgan drove back to Heighington, following Karen's directions to the Saunders's house.

'His wife, Doctor Saunders, works at the Heighington surgery,' Karen said. 'She's my GP actually, a nice lady.'

The Saunders lived in a large, detached stone house directly on the main road through Heighington, with no driveway or front garden. Three storeys high with large sash windows, it had been constructed in a time before cars existed, but the lack of a driveway and front garden didn't take away from its splendour.

'You can park around the back, I think,' Karen said, pointing to a side road.

DI Morgan pulled into Butts Lane and, after letting Karen out, he parked as close as he could to the imposing stone wall running along the lane.

He got out of the car and they looked up at the impressive house.

'That's what a GP's salary gets you these days,' Karen said. 'I should have studied medicine.'

CHAPTER THIRTEEN

The door was opened by Doctor Saunders, a petite woman with dark hair and warm brown eyes.

'Hi, Karen, come in,' she said.

Karen walked up the steps and through the front door, introducing DI Morgan as she did so.

'Matthew's in the living room if you'd like to go through,' Doctor Saunders said and shut the door behind them.

As Karen walked along the hallway, she glanced up at the stairs. There, peeking out through the banisters, was Danny. Karen smiled.

'Go back to bed!' Doctor Saunders said. 'It's way past your bedtime, Danny. I'll be up in a minute.'

The little boy sighed and turned away, sloping off to his bedroom as the adults went into the living room.

Matthew was sitting on the sofa. His hands were linked, and he was leaning over, resting his forearm on his knees, staring at the ground.

When they entered the room, he looked up. 'Hello. I didn't expect to see you again so soon. Is there any news on Sian and Emily?'

'Sit down, please. Can I get anyone a drink?' Doctor Saunders asked.

Both Karen and DI Morgan refused the offer. As they settled into cream armchairs on either side of the sofa, Doctor Saunders went to sit down beside her husband.

'There have been a few developments, but unfortunately we haven't found the girls yet,' Karen explained. 'We do have a couple more follow-up questions to ask you.'

'So you don't need to talk to Danny again?' Doctor Saunders asked.

'Not at the moment.'

'Good.' Doctor Saunders gave a sigh of relief. 'I think he's taken it quite hard. It's such a difficult concept to process at that age. He's feeling guilty that he didn't stop them or at least try to stop them.'

'There's nothing Danny could have done,' DI Morgan said.

'I know that. But convincing Danny is another matter. Our little boy is definitely a worrier. Isn't he, Matthew?'

Matthew licked his lips and nodded obediently. He seemed jumpy. Very nervous, in fact. When she'd spoken to him earlier, Karen had put this down to the fact he was suffering from the stress of the situation. His son had been the last person to see the two girls before they disappeared. Now Matthew Saunders had had some time to calm down, but he still seemed to be on edge.

'You can ask us whatever you want,' Doctor Saunders said. 'Anything, if it helps get those two little girls back. I can't imagine what their parents are going through right now.'

'Both Emily and Sian's parents are very distressed. I wondered if you could tell us how well you know them?' Karen asked.

Doctor Saunders's eyes widened, and she shook her head. 'Well, I barely know them. I saw them at the summer fête, but I think that was the last time. I'm the named GP for both Sian and Emily, but I haven't seen either of them recently.'

Karen focused on Matthew Saunders. 'Have you had many dealings with Sian or Emily's parents, Mr Saunders?'

The colour heightened in Matthew Saunders's cheeks. 'No, not really. I mean, obviously I pick Danny up from school, so I see them most days. That is, I see Leanne. Emily's mother used to let her walk home. To be honest, everyone at the school gates thought it was a bit off. I wish I'd said something now.'

'How well do you know Leanne Gibson?'

Matthew Saunders licked his lips again and shot a quick glance at his wife. 'We chat when we're at the school gates at the same time. Just small talk, you know.'

Karen gave a little cough and said, 'Doctor Saunders, would it be okay if I changed my mind and took you up on the offer of a cup of tea?'

The woman smiled. 'Call me Tanya. And of course. Can I get anyone else anything?'

DI Morgan shook his head. Matthew Saunders didn't answer.

'I'll give you a hand,' Karen said and followed the doctor out of the living room along the hallway and into the kitchen.

Karen had the distinct impression there was something Matthew Saunders wasn't telling them. Maybe he would open up if his wife wasn't sitting right next to him.

As Tanya filled the kettle, Karen asked, 'Cups?'

Tanya nodded to the cupboard above the fruit bowl. Karen grabbed two mugs and set them down on the counter beside the tea caddy.

'It's terrifying, isn't it? I don't know how you do it. It breaks my heart when I see kids ill or hurt in the surgery. That's nothing compared to what could have happened to those poor girls,' Tanya said as she tucked her dark hair behind her ears.

'We're hoping for the best obviously, but the longer the girls are missing . . .' Karen shrugged.

Tanya closed her eyes briefly and sighed. 'The poor little things. I tell you, my stomach has been in knots all night just thinking about the possibility Danny could have . . .'

Karen put a hand on Tanya's arm. 'You'll drive yourself mad thinking like that. Incidents like these are so rare.'

As the kettle came to the boil, Tanya nodded towards the fridge in the corner of the kitchen. 'Would you mind getting the milk?'

Karen opened the fridge and pulled the bottle from the door. She couldn't help noticing how tidy and full of healthy food their fridge was – a stark contrast to her own. She'd have to do an online shop at the weekend. She relied on the delivery service and didn't know what she'd do without it.

She hoped DI Morgan was managing to extract some information.

◆ ◆ ◆

There was a light sheen of sweat on Matthew Saunders's brow as DI Morgan looked at him intently.

'Was there something going on between you and Leanne Gibson?'

Matthew looked towards the doorway. 'Keep your voice down! Of course not. What gave you that idea?'

'Because when Leanne arrived at the school earlier today, she was quite unhappy to see you there.'

Matthew shook his head. 'She wasn't unhappy. She was just surprised. Look, all right,' he said and shifted a little closer to DI Morgan. 'We had a bit of a row about something a couple of months ago, and she hasn't quite forgiven me. It wasn't anything bad, honestly. Otherwise I'd have told you.'

'What was this row about?'

Matthew gave an uneasy chuckle. 'I can hardly remember now.'

'Try,' DI Morgan said.

Matthew groaned and rubbed a hand over his forehead. 'Fine. We'd organised a playdate. I was supposed to meet her for coffee with a couple of the other mums and I forgot. She took it personally. I told her not to be so silly, and things escalated from there.'

'Is that all?' DI Morgan asked.

'Yes, I told you it was silly. Something over nothing. She's probably still a bit peeved at me, that's all.'

DI Morgan nodded and smiled. He'd been a police officer for a long time, and if there was one thing he could usually tell, it was when someone was lying to him – and right now, Matthew Saunders was lying.

CHAPTER FOURTEEN

By the time they got back to the station, it was eleven p.m. The CID room was still buzzing. Sophie and Rick were busy going through leads received from the public appeal.

'How are you two getting on?' Karen asked, taking off her coat and throwing it over the back of her chair.

'I feel like I'm drowning in paperwork,' Rick said. 'Listen to this one.' He plucked a piece of paper from his desk and read, 'Mrs Patterson saw the girls at a McDonald's in Leeds ten minutes after they went missing.' He picked up another piece of paper. 'Mr Clarkson was certain he saw the girls at Manchester Piccadilly Station an hour before they went missing.'

'Well, at least that's an easy one to rule out – look on the bright side,' Karen said.

Rick groaned. 'I know people are only trying to help. But how are we meant to chase down genuine leads out of this lot?' He poked the pile of papers in front of him with his finger.

'With methodical police work. We'll get there. The superintendent's brought in a lot of bodies to answer the phones and prioritise. We just need one genuine sighting.'

Rick sighed heavily. 'I suppose you're right. I think I need another coffee.'

Karen looked over at Sophie. She was staring down at the papers on her desk. Her cheeks were flushed with concentration. 'How are you getting on, Sophie?'

The fresh-faced DC looked up. 'About the same as Rick, I'm afraid. I think my eyes are starting to glaze over.'

'Maybe take a coffee break. I could do with one too.' She turned to DI Morgan and was about to ask him if he'd like a coffee when the duty sergeant burst into the room.

'Sir, there's an update on the search. I couldn't put it through to your office. Do you want to take the call here?'

DI Morgan nodded. 'Yes, please.'

'Pick up that phone.' The sergeant pointed to the phone on Karen's desk. 'Dial six and then press line one.'

Everyone in the room turned to watch DI Morgan as he picked up the phone.

Karen realised she was holding her breath as she waited for the news.

After a few moments of murmuring yes and no, DI Morgan looked directly at Karen and shook his head. She felt deflated. No news. It was now more than seven hours since the girls had gone missing. They could have been taken anywhere by now.

DI Morgan put his hand over the mouthpiece and said, 'Nothing's been found in the vicinity of the glove except footprints, and they're far too big to belong to Sian or Emily.'

Karen trudged to the vending machine and brought back four coffees. They were weak and not altogether pleasant, but at least they contained caffeine.

Powered by the bitter coffee, they managed to plough on for another two hours before DI Morgan came out of his office again.

'All right, you lot are on the day shift, so you'd better be going home. I want you back here bright and early.'

Sophie rubbed her eyes and Rick smothered a yawn.

'You're right, boss,' he said, 'but I hate to go home knowing they're still out there.'

'Other officers will be working through the night, Rick. We're not giving up on them,' DI Morgan said. 'But you'll be no good tomorrow if you don't get any sleep, so scarper.'

'All right, you don't have to tell me twice,' Rick said, reaching for his coat. 'Come on, Sophie, let's go.'

As Rick and Sophie headed out of the office, Karen stood up and stretched. 'Are you going home too, sir?'

DI Morgan nodded. 'Soon. I just want to finish off a few bits, and I'll be back first thing tomorrow.'

Karen picked up her bag and reached for her mobile. 'All right. I'll say goodnight then. See you tomorrow. Bright and early.'

As Karen walked out of the open-plan office area and down the stairs, her legs felt like lead weights. It was horrible to be going home where she'd be safe and warm when she knew Emily and Sian were still out there somewhere. But DI Morgan was right. If they didn't get any sleep, tomorrow they wouldn't be able to function. And they had two little girls relying on them.

Karen drove her Honda Civic through Lincoln. At least driving home this late meant the traffic was light. There was barely a car to be seen as she crossed Pelham Bridge and drove straight on towards Canwick.

Somehow she was going to have to try and get her brain to calm down enough to sleep tonight. Right now, it was buzzing with suspects and theories. None of which were currently adding up.

DI Morgan had confided that he believed Matthew Saunders was still hiding something, and Karen had to agree that the man was acting strangely. Although she sensed it was not necessarily related to Emily and Sian's disappearance.

Then they had Sian's uncle, Nick Gibson.

Sian's mother had reacted strongly to the idea Nick had upset her daughter. Had it been more than a disagreement over an iPad? Karen sighed. In her current state, Leanne Gibson was not a reliable source. And apart from Nick's abruptness, Karen hadn't thought there was anything to suggest he was involved in the girls' disappearance.

She wondered if whoever had taken the girls had planned it. Or had Sian and Emily decided to leave school early on their own and then had a chance encounter with a predator?

Karen rubbed her tired eyes as she drove along Lincoln Road. Her house was a large five-bedroom detached on the main road through Branston. It had a long driveway and was set back from the road, so the noise from the traffic wasn't too troublesome.

She indicated and turned into her drive. The security light didn't come on. She groaned. The bulb must have blown, and she didn't have the energy to tackle it tonight. Typical police officer, she thought, dispensing advice but neglecting her own home safety.

She glanced over at the wheelie bins and groaned again. It was bin day tomorrow, and no doubt she'd forget to wheel them up the driveway in the morning so she'd have to do it now.

The night was cold. There would definitely be an overnight frost, and those poor girls were out there somewhere . . . At least she hoped they were still out there.

She brushed her hands together as she walked back towards the house, and was almost at the front door, reaching into a pocket for her keys, when there was a movement beside the holly bush.

Karen's stomach flipped over. She froze. There was somebody there in the darkness. Waiting for her.

She clutched the keys tightly, making sure one poked through her fingers, ready to use it in self-defence if she needed to.

She pulled herself up to full height and called out, 'Who's there?', trying to make her voice sound braver than she felt.

There was a shuffling sound and a blonde-haired figure stepped out from behind the bush. Karen held her breath before relaxing.

'Mary? What are you doing here?'

It was Mary Clarke, the victim of domestic abuse who'd shut the door in Karen's face not long ago. As she got closer, she could see the dried blood on Mary's cheek and her swollen lip.

'It happened again then,' Karen said in a dull voice.

'Yeah. I'm sorry.' Mary's voice sounded brittle. 'I hate to bother you, but I didn't know where else to go. I just couldn't go home.'

Karen sighed. This went against every rule in the book. She should phone the station and get someone to come out and take Mary's statement, get her cleaned up and farmed out to a hostel.

Despite knowing all that, Karen sighed and said, 'I suppose you'd better come in.'

She opened the front door and ushered Mary inside. After asking if she wanted to press charges before destroying any forensic evidence and Mary telling her she did not, Karen showed her the way to the bathroom.

While Mary was having a bath, Karen fixed them both some chicken soup. It was just tinned stuff, but it would have to do. Karen's stomach growled as the smell of the soup filled the air as she stirred the pan. It had been a long time since lunch.

The two women sat down together at the kitchen table.

'It can't go on like this, Mary,' Karen said. She paused with the spoon halfway to her mouth.

Mary wouldn't make eye contact, but she nodded. 'I know.'

'There are only two options. You press charges and get him out of your life, or you end up dead.'

Mary's hand shook, and the spoon clattered down into her bowl. She put one hand over her eyes and sobbed loudly.

Karen got up from the table, leaving her soup behind, and stood beside Mary with her hand resting gently on the woman's shoulder.

'I know you think I'm acting like an unfeeling bitch. But I hate seeing you like this. I want to help, but I can't if you don't let me.'

Mary took in a ragged breath, but she didn't reply.

Once Mary had stopped crying, Karen said, 'Fair enough, it's late, and I have to be up early tomorrow. The bed's made up in the spare room next to the bathroom. I'll leave you the spare key. I need to get going early tomorrow morning. So if you don't stick around, you can put the key back through the letterbox when you leave, okay?'

Mary nodded.

'But I strongly suggest you do not go back home. We can work something out. Get you a place in a women's shelter. A new job. A new life. A life without him.'

When she didn't get a response, Karen took the dishes and washed them in the sink. After she'd set the last dish on the draining board, she turned to see that Mary was now standing.

'Thanks for letting me stay,' Mary said.

'No problem,' Karen said, drying her hands on a tea towel as Mary walked towards the stairs.

Karen rolled her shoulders, trying to ease the ache between them. Sometimes there was so much bad stuff in the world, it felt overwhelming. She wanted to be reminded that most people were good but that wasn't easy in her job.

Her mind was still too alert to sleep, so she made herself a mug of hot chocolate and sat back down at the table, leaning back against the wall, crossing her legs at her ankles and stretching out.

The house was far too big. She and Josh had bought it almost ten years ago, and even then it had been a little big for the three of them. They'd joked about getting a golden retriever and giving the dog its own bedroom. Karen smiled at the memory. But now it was just Karen knocking around all alone. The garden was a ridiculous size as well. They'd bought the house because they'd loved the idea of Tilly running around in the garden having fun, climbing the apple trees and playing in the Wendy house. Karen looked out of the kitchen window. It was pitch black out there, but if she closed her eyes, she could picture her little girl squealing with delight as Josh chased her, spraying her with the garden hose on a magical day in the last summer they'd shared together.

It would be sensible to move somewhere more central, smaller, but she couldn't bring herself to do it for the same reason she didn't want to move away from Lincolnshire. She was scared that any distance she put between herself and her old life would make those precious memories grow fainter and fainter until they disappeared completely.

CHAPTER FIFTEEN

After a restless night's sleep, Karen got up early. She was in the shower by five a.m. and tiptoed around so she didn't wake Mary, who she assumed was asleep in the spare room.

She scrunched a little hairstyling foam through her hair. Fortunately, her dark hair was short and spiky and dried quickly. It was so much more convenient than having to blow-dry it every morning and one of the reasons she kept it short.

She plucked a pair of plain grey trousers from the wardrobe, selected a pale lilac cotton shirt and then shrugged on a grey cardigan. Layered clothing helped keep out the cold, and she'd need the extra warmth today. The weather app on her phone predicted a maximum temperature of six degrees.

She was about to go downstairs when she noticed the spare room door was wide open. She tiptoed across the landing and poked her head around the door. The bed was made up. The bathroom was empty too. There was no sign of Mary. She'd gone.

Karen quickly checked the other bedrooms. Mary had probably gone back home to her so-called partner, the man who beat her up.

'Why?' Karen muttered, hitting the side of her fist on the wall in frustration.

She knew domestic violence situations were complicated. And she was quite sure Mary's partner could be charming when he wanted to be. He probably told her it would never happen again, that he couldn't live without her. They always said that.

She'd offered her a way out on numerous occasions, and Mary had told her that her family was desperate for her to kick him to the kerb. It wasn't as though she didn't have support, but it seemed that wasn't enough.

Irritated and frustrated, Karen stalked away from the spare bedroom and stomped down the stairs.

She'd have to put it out of her mind for now. She needed to get to the station and focus on the case. She'd offered Mary help, but if the woman wasn't ready to accept it there was nothing Karen could do.

But there was something Karen could do for those two little girls.

She considered going straight to work without coffee, and then quickly decided that was a very bad idea. Even a few sips of caffeine would help. She spooned instant coffee into a cup and scrolled through her phone looking at social media, the local news and her emails as she waited for the kettle to boil. No developments had been reported in the press. Of course, that didn't mean the team hadn't uncovered anything new, only that the press hadn't got wind of it yet.

Karen finished making the coffee and took a couple of sips before throwing the rest down the sink. After grabbing her coat and bag, she left the house. It was still dark, and the security light switched on as Karen walked towards her car. It must have been playing up as she was sure it hadn't come on last night. She'd have to get someone in to look at it. Another thing to add to the growing number of jobs waiting for her attention. Her mind was full of the case and her to-do list, so when Christine called out to her over the fence, she jumped.

'Morning, Karen, love. I thought you'd be off early. Here you go.' Christine leaned over the fence that separated their front gardens and held out a thermal cup. 'Filter coffee. The cup keeps it hot.'

Christine was already dressed. She had trouble sleeping for more than five hours a night and was often up very early.

Karen walked over. 'You're an angel, Christine.'

'You just take care of yourself. Don't push too hard.'

Karen smiled. 'I won't.'

'I asked around, and people are talking about those two missing girls as you'd expect.'

'Did anyone see anything unusual?'

She shook her head. 'Nothing. There's the usual gossip, of course.'

'What are people saying?'

Christine pulled a face. 'Mostly moaning about the police. They remember Amy's disappearance and now two little girls have gone missing. People are shaken up by it.'

'That's understandable.' Karen turned away and then stopped. 'Christine, if you see a blonde-haired woman hanging about my place today, could you let her in?'

Christine looked surprised. 'Of course, I've got your spare key.'

She had a spare in case of emergencies and had let the British Gas man into Karen's house in the past, but Karen was aware the unusual circumstances needed explanation.

'Thanks. The woman's name is Mary. She's been a victim of domestic abuse and I've been trying to help her. It's like talking to a brick wall, though. The woman won't see sense.'

'I'll keep an eye out for her.'

'She may not come back.' Karen shrugged. 'And there's no reason to think her abusive partner will turn up here, but I wanted you to be aware of the situation just in case. I'm starting to think she doesn't want my help. It's so frustrating. We could have her in a safe house by now, rebuilding her life.'

Mary was entitled to privacy, but her turning up at Karen's door last night had changed things. Christine deserved to know the score, just in case Mary's good-for-nothing partner showed his face.

Christine smiled sadly. 'I know you want to fix her, but sometimes things can't be fixed. Sometimes all you can do is listen.'

◆ ◆ ◆

The dark Lincolnshire roads were almost empty so the journey up to Nettleham was swift. When Karen was halfway there, the caffeine kicked in and she managed to stop yawning.

It was just before six when she walked into the open office area. Detectives from the night shift looked up from their desks, nodded and muttered good morning. There was no sign of Rick or Sophie yet but she knew they'd be in shortly.

The light was on in DI Morgan's office and Karen walked over and rapped on the door. When she heard his voice, she pushed it open and walked inside.

'Morning. I hope you had a better night's sleep than I did,' she said.

DI Morgan stifled a yawn. 'I doubt it,' he said. 'The briefing won't be until nine.'

'Were there any developments overnight?' Karen asked.

'Numerous phone calls from the public and comments on social media. There was a potential sighting in Cherry Willingham which is being checked out, but I don't think it's going to lead us anywhere. An old lady reported children hanging around in her back garden last night in Heighington, but it turned out to be two teenage boys, who'd decided her shed was the perfect place to experiment with a bit of wacky baccy.'

Karen rolled her eyes. 'Great.'

'Unfortunately, this is what happens when we make an appeal, but we have to hope some of the information we get is worthwhile.'

'I wish there was a way we could sort the wheat from the chaff and make this a bit easier.'

'So do I.'

'I'm going to get myself a coffee from the vending machine,' Karen said. 'The way I'm feeling, I need to keep my caffeine levels topped up. Can I get you anything?'

DI Morgan pulled a face and gestured to the half-empty cup on his desk. 'Thanks, but I don't think I can stomach more just yet. Surely we can get some better-quality coffee in.'

'We used to have a proper machine in the mess room but it broke,' Karen said. 'I'll make a start on sorting through the leads.'

'Great. Last night, I was thinking things over and couldn't get my mind off how oddly Matthew Saunders behaved when we questioned him. We should speak to him again,' DI Morgan said. 'This time on his own. There's something about that man that makes me think he's hiding something.'

'I've got the same feeling about my visit to Nick Gibson,' she said. 'It's hard to judge if he had anything to do with his niece's disappearance, but he was a bit touchy.'

DI Morgan considered this for a moment before saying, 'Okay, we shouldn't rule him out just yet. Let's keep an eye on him.'

Karen agreed. It was too early to count anyone out, especially someone so close to one of the children.

'We'll need someone to speak to the girls' friends and the other children in the class,' DI Morgan said. 'There are twenty-five in Sian and Emily's class. Most of them were spoken to briefly yesterday, but we need to keep digging. They might have seen something or one of the girls might have mentioned something that could be relevant.'

'That's going to take a while.'

DI Morgan nodded. 'It will. But the school's opening today, and I spoke to Jackie Lyons. She's happy for some officers to come in and talk to one child at a time. The complication, of course, is that they need a guardian with them. At half seven, we should start ringing the parents to get their permission. If they're amenable, we can have a teacher present during the interview, or if they want, the parents can come to the school and attend the interview. It's possible some will refuse, but most people should want to cooperate and help as best they can.'

Karen hoped he was right. 'Okay, lots to do. I'll see you at the briefing.'

Karen left DI Morgan's office and walked through the general office space towards the vending machines in the corridor. She selected number twenty-three, white coffee with no sugar, and waited as the machine gurgled into life.

As Karen was waiting, she heard a chirpy voice behind her. 'Morning, Sarge.'

She turned around to see a tired-looking Rick grinning at her.

'Morning,' she said, reaching down to take the coffee out of the dispenser. 'Want one?' she asked, lifting it up.

Rick grimaced. 'No, thanks. I had some at home. Any news?'

They walked together back to the main office area, and Karen filled him in on the plans for the day.

'I've never been very good with kids,' Rick said, wrinkling his nose as he shrugged off his coat and flung it over the back of his chair. 'Are we going to go over the questions beforehand?'

Karen nodded. 'Yes, we'll do it after the briefing.' She blew over the top of her coffee before taking a sip.

'It was a cold one last night,' Rick said. 'It's horrible to think of those girls out there.'

Karen nodded. 'Well, we've got lots of leads to work on today. A whole heap of sightings have been reported. Bob McKenzie's coordinating the lines of enquiry. So you can get a bunch of paperwork from him and rule them out one by one. You should get through quite a few before the briefing.'

'Righto,' Rick said cheerfully, turning away and walking off to find Bob.

Sophie came in fifteen minutes later, and Karen gave her an update. She was pleased to see Sophie was a little more eager than Rick to take part in the questioning of the children from Moore Lane School.

Just before eight o'clock, the duty sergeant rushed into the office area. His cheeks were red, and he seemed out of breath.

'I've been trying to get through to DI Morgan,' he said, looking at Karen.

Karen turned, looked over her shoulder and saw the boss was on the phone in his office. 'If it's an urgent call you can redirect it to my line.'

'It's not a call. I've got a woman downstairs. She's a teacher at Washingborough Primary School.'

Washingborough was a village less than a mile away from Heighington. Karen waited for him to continue.

'She wants to talk to somebody about the missing girls. It turns out she thinks she saw a man hanging around her school yesterday, about lunchtime.'

Karen raised her eyebrows and stood up. 'And she's still downstairs now?'

'I showed her into interview room two. I thought you'd want to speak to her. You or DI Morgan.'

'I do. Thanks very much.'

Karen issued a few instructions to Rick and then scribbled a note for DI Morgan before walking into his office and sliding the note on to his desk.

He picked up the piece of paper and scanned it. It appeared to be an important phone call because he nodded and gestured for her to continue without him.

She grabbed her phone from her desk along with a notepad and pen and strode out of the office, along the corridor and then down the stairs to meet the teacher.

CHAPTER SIXTEEN

Karen opened the door to the interview room and found a nervous-looking woman sitting at the table. She had frizzy light brown hair, the type of curls that were impossible to tame.

She looked up at Karen as she entered the room.

'I understand you're a teacher at Washingborough Primary,' Karen said, offering her hand. 'I'm Detective Sergeant Karen Hart.'

The woman reached over the table to shake Karen's hand. 'You're working on the case of the missing girls from Heighington?'

Karen nodded and slid into a seat. 'That's right. What's your full name?'

'Tessa Grimes. I wasn't sure whether to get in touch. I didn't hear about what happened yesterday until early this morning when I checked Facebook, then I saw the email from our head teacher.' Tessa ran a hand through her unruly hair. 'The thing is, you always have to be on your guard these days, and it might be of no importance but I couldn't live with myself if I didn't tell you about it.'

'Of course,' Karen said, nodding encouragingly. 'You were right to come to the station. What exactly did you see?'

'Well, I didn't see much at all. I was on playground duty and one of the children came up and said that another pupil was at the front of the school, talking to a man. By the time I got there, he'd spotted me and started walking across the street. I don't think it was anything sinister but you do worry these days.'

'Which pupil was he talking to?'

'A year five pupil called Rachel Macintosh. I talked to her afterwards, of course. She didn't seem distressed at all and said the man was just after the time.'

'Why was Rachel at the front of the school?'

'Well, I'm not sure if you're familiar with Washingborough Primary, but there's a playground, and a bit of grass that leads down to the front. The children often play there. There are railings and gates, so the children can't get out. I don't think Rachel was ever in any danger. I spoke to our head teacher about the incident, and we were going to send a letter out to the parents today. So that everyone's on their guard. It can't hurt to be too careful.'

'I agree. Could you tell me what this man looked like?'

Tessa pulled a face. 'To be honest, I didn't get a very good look at him. I can't give you a good description. A couple of things that did stand out were his bright red hair and that he was very tall.'

Karen felt her pulse rate spike. 'Red hair?'

Tessa nodded. 'Yes, a vivid red. Very noticeable.'

'Could you estimate how old he was?'

'Let me see. I'd say he was probably mid-thirties, maybe a bit older.'

Karen leaned forward eagerly. 'This is really helpful. Thank you. Now, do you think Rachel and her parents would be happy with us talking to her this morning? Just to see if she can describe him or if he said anything else to her?'

'I'm sure they'd be more than willing to help. Everybody's probably heard about the poor missing girls by now. If it helps them get them home safely, I'm sure they'd be pleased to help.' Tessa put her palms flat on the table and studied the back of her hands. 'You just don't think this sort of thing could happen in our neck of the woods.'

'It is very rare,' Karen said. 'But it's good that you're alert. It's probably a good idea to stop the children playing near the gates.'

'You're right. I can't bear to think of one of our children being taken.'

Karen asked Tessa a few more questions, making careful notes. 'What time did this happen?'

'It was about twelve forty-five yesterday. The children were in the playground for their lunch break.'

Karen noted down the time. Had the same man who talked to Rachel then gone on to snatch Emily and Sian a few hours later? Or had they snuck away from school early and come across this red-headed predator?

Karen wrapped things up with Tessa Grimes and thanked her for her time. Tessa had given her the mobile number for Sarah Macintosh, Rachel Macintosh's mother.

Karen could barely wait to get out of the interview room and back to the office to inform DI Morgan of what she had uncovered. This could be the best lead they'd had so far.

Back in the shared office area, Karen grinned at Rick and walked up to his desk.

'You're looking pleased with yourself, Sarge,' Rick said. 'I take it that teacher had something useful to tell us.'

'She did indeed, Rick. She told me there was a man spotted at the gates of Washingborough Primary School yesterday lunchtime. That was just a few hours before Emily and Sian went missing.'

Rick nodded eagerly. 'Did you get a description?'

'The teacher didn't get a good look at him, but one thing she did say is that he had red hair.'

Rick let out a slow whistle. 'You're thinking of the Palmers again, aren't you?'

Karen shrugged. 'I'm not jumping to any conclusions. But Jasper Palmer does have bright red hair.'

Rick nodded slowly and widened his eyes. 'What did DI Morgan say?'

'I haven't spoken to him yet,' Karen said. 'I've got a job for you first. Are you familiar with Washingborough?'

Rick shook his head. 'I think I've passed through once or twice. But I don't know it well.'

'Well, the school is opposite the Co-op and thanks to a ram raid on the cashpoint last year, they've upgraded their CCTV system.'

A broad grin spread across Rick's face. 'So you're thinking we might have CCTV footage covering the school gates.'

'Exactly. With any luck, we'll be able to tell if it was Jasper Palmer. So I want you to get hold of the CCTV and go through the footage.'

Rick reached for his phone. 'Not a problem. I'll get straight on it.'

Karen gave him a thumbs-up and headed to DI Morgan's office to fill him in.

'Rick's looking into the CCTV footage now,' she told him. 'I'll ask Sophie if she'll give him a hand. I'm planning to go and talk to Sarah Macintosh and her little girl Rachel. She was the one who got the best look at him, so she might be able to give us a better description of the red-headed man. At the very least, we should be able to find out what he said to her, and that could reveal whether there's a link between the man talking to Rachel at the school gates and Emily and Sian disappearing a couple of hours later.'

DI Morgan nodded and threw his pen down on the desk. 'Excellent. This could be the breakthrough we need. If he was disturbed and wasn't able to abduct Rachel perhaps he went on to Heighington and Emily and Sian weren't quite so fortunate.'

'Do we have enough manpower to assign the interviews of the Heighington primary pupils to other officers?' Karen asked, remembering their original plan for the morning.

'Yes, it shouldn't be a problem.'

'I'll speak to the school now, then give Sarah Macintosh a call. After that, with your permission, sir, I'd like to put some pressure on Jasper Palmer.'

DI Morgan hesitated and then shook his head. He leaned back in his chair. 'I think it might be a bit soon. We should wait until the CCTV images come through. We can plan a strategy after that.'

Karen wanted to argue. She wanted to explain that when dealing with people like Nigel and Jasper Palmer you needed to turn up the heat, but she knew that wasn't the way DI Morgan operated. He liked logical, sensible procedural work based on evidence not gut feelings.

Karen managed to swallow her protests and nodded. 'Okay. That makes sense. I'll arrange to talk to the little girl and her mother and then we'll see what we get from the CCTV.'

'I think that's the best course of action,' DI Morgan said, and when Karen was almost at the door, he looked up and said, 'Good work, DS Hart.'

Karen smiled over her shoulder and then disappeared out into the office area to call Sarah Macintosh.

Karen drummed her fingers impatiently against her desk as she waited for Rachel Macintosh's mother to answer her mobile. After the first call rang out, Karen punched in the number again, and this time the phone was picked up on the third ring.

'Hello?' a female voice answered, sounding somewhat harassed.

'Hello, is that Mrs Macintosh?'

'It is, but if you're selling something, I'm not interested. I'm trying to get my daughter ready for school.'

'I'm not selling anything. My name is Detective Sergeant Karen Hart, and I'm calling from Nettleham Police Headquarters.'

Karen's words were met with a stunned silence on the other end of the phone, so she continued. 'I apologise for calling you so early, but I hoped to have a word with you and your daughter Rachel this morning.'

'Rachel? Whatever for?'

'Yesterday, when Rachel was at school, a man approached the school gates and spoke to your daughter. I believe Tessa Grimes, one of the teachers, told you what happened.'

'Yes, but it was nothing serious. Rachel said the man just asked what the time was. I mean, it did sound a bit odd, but do you really think she needs to talk to the police about it? I've given her the talk again about stranger danger and warned her not to talk to anyone hanging around outside the school.'

'I'm not sure if you're aware of the two little girls who went missing from their school in Heighington yesterday afternoon?'

Karen heard the woman's sharp intake of breath. 'No! I hadn't heard. God, how awful. Do you think it was the man Rachel was . . .?'

'We don't know. It's possible that it was a completely innocent encounter, but considering what happened just a few miles away a couple of hours later, we'd like to speak to Rachel. Of course, we'd like you to be present, and we're not going to do or say anything to upset Rachel.'

'Absolutely. I understand. When do you want to talk to Rachel?'

'As soon as possible. I wanted to ask where you think Rachel would be more comfortable. I could come to your house, or I could talk to her at school.'

There was silence as Sarah Macintosh thought for a moment and then she said, 'I think it might be better at school. If that's okay with you?'

'No problem. I could be at the school in about half an hour.'

'Okay.'

'Great, I'll see you soon. Thank you for your help.'

Karen hung up and called Tessa Grimes on her mobile.

'Hello?' The sound of traffic made her voice sound distant.

'Hi, Tessa, it's DS Hart.'

'Did I forget something?'

'No, I'm sorry to bother you again so soon. Were you driving?'

'Yes, but I've pulled into a lay-by. What is it?'

'I've just spoken to Rachel's mother, and she believes that Rachel would feel more comfortable talking to me at the school. I hoped we could meet her there in thirty minutes.'

'I suppose that would be all right, but we're not supposed to let students in early . . . You know, insurance reasons and all that.'

'This is very important, Tessa.'

'Yes, of course it is. Sorry, I'm sure it won't matter just this once.'

Karen put the phone down and felt a thrill of excitement. They were getting somewhere. If Rachel could identify the man at the school gates as Jasper Palmer, with any luck, Sian Gibson and Emily Dean's disappearance as well as Amy Fisher's eighteen-month-old missing person's case could be put to bed once and for all.

CHAPTER SEVENTEEN

Karen reached Washingborough Primary School in twenty-five minutes. She'd left the station in a rush, leaving DI Morgan to pass the news on to the superintendent.

Tessa Grimes waited for her at the entrance and smiled as Karen approached. She opened the big double doors. 'The head teacher's in her office if you'd like a chat beforehand?' Tessa suggested, closing the doors behind them.

Karen thanked her and said that was a good idea. It would help to talk to another teacher and get more information, and she was still a little early for her interview with Sarah Macintosh and Rachel.

Tessa showed her to the head's office and then excused herself, saying she was going to keep an eye out for Rachel and her mother to arrive.

The head teacher was younger than Karen had expected. With her sober black suit, slicked-back dark hair and pale make-up, Karen thought she looked like a character out of *The Matrix*.

The head stood up from behind the desk and held out her hand towards Karen. 'I'm Eleanor Trent,' she said. 'I was very concerned when Tessa told me about the incident yesterday. It's horrifying to think it could be related to the two girls going missing in Heighington.'

'Well, we don't know that for sure yet,' Karen said. 'That's why I wanted to talk to Rachel Macintosh.'

Miss Trent gestured to the chair in front of the desk. 'Please, sit down.'

Karen sat on the upholstered chair.

'We drafted a letter for all the children to take home.' Miss Trent pushed forward a sheet of paper.

Karen picked it up and quickly read the contents. It was a generic letter, full of warnings reminding parents that children must be aware of the risks of talking to strangers, with a paragraph at the end mentioning that a man had been seen hanging around the school gates.

Karen put the paper back on the desk. 'I think it's a good idea for parents to be alert.'

'Absolutely.' Eleanor Trent cleared her throat. 'The incident was concerning enough to prepare the letters, but it didn't strike me as anything too sinister at the time, and Rachel didn't seem distressed.' She frowned. 'Perhaps I should have done more, but I didn't want to overreact. I remember some years ago the police had a unit that visited schools to advise children on the dangers of talking to people they don't know. Do you provide anything like that?'

'We can definitely arrange that. There are officers assigned to go to schools on a rota, so I'll have a word and see if they can bump you up the queue.'

Miss Trent smiled. 'Thank you.' She glanced at the clock on her wall and said, 'I thought you could talk to Rachel in the staffroom. All the classrooms will be occupied. I've advised the teachers not to use the room because I didn't want you to feel you had to rush your conversation. We only have six teachers so it's not a huge space, but I think it'll be suitable for your purposes.'

She stood up and Karen did the same.

'Thank you.'

'Can I get you a coffee or tea?'

Karen shook her head. 'No, thanks.'

She followed the head teacher out of the office. The staffroom was a little further up the corridor on the right, and when Karen entered, she saw the head teacher had been right. It was small. There was an area for preparing coffee and tea; a little table; a rigid, uncomfortable-looking sofa; and two upholstered chairs that looked a little faded and tatty.

Once she was alone in the staffroom, Karen set about arranging the chairs so she'd be able to sit facing Rachel and her mother. She'd just moved one of the upholstered chairs to the left of the coffee table when the door opened.

It was Tessa Grimes, and behind her was a short, brown-haired lady, clutching the hand of a little girl.

They entered the room, and Tessa introduced them as Sarah and Rachel Macintosh. Karen smiled and made sure she kept her tone light as she asked them both to sit down.

Tessa said, 'If you don't need me any more, Detective, I'll get back to my classroom.'

'I'm sure we'll be fine, thank you.'

Tessa smiled. 'If you need anything before you go, the school secretary will help you. Her office is next door to the head teacher's.'

Karen thanked her again and then settled down into a chair and looked at Rachel and her mother. They looked terrified, which under the circumstances was certainly understandable.

'I just want to start by saying Rachel is here to help us. Nobody's going to get in any trouble, and anything you remember, however small you think it is, could help us. So it's important you tell me everything you remember.'

Sarah Macintosh gave Rachel a small nudge, and the child nodded.

Sarah had pale skin and light brown hair styled into a bob. Her eyebrows were so carefully arched that Karen suspected she must have drawn them on, or maybe had them tattooed. Rachel had the same shade of hair as her mother, but hers was long, halfway down her back.

She wore one pink clip pulling the top section of her fringe away from her forehead. Her skin was pale and tiny freckles dotted her nose.

'Did your mother tell you why I wanted to speak to you, Rachel?'

Rachel shook her head.

Her mother gave an exasperated sigh. 'Yes, I did. We talked about it on the way here.'

'I know, but I don't understand why she wants to talk to me,' Rachel muttered.

'I want to talk to you, Rachel, because you were the one who spoke to the man at the gate, and you got a good look at him. It's not because you're in any trouble, do you understand?'

Rachel nodded slowly.

'Have you seen the man before?'

Rachel shook her head.

'Did he tell you his name or ask for your name?'

'No, he just asked me what the time was.'

'And what did you say?'

'I told him I didn't know. It was lunchtime, but I don't have a watch.'

'Did he say anything else?'

Rachel hesitated and shot a sideways glance at her mother before replying, 'He said I had pretty hair.'

Sarah Macintosh smothered a gasp, and Karen could understand her reaction. The comment, a nice compliment under any other circumstances, had made her own skin crawl.

'Thank you, Rachel. That's really helpful. Now, can you remember what he looked like?'

The child chewed on her lower lip and swung her legs on the chair. Her shoes hit the wooden chair legs with a dull thud.

'Stop that, Rachel,' her mother said sharply.

'He was quite tall, and he had the same colour hair as Gillian.'

'Gillian?'

Sarah Macintosh removed her arm from her daughter's shoulders and reached down into her bag. 'Gillian is Rachel's cousin. My sister's daughter. I think I have a picture in my purse.'

A few seconds passed while Sarah Macintosh rummaged in her bag before pulling out an oversized black purse.

She unclipped it and one section fell forward, releasing a credit card holder jam-packed with photographs. She selected one and held it out for Karen to take a look.

'That's Gillian on the left.'

Karen looked at the pretty child. Her hair was a beautiful flame red but that wasn't what had made Karen's throat tighten. Her hair was exactly the same colour as Jasper Palmer's.

'Can you tell me anything else about his appearance?' Karen asked.

Rachel shook her head and said nothing.

'What colour were his eyes?' Sarah Macintosh asked, turning to her daughter.

'I . . . I don't remember.'

'What about the clothes he was wearing?' Karen prompted.

'He had on a long brown coat,' Rachel said. 'It was like the one Dad used to have when he went shooting.'

Sarah Macintosh explained. 'I think she means a wax jacket. You know the cape-like ones.'

Karen nodded. If necessary, they could show Rachel some photographs of various coats and see if she could pick one that resembled it.

'That's very helpful. Well done, Rachel.'

'What did he do to those other girls?' Rachel asked. 'Was it the same man?'

Sarah Macintosh looked horrified that her daughter had picked up on why they were so interested in the man she had spoken to yesterday.

'We don't know that yet, but we're trying to find out. That's why your description of him has been so helpful.' Karen smiled, and Rachel seemed to relax a little.

'Now, have you remembered anything else? Perhaps he asked you some questions?'

Rachel's eyes widened, and she shook her head firmly. 'No, he didn't say anything else.'

'Are you absolutely sure, Rachel? This is important,' her mother said.

Rachel's hands were on her lap and she twisted her fingers. 'I can't remember. I don't think so.'

'Well, you've been brilliant this morning, Rachel. Thank you very much.'

Rachel raised her head. 'Is that it? Is it finished?'

Karen nodded. 'Do you know where you're supposed to be now or shall I speak to the school secretary?'

As she spoke, the school bell rang out, and they heard the sound of a hundred children filing through the corridors.

Rachel got out of her seat, looking relieved. 'I know where my classroom is.'

Sarah Macintosh took her daughter to class, and Karen hastily gathered her things.

After stopping briefly to put her head around the school secretary's office door to tell her she was leaving, Karen headed quickly outside. She was eager to get back to the station and start gathering the evidence to tighten the net around Jasper Palmer.

If it were up to her, she'd head straight to the Palmer family farm now and bring him in. She couldn't wait see that smug smile wiped off his face.

Cathy Palmer sat at the table in the farmhouse kitchen. In front of her, spread out protecting the surface, were sheets from the local newspaper, and she was getting started on her favourite task. There weren't many household chores she enjoyed but cleaning the family silver had always felt like a treat. She remembered her mother doing it when she was young and she'd let Cathy help.

She dabbed a little polish on the soft cloth and began to buff the silver. It was a repetitive, meditative task and Cathy soon relaxed. Her father's breathing was steady as he slept beside the fire, and for once, Cathy could enjoy some peace and quiet. She still had an hour or two before she had to make a start on the next meal, and her father usually slept for an hour at a time, so he wouldn't be making demands for a while yet.

She steadily made her way through the items of silver, paying particular attention to the picture frames. There was a photograph of Cathy's grandparents, who'd run the farm before her father had taken over. She could barely remember them, even though they'd lived in the farmhouse when Cathy was a small child.

It all seemed like such a long time ago, a happier time. She thought of them as the good years, when her mother was still around and her father still smiled occasionally.

Cathy put down the cloth and pulled the old silver locket from beneath her clothing. She always wore it around her neck, discreetly hidden by high-necked blouses or jumpers. She didn't like to take it off.

Despite the fact that her father was almost certainly asleep, judging by his soft snores, Cathy didn't dare open the locket downstairs. She gave it a quick polish and was about to tuck it back beneath her blouse when her father gave a loud, startled snort and jerked in his sleep, knocking over a cup that had been sitting on the small coffee table beside him. It fell to the floor and smashed.

He turned the air blue with his swearing, and Cathy quickly got to her feet and rushed over to help.

'It's fine. It's just a cup,' she said. 'I'll clear it up and get you another cup of tea.'

'Why did you put it so close to the edge, you stupid girl?'

Cathy braced herself for more harsh words, and then she realised her father had gone strangely silent as she picked up the shards of the cup. Puzzled, she looked up and realised with horror he was staring at the locket dangling around her neck.

Before Cathy could react, he reached forward and grabbed the locket with a sharp yank, breaking the chain around her neck. He moved quickly for an old man who couldn't walk unassisted any more.

Cathy's heart was thundering in her chest as she waited for him to get started. He couldn't deliver the beatings any more, he was too weak for that, but she could still be a victim of his verbal abuse, and sometimes she thought that was worse.

She held her breath as his gnarled old fingers prised the locket open.

When he saw the photograph of her mother, his face screwed up. 'I told you to get rid of all the photographs,' he said through gritted teeth, and then to Cathy's dismay, he threw the locket into the fire.

She got to her feet, grabbed a poker and used it to search through the flaming pieces of wood. He laughed at her desperate attempts to retrieve the last photograph she had of her mother.

Eventually, she managed to hook the chain around the poker and flick the locket out. Glad it was safe, she reached for it, not considering the heat. She felt a searing pain as the hot metal branded the centre of her palm.

She cried out and dropped it, which only made her father laugh harder.

A sudden flash of anger overwhelmed her, and she gripped the handle of the poker, tempted to thrust the scalding metal into her father's chest and silence him once and for all.

CHAPTER EIGHTEEN

As Karen walked back to her car, she reminded herself to curb her enthusiasm. Both the superintendent and DI Morgan suspected she had an unhealthy interest in the Palmer family. Karen didn't agree. It was only that she cared deeply about this investigation. And even if Jasper Palmer hadn't been related to the Amy Fisher disappearance, she'd still have viewed him as a potential suspect in this case.

The super might talk about the dangers of being over-invested or emotionally attached, but Karen didn't believe it was possible to care too much. Something had happened to those two little girls. And something had happened to Amy Fisher. Unless the people who cared pushed hard to get to the truth, the culprit would get away with it. Over her dead body, Karen thought as she got behind the wheel of her Honda Civic. She was about to start the engine when her mobile rang. It was Rick.

'Rick, any news?'

'Hey, boss, I've got a result from the CCTV.'

Karen's fingers tightened around her mobile, and she held her breath waiting for him to continue.

'Don't get too excited. The CCTV captured a man at Washingborough Primary. But it only shows him from the back for the most part. For just a second, we get a glimpse of him from the side. It's definitely a man. He's tall and slim and he's got red hair. But I'm not sure we can ID him from the CCTV.'

Karen was silent as she processed the information. It wasn't the end of the world. They still had Tessa's account as well as Rachel's description. As far as Karen was concerned, that was good enough. They should bring Jasper Palmer in and apply some pressure.

'Are you still there, Sarge?'

'Yes,' Karen said. 'Listen, Rachel backed up what Tessa Grimes said. She got a really good look at him, so she might be able to ID him.'

She heard Rick suck his breath in through his teeth. 'You know that never goes down well, though, Sarge. A child ID won't be popular.'

'I know. But we could try Tessa Grimes first with a photograph of Jasper. We could show her a photographic ID parade.'

Rick sighed. 'Maybe that would work. Did Rachel give us anything else?'

'She confirmed he was wearing a brown coat and from the sound of it, it's some kind of hunting jacket, so that's something we can look into.'

'Right, that gives us something to go on. Are you coming back here, boss?'

'I am. Give me ten minutes, and we'll get together and talk this over.'

'Okay. Sorry I couldn't give you better news.'

'Don't worry, Rick. I think we're getting somewhere now. The CCTV images might not be enough on their own, but there are a lot of signs pointing to Jasper Palmer.'

'Yeah, boss. Look, about that . . .'

Karen frowned as she heard a muffled scratching sound on the phone, as though Rick had picked up his mobile and was moving with it. When he spoke again, his voice had more of an echo. She suspected he'd taken the call out into the corridor.

'This is probably none of my business, and you're not going to thank me for saying this but I'm going to say it anyway.'

'Go on,' Karen said.

'Well, it's just all this talk of Jasper Palmer. I understand he's a suspect – and don't get me wrong, I think he's a creepy bastard. But I know DI Morgan's getting worried about the fact you're continually focusing on the Palmers.'

Karen's first reaction was anger. If DI Morgan had mentioned anything to Rick about this, then that was pretty underhanded. She'd expected more of him than that.

'I don't like the idea of DI Morgan talking to you about how well I'm performing at my job.' To all intents and purposes, Karen was Rick's boss.

'No, don't take it like that. He hasn't said anything directly, but I can read the signs. Both he and the super are worried you're getting obsessed.'

'Obsessed?'

'Well, they didn't say obsessed in so many words. But they're concerned you might be a little bit blinkered, or biased. Anyway, I just thought I'd give you a heads-up, a bit of a warning.'

'You've worked with me for a long time, Rick. I do things by the book. I wouldn't rush into something without the evidence to back it up, but you have to admit Jasper Palmer looks mighty suspicious at the moment.'

'I agree.'

'So what's the problem?'

'Well, it's just you bring his name up a lot. Not just Jasper but the Palmer family, and I know you think they were somehow involved in Amy Fisher's disappearance.'

'I'd bet a lot of money on it, Rick.'

'Exactly. You're convinced they're guilty of that and so your history with the Palmers is influencing the way you're looking at this case.'

'So, I'm just supposed to ignore the fact that a man matching Jasper Palmer's description was seen a couple of hours before the girls went missing talking to another young girl outside a primary school?'

Rick groaned. 'I shouldn't have said anything. Look, I didn't mean to say you weren't doing your job properly. Please don't think that.'

'It's quite hard not to when you say things like that, Rick.' Karen took a deep breath and then said, 'I'm coming back to the station now. We'll discuss it there.'

She hung up, shoved her phone back in her bag and glared at it.

Rick was being ridiculous. She wasn't obsessed with the Palmers at all, but it was hard to ignore the possibility they were involved.

Nigel Palmer was weak and infirm, but maybe he had his son doing his dirty work. It had always puzzled Karen how Amy Fisher, a strong, healthy nineteen-year-old, could have been overpowered by a man like Nigel Palmer. Eighteen months ago, he hadn't been as ill as he was now, but it was still a conundrum.

She'd considered the possibility that Amy had been drugged, but now she strongly suspected Nigel wasn't acting alone. Perhaps the son shared his father's sick obsession with young girls. Perhaps Jasper acted as the muscle, and Nigel Palmer was the brains behind the operation.

She didn't enjoy Rick talking to her like that, but she appreciated his candour. She'd have to be on her guard now when talking to DI Morgan and the superintendent. She couldn't take the risk of getting shunted off this case. Not if it was her chance to bring the Palmers down once and for all.

◆ ◆ ◆

Fortunately the traffic was light and Karen made good time getting back to Nettleham HQ. She'd given herself a talking-to in the car. She'd play it cool and not give away any signs that she was desperate to haul Jasper Palmer in for questioning.

DI Morgan was an excellent officer. Karen had no reason to believe he wouldn't come to the same conclusion as she had about the Palmers. She just needed to bide her time and not lose her temper.

She was striding along the third-floor corridor towards the office when one of the doors opened and Rick stuck his head out.

'Sarge, we're in here.'

They were in AV room one, where the audiovisual equipment included several large computers and playback devices as well as other technical gadgetry.

DI Morgan and Sophie were already seated around a computer screen. Karen and Rick joined them. They were looking at CCTV images taken from the recording. Rick reached for the mouse and began flicking through the freeze-frames.

Karen leaned forward, her fingers gripping the back of Sophie's chair. The images weren't great quality. They were a bit dark and grainy and the colours were unsaturated. It was clear the man captured on the CCTV had red hair, but Karen had to admit it didn't appear quite as bright red as Jasper Palmer's. Judging his height in relation to the school gates, he looked a little shorter than Jasper Palmer. Karen's stomach dropped. Maybe he was slouching?

'Do you get a view of his face at all?' Karen asked.

Rick peered at the computer screen and clicked on the mouse, scrolling through the images until he had one of the man in profile.

It wasn't good enough. Rick had been correct. There was no way they could identify Jasper Palmer from this.

Disappointment curled up and sank like a stone in Karen's stomach. But this didn't mean it was the end of the road. They still had descriptions from Tessa and Rachel, and if they could get an identification that way, it would be good enough.

'How did you get on with Rachel Macintosh?' DI Morgan asked.

'Good. She was a bit subdued, but I think it was just the stress of the situation. Plus, of course, her mother was very worried and that can always rub off on children.'

DI Morgan nodded thoughtfully. 'The suspect didn't say anything to Rachel?'

'He asked her the time and told her she had pretty hair.'

Sophie shivered. 'That's a bit creepy.'

'And did the teacher remember anything else?'

Karen shook her head. 'She got a brief glance but didn't speak to him. She knows he's got red hair.' Karen turned and looked back at the CCTV image. 'It could be him.'

The words slipped out before she could stop them. So much for playing it cool.

DI Morgan narrowed his eyes. 'You mean Jasper Palmer?'

Karen took a deep breath and turned to face her boss. 'That's right.'

She was starting to push her luck. The last thing she wanted was DI Morgan thinking she was unstable, but she had to make him see there was a strong possibility that Jasper Palmer had abducted the girls. But maybe she *was* looking for patterns when there were none to be found. Sound judgement was so important for a police officer and before the accident Karen had never doubted her own. She'd been wrong to think there was something sinister behind the car crash that killed Josh and Tilly. Was she wrong now too?

DI Morgan looked back at the image. 'The man's hair looks darker than Jasper's. Almost auburn in this picture.'

Karen considered his point. 'But the picture quality is terrible. Look at the colour of the grass. That looks dark too. Besides, he could have some gel on his hair or something. Maybe it was wet. Had it been raining?' Karen tried to think back to yesterday lunchtime.

DI Morgan shook his head. 'It was cloudy and overcast, but it wasn't raining.'

'Look, I think we should invest some manpower in searching the Palmers' property. They have numerous outbuildings and barns scattered all over their land. It can't hurt to take a good look.' She caught a glance pass between DI Morgan and Rick, and Karen felt her temper build. Did they think she'd lost perspective on this case? Maybe she had. There was no hard evidence pointing to Nigel Palmer or his son so why couldn't she let it go? The looks on their faces reminded Karen she still hadn't booked an appointment with her counsellor.

Sophie seemed the only one who hadn't picked up on the tension. She shrugged. 'The Palmers have provided keys every time we've asked them. All their outbuildings have been included in the search.'

Karen noticed she was wringing her hands and shoved them in the pockets of her trousers. 'Don't you think it's a coincidence that Jasper Palmer was the one who found the glove? On his land? I can't help feeling he's laughing at us. Playing some kind of sick game. We should bring him in.'

DI Morgan grimaced. 'It's too soon. If he's involved, we don't want the rest of the family panicking and hiding evidence. We'll talk to him, though.'

'Great,' Karen said. 'We should talk to him as soon as possible. Afterwards, we can show a picture of Jasper to Tessa Grimes. Hopefully she can identify him, so we don't have to rely on Rachel Macintosh's ID.'

'Right, you try and track him down. He could be working anywhere on the farm today.'

Back at her desk, Karen located the number for the Palmer farm. There was every chance Jasper had his mobile on him while working in the fields, but Karen didn't have his number.

She dialled the farmhouse, and on the fourth ring a female voice answered.

'Hello, Cathy, is that you? This is DS Karen Hart.'

There was a pause on the line before Cathy answered. Her voice sounded reedy and thin. 'Yes, is something wrong?'

'I need to speak to Jasper, Cathy. It's important, and I wondered if you could tell me where he's working today.'

Again there was a long pause. 'I'm sorry. I'd like to help. But Jasper doesn't like the police and he'd be angry if he knew I was talking to you.'

Karen leaned back in her chair. 'I know that Jasper and your father have had difficulties with the police in the past, but this isn't just about them, Cathy. It's about the two little girls that went missing. It's really important I talk to him.'

Cathy said nothing.

Karen tried another tack. 'Do you have Jasper's mobile number? Does he have his phone with him today?'

'I couldn't give you that. Jasper would be furious.'

Karen wanted to shake some sense into the woman. Did she really allow her father and brother to dictate her every move?

'Okay, Cathy. Either you tell me where Jasper is today, or I'll have to come to the farmhouse and sit there until he comes home.'

'I want to help, but he's going to be so angry.'

'You don't have much choice, Cathy. Either you tell me where he is and Jasper is angry with you. Or you don't tell me where he is, I turn up at the farmhouse, and when Jasper gets home, he'll be angry with you anyway.'

Cathy let out a shaky little noise and Karen felt a pang of guilt. But she pushed those feelings away. She was bullying Cathy, but she had to. If getting Jasper to talk meant they were closer to getting those two girls back and finding out what happened to them, then it was worth upsetting Cathy Palmer.

'Okay, he's cutting back hedges again, this time at the edge of Washingborough. He could be in any of the four fields along Tranmere Lane.'

'Thanks, Cathy. You've been really helpful. And I promise I won't tell Jasper you told me he was there. I'll make it look like we happened to find him ourselves, okay?'

'Oh, thank you!' Cathy sounded so pathetically grateful that Karen suffered a second pang of guilt as she hung up.

CHAPTER NINETEEN

Cathy had been telling the truth. They found Jasper in the third field they passed along Tranmere Lane. The wide, open sky was crystal blue, and without cloud cover the temperature had plummeted.

DI Morgan was driving one of the fleet cars, and when Karen pointed out the green tractor with a large red cutting attachment, DI Morgan slowed the car to a crawl. The tractor was easy enough to spot from the road but it was hard to make out who was operating the machine.

DI Morgan stopped the car in a layby beside the grass verge. Karen was determined to stand back and let him lead the questioning. She planned to watch Jasper Palmer like a hawk for any telltale signs he was lying or hiding something.

Due to Rick's comments earlier, she was starting to feel paranoid. Perhaps she was letting her desire to bring down Nigel Palmer get in the way of good, steady police work.

They waved at the tractor, but the driver was either oblivious to them standing on the other side of the hedgerow or simply determined to ignore them. The rumble of the engine meant he couldn't hear them calling out to him either.

DI Morgan pointed out a gap in the recently shorn hedge a short distance away and they made their way towards it. The tufts of grass were slick and the ground was bumpy as they navigated the verge but they finally made it through the hedgerow, Karen wincing as she scratched her hand on a sharp thorn.

The hedge was a native mixed hedgerow, a jumble of spiky hawthorn and blackthorn, entwined with hazel and some other plants Karen didn't recognise.

Once past the hedge, they trudged along a strip of uncultivated land that skirted the recently ploughed earth in the field. The long grass clung to Karen's ankles and soaked the bottom of her trousers. DI Morgan strode ahead of her towards the tractor, waving his arms to attract the occupant's attention.

Karen felt a smile tug on her lips when she saw it was indeed Jasper Palmer operating the controls. He didn't look very happy to see them.

Her contentment was short-lived. Ahead of her, DI Morgan let out a startled cry. At first, she thought he'd been hurt. Traps were outlawed, but two years ago she'd seen the aftermath when some poor chap's leg had been mangled in an illegal animal trap.

But then she saw what had made DI Morgan jump with fright and inappropriate laughter bubbled up in her throat.

She heard the familiar squawking alarm call and then saw a jumble of reddish-brown feathers flapping in front of them. They'd startled a pheasant. There were plenty around here. Karen even had one that roosted in her garden. She lived beside an open field, and the male pheasant – she'd named him Peter – liked to roost in the lime tree in her garden. He always made his way home at dusk. Last year, Karen had been worried about Peter. She hadn't seen him for a while, and when she'd mown the grass before the start of winter, she'd been horrified to find some long tail feathers. Fearing the worst, Karen had assumed he'd been eaten by a fox or maybe an overly large farm cat. Christine had found Karen's reaction very funny and kindly informed her that male pheasants shed their tail feathers and it was nothing to worry about.

Sure enough, the next evening at dusk, Peter had squawked and ambled his way happily across the garden to his usual roosting spot.

Karen had grown quite fond of him, but from the way DI Morgan was now glaring at the pheasant scurrying away towards the open field, she guessed he didn't feel the same about this particular bird.

'Did it startle you, sir?' Karen asked, unable to resist a grin.

'I think the fact I nearly jumped a foot in the air was a pretty good indication that it did startle me, thank you, DS Hart.' To his credit, he returned her grin.

'Looks like Cathy was right,' Karen said, nodding at the cab of the tractor where Jasper sat scowling behind the windscreen.

DI Morgan gestured for him to cut the engine and climb down.

Slowly, and with a sulky expression, Jasper did as he asked. He opened the small door to the cab and jumped down, landing with a thud. 'What is it? I'm at work.'

He wore a worn-out checked shirt tucked into dark jeans. His boots were covered in mud. He glowered at them, and his bright eyes blazed. He had a reputation as a ladies' man around these parts though Karen could not see the attraction, but that was probably because she saw so many similarities with his father.

'We'd like a word,' DI Morgan said.

'I didn't think you'd come out here to offer me a cup of tea,' Jasper said sarcastically.

He smirked at Karen and then leaned back against one of the enormous tractor wheels, casually watching them and waiting. The irritated look on his face had disappeared and had been replaced by his usual cocky expression.

Karen couldn't help thinking he believed he was getting one over on them.

'Where were you yesterday lunchtime?' DI Morgan asked.

Jasper ran a hand through his red hair, ruffling it, and frowned. 'I thought the girls went missing in the afternoon?'

'Answer the question, please.'

'I was working on the field. Like I told you, I've been cutting back the hedgerows. This is the time of year we like to do it. It takes a long time. We used to hire help in, but now . . .' Jasper shrugged. 'I like to do it myself anyway. The others always cut it too short or leave it too long. It takes an experienced man to handle a machine like this.' He rubbed the side of the tractor, fingering the green paintwork. And then he looked at Karen with what could only be described as a leer.

She didn't react. She'd dealt with worse in her time. If he thought that was going to intimidate her, he'd better think again.

DI Morgan pressed on. 'Do you have anyone who can corroborate that?'

'I don't know, but surely any person passing by the fields would have seen me. There was a lot of traffic on Station Road when I was working there.' He sighed. 'I had Brian helping me in the afternoon.'

'Did you go into Washingborough yesterday, Jasper?' Karen asked. She couldn't help herself. She'd intended to leave all the questions to DI Morgan, but she couldn't stand by, watching his arrogant stare as though he was enjoying watching them rush about like headless chickens. She was desperate for answers. Desperate to find out what had happened to those little girls.

'Washingborough? No, but I do go to the Ferry Boat sometimes,' he said, referring to the pub. 'They do a lovely fish and chips. Maybe you could meet me there one night.' He gave Karen what she assumed he thought was a charming smile.

Karen rolled her eyes. 'But you didn't go to the Ferry Boat yesterday.'

'No, officer. I didn't go to Washingborough at all yesterday,' he said mockingly.

Karen clenched her fists tightly and shoved them into her jacket pockets. 'That's funny. We've got a witness who says they saw you in Washingborough yesterday.'

DI Morgan shot her a warning look, but it was too late.

Jasper laughed and that was the last straw for Karen. 'I don't think we're getting very far here, Jasper. Maybe you should come to the station and answer our questions there.'

Jasper stopped laughing abruptly. 'What is all this? Are you trying to fit me up?' He looked at DI Morgan. 'You should keep an eye on this one. She's a bit loopy.' He moved his hand in tight circles by his temple. 'She's got a bee in her bonnet about that other girl that went missing. She thought it was my dad.' He barked out a laugh. 'I mean, he's on his last legs. What chance would he have against a feisty girl like Amy?'

'Feisty?' Karen's voice was as cold as ice. 'Why do you describe her as feisty? Did she turn you down? Maybe she didn't appreciate your advances. You don't like women saying no to you, do you, Jasper?'

Jasper grinned. 'You've lost the plot. I liked Amy. We got on. I was as surprised as anyone when she disappeared. I've told you all that before, but you don't listen.'

'It would be better for you if you told us the truth, Jasper. Were you in Washingborough yesterday?' DI Morgan asked.

He laughed and shook his head. 'Don't tell me you've fallen for this loopy cow's theories, have you?'

'Right, that's it. You're coming with us,' Karen said.

'You're arresting me?' Jasper wiped his hands on a rag and then chucked it back into the cab of the tractor.

'No, Jasper,' Karen said. 'We're not arresting you. But I'd like you to accompany us to the station. We can ask you questions, and you can have your legal representative present if so desired. If you don't come in and talk to us now . . . Well, that looks bad for you, doesn't it?'

'Pull the other one. I am not stepping foot inside a police station unless I have no choice. Why should I? You're just out to get some easy pickings and piss off down the pub with your colleagues and talk about how you solved the case. Well, detective, you're barking up the wrong tree. I have no idea where those girls are, and you're wasting time with me. Why don't you talk to Emily's father? Dennis Dean, he's got his fingers in an awful lot of pies around here.'

'What do you mean by that?' DI Morgan asked.

'Ask anyone. Even she knows.' Jasper jerked his chin in Karen's direction. 'He's a nutter. If you want my opinion, he's probably pissed off the wrong bloke, who's decided to teach Dennis a lesson by taking the girls.'

'That doesn't make any sense, Jasper,' DI Morgan said. 'If that were the case, they'd only take Emily.'

Jasper shrugged. 'Maybe something went wrong. Anyway, as lovely as it's been talking to you, I need to get back to work, and I suggest you two do the same. Stop wasting taxpayers' money. And go catch some real criminals for a change.'

Blood boiling, Karen watched him climb back into the tractor.

She was angry. Furious with Jasper Palmer, but also annoyed that DI Morgan hadn't backed her up and demanded Jasper accompany them to the station. But that was unfair on DI Morgan. It was her own fault for pushing too hard too soon. What was it about this case that had turned her normally level-headed nature upside down? Was she sliding back to that dark, paranoid place she'd inhabited after the accident?

She couldn't dispute the facts. They didn't have enough evidence to charge him. They needed to get a proper identification and build the case step by step.

But right now, all she really wanted to do was lock Jasper Palmer up and throw away the key.

CHAPTER TWENTY

Karen and DI Morgan spent the afternoon following up endless futile leads and checking in with the search parties. They weren't getting anywhere. It was almost as though the girls had vanished into thin air.

Back at the station, Karen tried to work out how the girls could just have disappeared. Maybe they'd been taken away by road. Karen pulled up a map of the local area on her computer. Vehicle access in the immediate area surrounding Moore Lane School was limited to two roads: Moore Lane itself or Longwater Lane at the back of the woods. There were numerous houses along both roads. Someone should have seen something at that time of day.

On the other hand, if the girls had wandered across the open farmland, they could have walked unspotted for some time. But the school had been quick to alert the police, and the search had been initiated in less than an hour. It took time to organise an official search. But there were uniformed officers and local people searching the farmland before the hour was up.

DI Morgan had checked in with both girls' families, and Karen was glad she didn't have that job this afternoon. It was always difficult to see the harrowing after-effects of crime in victims and their families, and in this case Karen felt it particularly keenly. Although her own daughter had been just five years old when she'd died, had she been alive now she would have been the same age as Emily and Sian.

Karen refused to let her mind wander. She couldn't bear imagining what Tilly's face would look like now if she hadn't been so cruelly taken away.

Instead, Karen leaned forward at her desk and opened the folder containing the screenshots of the CCTV images. If she looked at the images in a certain way, there was a definite resemblance to Jasper Palmer.

Karen had caught up with Tessa Grimes earlier, but unfortunately, Tessa told her she hadn't seen the man long enough to say whether it had been Jasper.

Karen hadn't wanted to ask Rachel. It would leave the case open to criticism. Children were never looked on as the most reliable of witnesses, and it was always preferable to get an adult, someone who could sign a witness statement and understand the gravity of what they were saying when they made an identification.

But two girls' lives could be at stake, so reluctantly, knowing that it could cause a lot of trouble, Karen had shown Rachel a picture of Jasper Palmer. She'd held her breath as she waited for Rachel's response, ignoring that little voice in her head telling her she was pushing too hard again and losing perspective. It had all been for nothing, though. The little girl shook her head and said she couldn't remember. Karen had given her mother her contact details again and asked her to get in touch if Rachel remembered anything else.

Outside, the sky had clouded over and rain had started to fall, steady and relentless The people manning the search would be drenched through to the skin as they carried on, hoping that against all the odds they'd find something to help them track the girls. But there had been nothing since Sian's glove. No trace of the girls at all.

The case already weighed so heavily on the officers involved that it was hard to believe it was only the second day. Rick Cooper's usual banter in the office had come to a complete halt as he sat frowning down at various sheets of paper detailing leads that had come in from the general public and filtered up to the main CID room. You never knew which tip-off was going to be a promising lead or which one would be a waste of time and have you running around in circles while the real perpetrator got further and further away.

Sophie was looking down at her desk just as intently as Rick, her cheeks flushed as she read through some printed notes and then reached for the phone.

Karen pushed her chair back, intending to grab another coffee, but she paused to stare again at the image of the red-haired man outside Washingborough Primary School.

Was it him? Was it Jasper Palmer? She frowned at the image, willing something to jump out at her, something they'd missed, but it was no good. She just couldn't be sure.

A few hours later, DI Morgan had noticed his team were flagging, and when the night shift came on, he insisted they all left by ten p.m.

Karen hated to admit it, but it seemed like this case could go on for a while. It was looking more and more likely that they wouldn't find the girls alive.

There were some terrible statistics about child abductions. The most worrying to Karen was that they were on the increase. Most cases didn't end in murder, though. Many of the children were targeted, abused and released quickly.

A larger percentage of the reports that came in were the result of parental abduction. A parent, often born in another country, would take the child abroad without permission and not bring them back. There wasn't much the police in the UK could do about that.

The most horrendous cases, the stuff of parents' nightmares, were the abductions followed by murder. In some instances, the child was killed very soon after they were taken.

Karen hated to think about that. The idea that Emily and Sian were out there somewhere, still alive and hoping to be rescued, kept her going.

◆ ◆ ◆

At ten thirty p.m., Karen pulled into her driveway. She took a careful look around to make sure nobody was hiding in the shadows tonight, but the driveway was empty. She returned her empty bin to its usual spot at the side of the house and then headed inside.

She took her jacket off and washed her hands, staring out of the dark kitchen window into the garden. In the distance, the mast at Donington-on-Bain was glowing red. The Belmont transmitting station was twenty miles away but dominated the skyline at night with its aircraft warning lights. Some years ago proud locals had unsuccessfully campaigned against a decision to shorten the mast.

When she was four, Tilly had asked about the strange red object in the sky. Karen had tried to give a lesson on perspective and distances but failed miserably. Her husband had chuckled at her long-winded attempt to explain that it might not look very big, but that was because it was a long way away, and if they stood next to it, it would be very big indeed.

She left the kitchen and went into the small room at the front of the house that used to be Tilly's playroom. Karen now used it as a study. From the bottom drawer of the desk, she pulled out a blue A4 ring binder. She took a deep breath and opened it. Inside, there were pages and pages of research into the road traffic accident that had killed Josh and Tilly. Sentences had been marked with a bright yellow highlighter and rings from coffee cups decorated some of the printed sheets from the nights when Karen stayed up until the early hours of the morning, poring over her findings, desperately looking for answers.

She didn't find any answers because there was nothing to be found. There was no conspiracy, no patterns, no justice to chase. Just death. Just a tragic accident. She flipped through the sheets, feeling guilty. At one of the last sessions she'd had with Amethyst, Karen had told her she'd destroyed the folder and put her investigations to bed once and for all. She'd told Amethyst what she wanted to hear. It wasn't a big lie. Karen understood she'd been way off course but couldn't bring herself to get rid of the folder. Not yet.

With a lump in her throat, Karen put the folder away, went back into the kitchen and looked at the miserably bare contents of the fridge. She should have picked up a takeaway on the way home or had some of the pizza Rick had ordered at the station, but when it arrived her stomach had still been churning from the run-in with Jasper, and she'd turned down a slice of spicy pepperoni.

She pulled a chunk of cheddar out from the back of the fridge and checked it for spots of mould. After a quick sniff, she decided it would probably be okay. She'd had the foresight to freeze a loaf of brown bread earlier in the week and she took out a couple of slices and chucked them under the grill before slicing the cheese.

As the toast cooked, she leaned against the cupboard next to the oven, enjoying the warmth of the grill. She had the heating set to come on at five o'clock and go off at nine, so the house was already cooling down. She nipped into the utility room and punched a few buttons to change the timer. While this case was running, it was stupid to have the heating come on at five when she wasn't here. She set it to come on earlier in the morning too, knowing she'd have another early start.

She made her way back into the kitchen just as the toast was starting to turn golden brown and quickly turned it over on the grill. She piled the top half with cheese and then pushed the grill tray back under the heated red bars until it began to bubble.

To her surprise, her mouth watered as she cut the toast in half and melted cheese pulled away in stringy sections. She added a dollop of Lincolnshire chutney, handmade by Christine, and sat down to eat at the kitchen table. Karen found dinnertime unbearably lonely. Maybe she wouldn't have minded so much if she'd always been on her own, but she didn't like the silence of sitting there and had taken to watching TV while she ate. Of course, there were other times when she missed Josh and Tilly keenly. Even now, five years later, she'd turn over in bed and be surprised when her arm reached out and encountered nothing but the cold side of the duvet. It was that moment between waking and being asleep that hurt the most, the few seconds when she forgot all about the accident.

When Karen first started seeing her counsellor, she'd been surprised when Amethyst had told her seeing other families and children might bring back painful memories, but Karen found the opposite was true. She loved to see happy children.

Six months after she lost her family, Karen had been standing in line at the Tesco checkout when the woman queuing behind began to shout at her little girl until she cried. Karen had wanted to shake the woman until her teeth rattled. Thankfully she'd had the presence of mind to move her basket and go to another checkout.

The child didn't look neglected, and the mother was clearly just at the end of her tether after a stressful shop with a three-year-old prone to tantrums, but Karen wanted to shout at her, to say to her, 'You'd miss this if it were taken away. It's driving you crazy right now, but you'd miss it so much that it hurts. You'd give anything for another tantrum.'

Lost in a daydream, Karen was surprised when she looked down and saw her plate was empty. She brushed the crumbs from her hands and put the plate in the dishwasher.

Then she grabbed the washing from upstairs, stuffed it into the machine and set it to run on a quick cycle. Deciding she really should stay awake long enough to hang the washing out, she walked into the sitting room, sat down on the grey sofa and reached for the cream throw to cover her legs.

Feeling sleepy, she opened the messenger app on her phone, tapped on the family group and felt a twinge of guilt when she scrolled through a whole day's worth of messages from her mum, dad and sister. She smiled at a photo of her niece, Mallory, grinning widely and showing off the gap in her front teeth. It was captioned:

Tooth Fairy tonight!

She tapped out a quick reply. She'd give her parents a call tomorrow. She knew they worried about her.

Easing herself back on to the cushions, she switched on the television and muttered to herself, 'Just don't fall asleep.'

It didn't work. Karen was asleep within seconds, but the shrill ring of her mobile broke through her hazy dream, and she sat up. Grabbing her phone, she blinked at the screen and saw it was an unknown number.

'Hello?' Karen's voice sounded thick with sleep, even though she was sure she'd only closed her eyes for a few seconds.

'I'm sorry to disturb you so late. This is Sarah Macintosh, Rachel's mother.'

'Right.' Karen got to her feet and clamped the phone to her ear.

Walking back into the kitchen, she glanced at the digital clock on top of the oven. It was after eleven p.m. What could be so important that Sarah needed to call her now?

'It's not a problem,' Karen said. 'I've not been home long actually. Is there something wrong?'

Sarah let out a shaky breath. 'Yes, I think there is. I'd have waited until morning, but it's just that Rachel was so upset, and I know it could be important because of those two little girls that went missing.' Sarah sounded on the verge of hysteria.

'You did the right thing by calling me. Now, tell me what's happened.'

'Well, it was Rachel. She couldn't sleep, you see. I just thought she was upset because of today and everything. So I insisted she go back to bed, and then when I went to check on her, I noticed she'd been crying. So I went in and told her she needed to tell me the truth, tell me what was bothering her. She wouldn't, though. She kept telling me that she couldn't, that she wasn't allowed.'

'Did you manage to find out what was upsetting her?'

'Yes,' Sarah said. 'Look, it's really difficult to explain on the phone. Do you think you could come to our house?'

Karen's mind was spinning as she jotted down the address. 'I'll be there soon, Sarah. Try not to worry. We'll get to the bottom of this.'

'Thank you. I do appreciate it. I know it's really late and this must be your personal time.'

'Really,' Karen said, grabbing her jacket and folding it over one arm while looking around for her keys, 'it's not a problem.'

'I don't know what to think. She's never behaved like this before. It's completely out of character.'

Karen was almost at the car when something Sarah said made her pause.

'I'm so terribly sorry, but it seems Rachel wasn't telling the truth when she spoke to you earlier. She fed us both a pack of lies.'

CHAPTER TWENTY-ONE

Fifteen minutes later, Karen pulled up outside the Macintosh family home. Constructed from sand-coloured stone, it was an old detached building at the end of a narrow country lane. There were only four other houses on the lane, which overlooked fields on both sides. During the day, the residents would have a lovely view of arable farmland and sweeping skies, but at night it felt isolated. There were no street lights, and Karen shivered as she switched off the engine.

She'd parked beside a large ash tree. When she shut the door, a tawny owl gave a *ke-wick* call. The noise startled her, and she looked upwards, but despite repeating its call, she couldn't see the owl in the dark branches. She locked the car and hurried towards the Macintoshes' front door. She wasn't superstitious, she told herself, just on edge.

Rachel's mother answered the door before Karen even had a chance to knock.

'Thanks for coming,' she said, opening the door wide.

'No problem.' Karen stepped into a brightly lit hall. The warm wooden flooring and pastel wallpaper made the house cosy and inviting.

'Rachel's in her bedroom,' Sarah said over her shoulder as she began to climb the stairs. 'My husband's away on a business trip in Prague. I haven't told him about any of this yet.'

Karen followed her upstairs.

Rachel was sitting propped up against the pillows in her bed. The room wasn't small, but it seemed so due to the vast number of toys crowding every surface and the oversized wardrobe that dominated the room. Rachel's bed was set back against the wall, covered with a swirly-patterned pink duvet.

The little girl looked up at Karen. Her eyes were red, her skin blotchy, and it was obvious she'd been crying.

'What do you have to say to the police officer, Rachel?' Sarah Macintosh said sternly to her daughter.

Rachel's lower lip wobbled, and her eyes grew glassy as she shook her head.

'We talked about this, Rachel. You need to tell the truth.'

Karen felt her stomach tighten and her skin prickle in anticipation. If Rachel positively identified Jasper Palmer, it could be the breakthrough they needed. She held her breath as she waited for Rachel to answer.

Without raising her head, Rachel mumbled, 'I'm sorry.'

'Why are you sorry, Rachel?' Karen asked, desperate for answers but not wanting to push the little girl, who was obviously very upset.

Rachel sniffed and shot a look at her mother. 'I didn't tell you the whole truth earlier when I said I didn't recognise the man.'

'It's important you tell me the truth now, Rachel. You understand that, don't you?'

Rachel nodded and stared down at the duvet.

'Show the policewoman your arms,' Sarah Macintosh ordered.

Karen frowned as slowly Rachel pushed back the sleeves of her unicorn pyjamas. There were dark, ugly bruises on both arms, small in size but painful-looking.

This was an unexpected development. 'How did she get these?' Karen asked, looking up at Mrs Macintosh.

'From another girl in her class, Molly Greenwood. She's been bullying Rachel.' .

Momentarily at a loss as to what this had to do with the man at the school gates, Karen turned her attention back to Rachel.

'And is this why you didn't want to tell the truth when I spoke to you?'

Rachel gave another sniff, wiped her nose on the back of her hand and nodded.

'Tell the police officer about Molly,' Sarah Macintosh prompted her daughter.

'Molly said I wasn't allowed to tell anybody. She said if I did she'd beat me up and tell everyone not to talk to me.'

Slowly the pieces were falling into place. 'And Molly knows the man at the gate?' Karen asked.

Rachel nodded. 'It was Molly's dad. He left Molly's mum, and she won't let him come home, so he came to the school to see Molly, but he's not supposed to. Molly didn't want me to tell you in case he got into trouble.'

Before Karen could ask another question, Sarah Macintosh cut in. 'It's been all around the village. He was violent, and Lydia Greenwood has an injunction against him. He's only supposed to see Molly under supervision.'

'And what is Molly's father's name?'

Sarah replied, 'Les Greenwood. He has a problem with alcohol too.'

'Right, so the man at the gate was Les Greenwood, Molly's dad. Is that what you're telling me, Rachel?'

Rachel wrapped her arms around herself and nodded again. 'Yes,' she replied in a small voice.

Karen felt a wave of frustration. Not only did she not have the evidence she wanted against Jasper Palmer, but it looked as though they'd been chasing a false lead.

Karen smiled and stood up. 'Thank you, Rachel.'

'You won't tell Molly I told you, will you?' she asked anxiously as Karen walked towards the door.

'Molly shouldn't be hurting you, Rachel. She's the one who'll be in trouble, not you.' Karen turned to Sarah Macintosh. 'You'll be reporting this to the head teacher?'

Sarah nodded firmly. She lowered her voice and led Karen out of Rachel's bedroom. 'Absolutely. I'm furious. What'll happen now?'

'We'll have to speak to Les Greenwood, but I'd guess he did go to the school to talk to his daughter.'

'I was furious when Rachel told me what Molly had been doing to her, but I do understand the girl's been going through a rough patch. I'm going to talk to the head teacher but also Molly's mother. We've always got on well in the past, and I think she'd want to know so she can nip Molly's behaviour in the bud,' Sarah said as they made their way down the stairs.

When they reached the front door, Sarah asked, 'Would you like a drink or something before you go?'

Karen looked at her watch. 'No, thanks, I'd better get going. Do you by any chance have an address for Molly's mother or father?'

'I have Molly's mother's address. I'm not sure where Les has been living. Do you want me to get it for you?'

'That would be great.' Karen followed her through a small sitting room and then into a large kitchen.

Sarah plucked a piece of paper covered with cartoon balloons from under a magnet on the fridge and handed it to Karen. 'It's Molly's birthday party next week, and their address is on the invitation.'

Karen took a photograph of the invitation using her phone and then handed it back to Sarah Macintosh.

'Thanks,' Karen said. 'You've been very helpful.'

Karen was polite while she was still inside the house, but as soon as the front door closed behind her, she turned the air blue and stalked towards her car. She could feel Jasper Palmer slipping through her fingers. Chasing the man seen outside Washingborough School had been a waste of time.

Once inside the car, she pulled out her mobile to fill in DI Morgan, apologising for calling so late. He promised her he'd let the duty officer know so no more time was wasted. They would still need to follow up with Les Greenwood just to confirm Rachel's story.

After she'd hung up, Karen put the phone in the circular cupholder in front of the handbrake and leaned her head back on the headrest. Somewhere out there were two scared little girls, and they didn't seem to be getting any closer to finding them.

◆ ◆ ◆

DI Morgan had only just put the phone down after speaking to the inspector in charge of the night shift when his doorbell rang.

He was renting an old two-bedroom terraced house in Canwick on a short-term basis until he'd decided whether he wanted to settle in Lincolnshire for the foreseeable future. As he walked along the dark, narrow corridor with its flagstone floor, he shivered at the draught that crept around the front door. The windows were just as bad. The house had character but was absolutely freezing.

He'd put on a thick, fisherman-style jumper when he got home and changed into a pair of comfortable, faded jeans.

He glanced at the Omega watch on his wrist and saw that it was almost midnight. Who would be ringing his doorbell at this time?

It had to be something to do with work. He hadn't got to know any of his neighbours. He worked long hours and wasn't exactly sociable. He kept telling himself he'd go to the local pub and get to know people, but he hadn't had much time for that yet.

He opened the door and saw a woman shivering on his doorstep.

'Julia, what are you doing here?'

She gazed up at him through a thick fringe. 'Aren't you going to ask me in, Scott?'

He took a step back and opened the door wide. 'Of course, sorry. I wasn't expecting you. We cancelled our date, didn't we?'

Julia stomped past him into the narrow hallway, and he shut the door behind her. He noticed she hadn't brought an overnight bag. He looked at her in confusion and waited for her to explain.

'*You* cancelled our date, Scott.'

'Oh, I see. I'm sorry. But I really didn't have a choice. We have a big case on at the moment.'

She put her hand up to stop him talking. 'I'm driving. So I can't have a proper drink, but you could at least offer to make me a coffee.'

'Of course.'

He led the way into the kitchen.

Julia still lived in Oxford, but he'd thought she was happy for them to continue with things as they were. He'd met her eight months ago. She was a solicitor, hard-working and ambitious, and wasn't interested in a long-term relationship. *Let's just have some fun*, she'd said and that had sounded appealing to DI Morgan.

But from the bad-tempered look on Julia's face tonight, fun was the last thing on her mind.

DI Morgan filled the kettle and flicked the switch before retrieving a couple of mugs from the cupboard. 'Is instant okay?'

Julia rolled her eyes and pointed at the coffee machine she'd bought for his birthday. 'What's wrong with that?'

DI Morgan put his hands in his pockets and looked sheepish. 'Nothing. I just ran out of ground coffee. I haven't had time to go to the supermarket. Like I said, it's this case and—'

'I didn't come all this way to talk about your current case, Scott,' Julia said coldly. 'I suppose instant will have to do.'

Feeling wrong-footed, DI Morgan spooned instant coffee granules into the mugs and retrieved the milk from the fridge. She was angry with him, that much was clear, but he had no idea why. He'd cancelled their date but had given her ample notice. He'd sent the email yesterday. It occurred to him that perhaps she hadn't received it.

'Did you get my email?'

Julia's face tightened and she pursed her lips together.

There was an awkward silence as he waited for her to answer and then he decided to get on with making the coffee. He poured hot water into the mugs.

While he was adding the milk, Julia said, 'I did get your email. And that's what I want to talk to you about.'

DI Morgan nodded as he handed her a steaming mug. 'I should have called, shouldn't I?'

'Yes, at the very least.' She shook her head. 'This isn't working, Scott.'

DI Morgan picked up his own cup and chose his words carefully. 'I thought everything was going okay. There are bound to be some road bumps in a long-distance relationship.'

'It's hardly a relationship. I see you barely twice a month, and it's all so . . .'

She looked around, searching for the right words, and waved a hand. 'It's all so businesslike.'

Scott took the time to sip his coffee, feeling out of his depth.

'Take tonight, for example,' Julia said. 'You were supposed to be having a couple of days off so we could spend some time together, and out of the blue, I get an email informing me you have to work. You don't even bother to call me.'

'I'm sorry,' DI Morgan said carefully. 'I should have been more considerate.'

'It's just not going anywhere,' Julia said.

'Where did you want it to go?' DI Morgan said, genuinely perplexed.

Julia put her coffee down on the kitchen counter. 'You really are impossible.'

'I don't know what I've done wrong, Julia. You said you weren't interested in a long-term, committed relationship.'

'I know what I said. But I didn't expect it to be like this. I need something more.'

DI Morgan nodded slowly. 'I see. Well, I could try—'

'We have tried, Scott, but until you deal with your problems, you'll never be able to open up and have a proper relationship.' She sighed. 'What happened to you? I know something did, but you never talk about it.'

DI Morgan tensed. 'There's no point talking about the past. Why don't we take some time to—'

'No, it's not going to work. You're too cold and contained.' She looked away, unable to meet his gaze.

'You've met someone else,' DI Morgan said.

'That's not the point. That isn't what I came here to talk about.'

'Isn't it?'

'No, and don't try to shift the blame on to me. We're breaking up because emotionally you don't give me anything, and you never give any thought to my feelings.'

'So we're breaking up?'

'Yes.' Julia ran a hand through her hair and sighed. 'This isn't going how I planned. I was supposed to be angry with you, but you're just looking at me like you're confused.'

'That's because I am confused. I thought things were fine.'

'Well, they're not.'

'Is there anything I can do to change that?'

Julia shook her head. 'No, it's just who you are, Scott. And it's not enough for me.'

'You came all the way to Lincoln tonight to tell me that?'

She turned on him and her eyes narrowed in irritation. 'Yes, because that's the decent thing to do. Let somebody down in person. Did you think I'd do it over email?'

'I'm not sure what you want me to say.'

Julia's shoulders slumped, and she sighed. 'And that's the problem, Scott.'

CHAPTER TWENTY-TWO

The following morning, DC Rick Cooper was running late. Everything was against him. He'd intended to get to work early and go through a few more reported sightings of the girls. Most of them were probably cases of mistaken identity, but they still had to be examined in detail before they could be ruled out. But at this rate, he wouldn't be there early. He wouldn't even be on time.

'Come on, Mum,' Rick said, leaning on the kitchen table. 'You know I have to go to work.'

His mother sat shivering in her wheelchair, but she refused to put on her pink dressing gown. Rick hadn't expected his mother to wake an hour earlier than normal this morning. It had royally scuppered his plans for an early start.

'You can't leave me here,' she insisted. 'Not again.'

Rick took a deep breath and tried to keep his patience. 'Look, you're going to catch your death. Let me help you with your dressing gown, and then I'll make you a nice cup of tea before Lauren gets here.'

Rick glanced at the clock. His sister, Lauren, wasn't due for another half an hour.

'No, I don't want my dressing gown. There's something wrong with it.'

Rick frowned and looked down at the pink fleecy dressing gown. He'd bought his mother this one a couple of months ago because her older one had been made of a heavier material and really wasn't suitable. The fleece one was much better. It washed and dried quickly and was lightweight but still kept her warm.

'What's wrong with it?'

'It's got bits on it and they itch me.'

Rick turned it over in his hands, examining the fleece for any areas that could irritate her skin. But it looked perfectly fine to him. His mother had been wearing it for the last two months without any complaints.

Feeling he was losing the battle, Rick put the dressing gown over the back of the kitchen chair, wishing he hadn't already put the old one in the local charity clothes bin.

'All right. We'll leave the dressing gown. What about a cup of tea to warm you up?'

His mother pushed her grey-streaked hair back from her face and nodded. 'Go on then.'

Rick flicked the switch on the kettle and then set about making them both some toast.

He pushed his mother's wheelchair up to the table. 'Are you comfortable enough there or do you want me to help you into a chair?'

'Of course I want to sit in a chair,' she said, looking at him as though he'd lost his marbles. Even though, according to Lauren, she'd wanted to stay in her wheelchair for dinner last night, saying it was more comfortable.

Rick helped his mother out of the wheelchair and into one of the hardback chairs beside the table. He felt a fluttery panic in his chest when he noticed how light she was. Her bones felt so fragile he feared they might snap if he held her too tightly.

'Do you need a cushion, Mum?'

His mother shook her head, picked up a piece of toast and dug in.

Rick was relieved to see her eat. For some time, her appetite hadn't been great, and she'd been losing weight at a rapid clip. The doctors weren't much help, only prescribing a few gloopy, unappealing milk-shakes to try and bulk her up.

They ate their toast in silence, and when his mother had cleared her plate, Rick decided to try again. 'I'm working on an important case at the moment, Mum. That's why I need to be at work early and stay quite late. But Lauren's going to stay longer this week to look after you. You'll have a great time. Maybe she can dig out the puzzles again.' Rick smiled.

His mother narrowed her eyes. 'No, I'm not having her in my house.'

'Lauren is your daughter, Mum,' Rick said gently. Just last week his mother had thought Rick was his uncle Terry, and she'd insisted she'd never seen Lauren before. But that episode had been short-lived, and Rick desperately hoped it was a one-off.

'I know who she is,' his mother said bossily, sounding more like her old self. 'But I'm still not having her in my house.'

Now Rick was really confused. 'Why not? Lauren always looks after you during the day.'

'I don't need looking after. I'm not a child,' she snapped.

Rick didn't quite know how to respond. His mother had always been close to Lauren, and she'd been so proud of them both.

'She wants to get rid of me. She wants to see me dead and buried so she can get her hands on this house.'

Rick's jaw dropped open, and a moment passed before he could gather his wits to reply. 'Don't be ridiculous. Lauren would never do that.'

'Don't speak to me like that. I'll have you know, she tried to kill me yesterday. She just waits until you're not here.' She leaned forward over the kitchen table. 'She tried to give me too many tablets.' She winked at Rick. 'But I'm not stupid. I don't take them. I just pretend and then spit them out when she's not looking.'

'Mum, you need those tablets. The doctor prescribed them.'

Was this why she'd been getting worse? He knew it was coming, of course. The doctor had told them she wasn't going to get any better. There was nothing reversible about early-onset dementia, but Rick had been shocked at how quickly she'd deteriorated. If she hadn't been taking her pills, that was one possible explanation.

Rick thought maybe he should be in charge of the medicine from now on.

'All right,' he said. 'How about I give you your tablets?'

His mother thought about that and then nodded. 'All right, boy. I know you've only got my best interests at heart.'

She gave him a smile that reminded him of how his mother used to be. And to his horror, Rick's eyes filled with tears. He quickly walked out of the kitchen and along the hallway to the downstairs bathroom.

They'd fitted a small lock on the bathroom cabinet, just in case. When his mother used to take her tablets on her own, Rick always feared she might take too many one day because she'd forgotten that she'd already taken some. He unlocked the cabinet and selected the three bottles of pills and then carried them back into the kitchen.

He knew Lauren had a regime. She had a special tablet holder with the days of the week marked on it. At the start of every week, Lauren carefully allocated the medication in the appropriate doses for each day. She'd be irritated at Rick for messing up her system, but when he explained what their mother had said, surely she would understand.

Although he wasn't sure how he was going to tell her something like that. It wasn't something you could put diplomatically. *Sorry, Lauren, your own mother thinks you're trying to kill her . . .*

He lined up the individual pills on the table. Last week she'd had some difficulty swallowing, but she'd had no problem eating the toast this morning so he hoped she'd be able to gulp down the tablets without any issues.

He passed her a glass of water and then watched her take each one.

When she was finished, he demanded that she open her mouth and lift her tongue so he could make sure she hadn't been pretending to take them.

She looked hurt. 'I wouldn't try to trick you.'

Rick sat down and prepared to talk things through with his mother. He had to get it through to her that Lauren wanted to help and would never try to hurt her. But before he'd made much progress, his mobile rang.

It was DS Hart. Damn.

He glanced at the clock on the kitchen wall. So much for being early.

'I'll be back in a minute, Mum,' Rick said, picking up the bottles of tablets so they were out of his mother's reach. He walked out into the hallway and answered the phone. 'Hello, Sarge.'

'Rick, I wondered how far you'd managed to get with the background check on Molly Greenwood's father, Les Greenwood. I left a message last night.'

'I'm sorry, Sarge. I haven't had a chance yet.'

There was a pause, and then Karen said, 'I thought you were supposed to be getting in early this morning to get a head start on things.'

'That was the plan,' Rick said, stuffing the tablets back in the medicine cabinet and trying to lock it with one hand. 'But I'm running late this morning.'

He could hear the impatience in Karen's voice. 'For goodness' sake, Rick. You could have told me. I'm waiting for that information. I'm sitting outside the Greenwoods' house now, and I've got no background.'

Rick grimaced. 'I'm sorry, boss.'

'And what's so important it's made you late for work? Did you sleep through your alarm again?'

157

'Er, something like that.'

Rick didn't know why he didn't tell DS Hart the truth. As far as bosses went, Karen was very understanding and wouldn't hold it against him if he told her the real reason he was late. But Rick didn't want anybody's pity.

'You went out drinking last night most likely,' Karen said coolly. 'You've probably got a hangover and overslept, is that right?'

She took Rick's silence as a guilty response. 'This is vital work, Rick. Those two girls are still missing.'

'I know, boss. I'm sorry. I'll be in as soon as possible.'

'Make sure you are,' Karen said and hung up.

Rick called Sophie, who was already at her desk. Of course she was. *Sophie Jones, the perfect detective constable, a shining example to everyone else*, Rick thought moodily.

He hated to ask her for help, but he didn't have much choice. 'Sophie, I need you to do me a favour. Sarge needs a background check on Les Greenwood, particularly looking into his criminal history and what contact he's allowed to have with his daughter. We think it was Greenwood we caught on the CCTV. I'll forward you the email with everything we know about him so far.'

'Not a problem. I'll start work on it now. Are you coming in or do you want me to send the information to you?'

'I'll be in soon, but if you could send the information directly to Karen as soon as possible, that would be great.'

As he was talking, he heard the front door open, and his sister, Lauren, appeared at the end of the hall. He gave her a quick wave and then went back to his phone call.

He finished talking to Sophie and had just hung up when there was an almighty racket from the kitchen.

His mother was screaming blue murder. 'Get off me! Don't you touch me, get away!'

Rick rushed into the kitchen.

His mother had picked up a plate and was brandishing it at Lauren.

'What on earth is going on? Why are you trying to hit Lauren?' If he hadn't been so worried, it would have been funny. He removed the plate from his mother's hand and put it in the sink.

Then he turned to Lauren and saw she was trembling.

'She wouldn't have hurt you,' Rick said. 'It was only a plate.'

Lauren shook her head and walked past him out of the kitchen.

'Good riddance,' his mother said.

Rick pinched the bridge of his nose and felt a tension headache building behind his eyes. He left his mother in the kitchen and went to find Lauren.

She was sitting on the sofa in the living room, staring down at her lap. Rick sat beside her.

'I can't do this any more, Rick.'

'I know it's difficult.'

'It's more than difficult. It's impossible. I can't take it. She just accused me of trying to kill her.'

Rick grimaced. 'I'm sorry. I should have warned you. It's something she said this morning. Look on the bright side – she'll probably have forgotten about it by lunchtime.' He smiled, even though he knew the joke wasn't appropriate. As a police officer, black humour had helped him through some difficult times.

'It's too much for me, Rick. I can't take it. It's all right for you, you only get it at night and she's asleep most of the time.'

Rick paused before answering. His gaze fell on a photograph on the mantelpiece. His mother and father smiled out from the frame. The picture had been taken on their thirtieth wedding anniversary. He hated to think that the kind, strong, caring woman in that photo was slowly slipping away.

Maybe Lauren was right. Things had been getting worse, and she definitely had the short end of the stick, though it wasn't easy for Rick either. He didn't have much of a social life, having to stay in and look after his mother all the time, although he played up his Romeo reputation at the station. Whenever he was invited for drinks after work, he told everyone he had a date, living up to the ladykiller role, but it was far from the truth. Rick was usually at home making his mother a cup of cocoa by nine p.m. most nights.

Occasionally he'd have to work late or do a night shift, which meant Lauren would swap around with him. It wasn't easy for her, though. She had her two young children to think about. In the beginning, she'd brought them back here after school to spend time with their grandma. The two boys had been marvellous and coped really well considering their young ages. Even when their grandmother had demanded to know who they were, they patiently responded and won her over with their childish chatter.

'Maybe I can try and cut back on the overtime once this case is over. It's a big one, you see, and more demanding than usual. I know you get the worst of it, Lauren. But I promise to pull my weight a bit more once this case is off my plate.'

Lauren shook her head. She got to her feet and wandered off into the hallway. Rick frowned. He'd never seen his sister like this before. She was close to the end of her tether and it scared him. She came back into the room, holding her bag. After rummaging inside, she pulled out some sheets of paper and handed them to Rick.

'What's this?' he asked, flipping through them.

'It's a specialised care facility for people with dementia. We just need to sign the paperwork.'

Rick dropped the papers on the sofa next to him and stood up. 'No way. Absolutely not.'

Lauren's face crumpled and she looked as though she might start to cry.

Rick closed his eyes and ran a hand through his hair. 'Look, I do understand how hard it is. I tell you what, why don't I organise some help to come in a couple of days a week? That should take the pressure off you a bit.'

'I don't know, Rick. I think we've already left it too long.'

Rick took her hands in his. 'Please, Lauren. Let's see how things go with a bit of extra help, and then we can make the decision, all right?'

Lauren took a long time to respond, but eventually she nodded.

When he went back into the kitchen, Rick saw his mother had fallen asleep. He carefully lifted her out of the chair and carried her to her bedroom. After lowering her on to the bed, he tucked her under the covers.

He kissed her on the forehead and said, 'See you later, Mum.'

Then he left for work, feeling like the weight of the world was on his shoulders.

CHAPTER TWENTY-THREE

Karen was in a bad mood. She had hoped to speak to Mrs Greenwood and her daughter, Molly, before school. If the sighting of the red-haired man at Washingborough Primary was completely unrelated to Emily and Sian's disappearance, she wanted it off her plate as soon as possible. But she'd been trying to cram in too much. To top it off, Rick hadn't come through with the background information.

It was unlike him. She'd been too harsh on the phone and she knew it. He'd probably had a skinful last night, but that wasn't an uncommon way for police officers to unwind when they were in the middle of a stressful case.

Of course, she couldn't just stand by and let it become a regular occurrence, but she could have been more understanding. She could have let him talk to her rather than biting his head off.

The job was a constant challenge to every officer's mental health. DI Morgan was a good policeman, but he wasn't the warm, fuzzy, let's-have-bonding-sessions-and-a-group-hug type. She wasn't much better, but as DI Morgan was unlikely to fill the pastoral role the younger officers needed, it would be up to her to take care of the junior detectives' needs.

She was sitting in her car outside the Greenwoods'. It was a semi-detached house with a pleasant front garden. It probably looked nice in the summer with roses in bloom, but now they had lost most of their leaves.

Since she was already there, Karen decided to speak to Molly's mother. She didn't like going in without some background information, but in this case she'd have to make an exception. She was pretty sure the whole thing was going to end up being a dead end anyway. Les Greenwood had been hanging around the school to see his daughter. He wasn't about to become the number one suspect in their search for the missing schoolgirls.

Karen locked the car and walked up the small garden path towards the red front door. She pressed the doorbell and a cheerful chime rang out. A small dog yapped on the other side of the door. There was a six-inch-wide strip of frosted glass running along the side of the door, and Karen could just see a small furry shape bouncing up and down.

A moment later, the little dog was scooped up and the front door opened.

Holding a Yorkshire terrier, the woman facing Karen looked to be in her early thirties. She wore no lipstick and her lips looked strangely pale against her perfectly tanned skin. 'Can I help you?'

Karen showed her ID, then quickly said, 'It's nothing to worry about. I just needed a quick word with you, Mrs Greenwood.'

The woman's mouth fell open, and she took a moment to gather herself. 'Sorry, of course – come in.' She shut the front door behind Karen and put the dog down in a room off the hall before shutting him in. 'Please, come through.'

Karen stepped into a pokey little kitchen. It was nicely decorated but there was only one narrow window, and every counter was covered with electrical items, giving the impression of an overstuffed showroom.

Mrs Greenwood squeezed past her. 'Is it Les? Has he done something?'

'Why do you say that?'

She shrugged. 'I don't know why else you'd be here. I don't usually get visits from police officers before eight thirty in the morning.' She tried to make a joke, but her smile didn't quite take hold.

'It's actually something that happened at your daughter's school. Two days ago.'

'Molly? What happened?'

'I suppose you've heard about the missing girls from Heighington?'

The woman nodded and folded her arms across her chest. 'Yes, I did. It's awful. Is there any news?'

Karen shook her head. 'We had reports that a man had been seen hanging around Molly's school—'

'Oh my God,' the woman interrupted.

'—but we don't think it's related to our enquiry at this stage. We think it was Molly's father.'

'At her school?' Mrs Greenwood's cheeks flushed pink. 'But he's not allowed to see her without supervision. Why didn't one of the teachers stop him?'

Karen continued, 'He was seen by the school gates and spoke to another pupil at the school. When he was spotted by one of the teachers, he headed off straightaway. We caught this image on CCTV and wondered if you'd be able to identify him from this.'

Karen set the printouts down on the kitchen counter. Mrs Greenwood picked one up and studied it before moving on to the next sheet. 'It looks like him. Yes, I'd say I'm sure that's him. It's Les.'

'Thank you,' Karen said. 'Do you have a recent photograph of Mr Greenwood?'

'There's probably a few in the old albums but they won't be recent.' She frowned and tapped a finger against her chin. 'I know where I can find one. The computer. Do you want me to get it now?'

'Please. That would be very helpful.'

While Mrs Greenwood went to find the photograph, Karen checked her messages on her phone.

'I hope you're going to have a word with him and tell him to stay away from the school,' Mrs Greenwood said as she came back into the room holding a laptop. 'He knows he shouldn't be there.'

Karen felt a pang of sympathy for Molly as she looked at a selection of photographs of the young girl and her father. It was definitely Les Greenwood in the CCTV footage.

She thanked Mrs Greenwood and then said, 'There is one other thing I think I should mention. This isn't a police matter, but Molly was threatening another child.'

Mrs Greenwood looked outraged. 'Molly wouldn't do that.'

'The other child spotted Les at the school, and Molly was threatening her to keep her quiet. The child has some bruises on her arms from where Molly pinched her. I think Molly was worried that her father was going to get into trouble.'

The woman put her head in her hands. 'Oh God. I've done my best to keep her out of it, but she doesn't understand. She still loves him. She can't see him for the alcoholic waste of space everybody else can.'

Karen wasn't about to dole out any advice but she hoped the woman would talk to Molly. Whatever Les Greenwood had done, he was still Molly's father.

Karen finished up by asking a few more questions and then prepared to leave so Mrs Greenwood could take Molly to school.

As she stood on the front step, Karen added in a low voice so Molly wouldn't overhear, 'Please don't mention this yet to your husband. We're going to be talking to him this morning.'

Karen crossed over to unlock her car and slid into the driver's seat. Her phone started to ring.

It was Sophie. 'Hello, Sarge. Rick asked me to do some background for you. The stuff on Les Greenwood?'

Karen frowned at the thought of Rick fobbing his work off on Sophie, but she supposed at least it meant she got what she needed. 'Great, thanks, Sophie. Did anything turn up?'

'I've emailed it to you. Nothing stands out. I've confirmed his address, and he's had a couple of arrests for drunk and disorderly. Uniform have been called out to Mrs Greenwood's address a couple of times over the past year due to domestic disturbances, but there are no records to suggest he'd be a threat to children. Due to his drinking and Mrs Greenwood getting a hotshot lawyer, he's only allowed to see his daughter on supervised visits at the moment. I've spoken to the social worker and from the looks of things, he's going to be allowed full visitation rights soon. She doesn't believe he's a danger to his daughter or any other child. He just has a problem with drink.'

'Thanks, Sophie. I think it's pretty obvious that it was Les Greenwood at the school. I was hoping to call on him this morning before he left for work but I've run out of time. I'm coming back to the station now. I'll assign someone else to follow up. We've got bigger fish to fry.'

By the time she arrived at Nettleham, Karen was thoroughly fed up. It had taken her nearly an hour to get there after leaving the Greenwoods' house. Two lorries had crashed going up Lindum Hill, and the centre of Lincoln was logjammed. She gave a brief nod to the duty sergeant on the desk and then used her access card to get into the secure area of the police station.

Karen took the stairs rather than the lift and then strode down the corridor into the open-plan office area. Pleased to see Rick was now at his desk, she said good morning to him and Sophie and then headed to see DI Morgan.

There was a long rectangular window in the door to DI Morgan's office. Karen paused beside it and saw he was alone. She rapped on the door before pushing it open.

DI Morgan looked up. 'Karen, how did you get on?'

Karen sat down. 'I spoke to Molly's mother. It seems highly likely that the man outside Washingborough Primary was Les Greenwood and his only motive was wanting to see his daughter. I was planning to talk to him this morning, but I thought it would be a better use of the time to follow up on more promising leads, and then I ended up sitting in traffic for an hour.'

DI Morgan nodded. 'Yes, I heard about the jam on Lindum Hill. Half the station use that route in the morning. I agree with you, though. I think we can pass Les Greenwood on to another officer.'

They chatted for a little longer, and after DI Morgan had brought Karen up to date, she went back to the main office to catch up with Rick and Sophie.

'I think I may have something interesting here,' Rick said as Karen stopped by his desk.

Rick was hunched over with one elbow on the desk, resting his chin on his hand. He stared down at a sheet of paper.

'What is it?'

'We've had a call from a man called Mark Goodman. He has a daughter called Phoebe, and he's got something to tell us about Nick Gibson.'

Sophie perked up at this and looked up from her computer screen. 'Sian's uncle?'

'Yes,' Rick said nodding, still looking at the sheet of paper. 'According to Mr Goodman, Nick Gibson took some photographs of his daughter, Phoebe, when she was underage. It sounds like a strong lead, Sarge. Shall I give him a ring and get him to come in?'

Sophie jumped up from the desk to read the piece of paper over Rick's shoulder. 'I could do it. I know Rick's got a lot of other things on at the moment.'

Rick frowned and moved the piece of paper away from Sophie. 'Oh no you don't. I've been through a mountain of leads to get to this one. You can't just cherry-pick the best ones, Sophie.'

'Cherry-pick? I was just offering to help.' Sophie tried to look affronted but Karen saw the eagerness in her eyes.

Karen leaned over Rick's desk and quickly scanned the text, absorbing the main points. 'Interesting.'

'I'll call him now,' Rick said. 'I take it you'll want to speak to him yourself, Sarge?'

'Yes, ask him to come in as soon as possible. If what he has to say has a bearing on our current case, it'll be good to have him at the station in case we need to follow things up.'

'That's just what I was thinking,' Rick said and reached for the phone.

'You'll need someone else in the room when you question him,' Sophie said. 'It would be a very good opportunity for me to get some experience.' She looked at Karen with puppy-dog eyes.

Rick glared at her. 'You've only been on the job a few months. I uncovered the lead, and by rights I should be in the interview with Mark Goodman.'

'You're both being ridiculous,' Karen said. 'Rick has more experience and he'll join me in the interview.'

Sophie's face fell.

'I'm sure you've got a lot to be getting on with in the meantime, Sophie,' Karen said.

As Sophie sloped off back to her desk, Rick grinned. 'I'm glad you saw it from my point of view, Sarge.'

Karen narrowed her eyes. 'Don't get too cocky, Detective Constable. I'm getting tired of the sniping between you and DC Jones. You should be helping her, not arguing with her.'

Rick looked repentant and nodded. 'Sorry, boss.'

CHAPTER TWENTY-FOUR

Less than an hour later, Mark Goodman arrived at Nettleham station and was shown into interview room three.

Karen and Rick joined him and got the formalities out of the way. They were not planning on recording the interview, but it was good to know the equipment was in place if needed.

'We understand you called the hotline with some information, Mr Goodman,' Karen said.

Mark Goodman, a balding man with a pot belly and small, dark brown eyes, nodded. 'I did. As soon as I heard those two girls were missing, I knew I had to phone the police and let them know the truth about Nick Gibson.'

'We appreciate you coming forward,' Karen said. 'If you could explain in your own words, please.'

'I did already explain this on the phone,' Mark Goodman said.

'If you could repeat it for our benefit, sir, that would be most helpful,' Rick said. 'We don't want to get anything wrong.'

Mark Goodman nodded and fiddled with his shiny blue tie, which was well worn and had a small stain at the bottom. 'Yes, well, I'm glad you're taking it seriously this time. When I went to the police after it happened, they didn't want to know.'

'When what happened?' Karen asked.

'It's about my daughter, Phoebe. She was fifteen when Nick Gibson took an interest in her. She was young and naive, and he took advantage.'

Rick made a note on the pad in front of him. 'I see, and how did your daughter know Nick Gibson?'

'They were both in an amateur dramatics society, working on a production of *The Taming of the Shrew*. I should have noticed something was wrong – Phoebe seemed so excited about it at first but then became very withdrawn after a few weeks.'

Karen said nothing but nodded encouragingly.

'Well, it was then that I found the photograph. It was a Polaroid, and it showed Phoebe, lying on a bed.' His mouth quivered a little, and then he said, 'She didn't have any clothes on. Of course, I hit the roof, but when we talked it over, she explained to me that Nick had talked her into allowing him to take the photographs and then he'd threatened to show them to people if she told anyone.'

'And Phoebe was fifteen at the time?' Karen asked.

'Well, that's the thing. I know she was fifteen because Phoebe told me it had happened months before I found the photograph, but by the time I went to the police, Phoebe had passed her sixteenth birthday. She was scared, and so she told the police officers that they'd been in a relationship, and the photographs were consensual, but I know that wasn't true. Phoebe wasn't like that. She wouldn't have just agreed to have those kinds of photos taken. He must have threatened her with something.'

'When did this occur?' Karen asked.

'Nineteen ninety-five.'

Karen mentally calculated that would make Nick Gibson only a year or so older than Phoebe.

'Do you think Phoebe would mind talking to us about this?' Rick asked.

The man pulled a face. 'She won't talk about it. She's put it behind her now and moved on. In fact, she hates it if anyone even mentions anything about Nick Gibson.'

They asked Mark Goodman a few more questions, and Karen got the sense that Phoebe and Nick had had some kind of relationship when she was underage and that it had ended badly. She didn't like the idea of anyone taking naked photographs of a fifteen-year-old girl, but if Nick himself was only sixteen at the time, she didn't think it necessarily made him a serial child predator.

They thanked Mark Goodman for his time, and after he left, Karen turned to Rick. 'What did you make of that?'

'I think we need to speak to Phoebe,' Rick said. 'We're only hearing things from her father's point of view, and he's obviously dead set against Nick Gibson. I don't blame him for that, but I don't think there's enough evidence to suggest Nick Gibson has an unhealthy interest in his young niece.'

Karen nodded. 'I agree. Still, we'll need to have a good look at Nick Gibson's background. If it's all right with you, I'll ask Sophie to call and speak to Phoebe.'

Rick looked hurt. 'Why? I could do it.'

'I know you could, but Sophie was right when she said she needed more experience. I also think Phoebe might feel more comfortable talking to a woman.'

Rick shoved the chair under the desk and walked around to follow Karen out of the interview room. 'I suppose you're right,' he said grudgingly and switched the light off behind them before closing the door.

◆　◆　◆

Sophie was pleased as punch to get the task of phoning Phoebe Goodman. And she made quite a song and dance about it, irritating

Rick as she picked up the phone and prepared to dial, giving him a smug grin.

Karen rolled her eyes. She wished the two of them would learn to work together and stop being so competitive. If it got much worse, she'd have to mention it to DI Morgan.

Sophie spoke to Phoebe for ten minutes and when she'd finished, she came over to Karen's desk.

'She tells quite a different story to her father. Phoebe admitted having a relationship with Nick Gibson, but she said she was almost sixteen, and Nick was only a year older than her. She never got over the embarrassment of her father finding the photograph and admitted she probably led him to believe it was more Nick's fault than hers. She told me the photographs were consensual and that there hadn't been any hard feelings between her and Nick.'

Karen nodded. 'I suspected as much.' She leaned back in her chair and tapped her pen on a desk. 'Did she agree to speak to us in person?'

'Yes, but she took some persuading. She said she didn't want to dredge it all up again, but when I told her it was very important for us to get the full story, she agreed. I did hint that if she didn't speak to us, we'd be focusing our enquiry on Nick. That was when she agreed to come in.' Sophie looked at her watch. 'She promised to come to the station after she's finished work. That'll be about five thirty.'

Karen smiled. 'Good work. I'll go over some interview questions before she gets here to make sure we get the whole picture, and you can ask the questions if you like.'

Sophie beamed. 'Absolutely, Sarge. I won't let you down.'

Over Sophie's shoulder, Karen noticed Rick mimicking her words and pulling a funny face. She sighed. Honestly, it was like being back at school.

DI Morgan leaned forward at his desk, resting his elbows on the paperwork scattered in front of him when Karen told him what Phoebe had said.

'I'm not convinced Nick Gibson is involved but it's certainly something we can't ignore. We'll apply for a warrant and I want to have his place searched. We need all of his electronic devices analysed. In my opinion, we need to play it safe. I don't want to take any chances here.' He turned to Karen. 'Are you happy to take the lead on this?'

Karen looked up, surprised. 'Yes.'

DI Morgan nodded. 'Good. You should take Sophie with you. It'll be good for her.'

'I agree,' Karen said. She pictured Sophie bouncing off the walls in delight. It would be a good experience for Sophie, but Karen wished the junior detective could contain her excitement just a little.

'I'll touch base with the families,' DI Morgan said. 'I need to talk to Thomas Gibson and find out if he knew about the photographs his brother took of Phoebe. I'll try to be as gentle as I can, but I want to find out whether they had any reservations about Sian spending time with her uncle.'

Karen didn't envy him that task. She appreciated the fact that he'd given her the responsibility of overseeing the search of Nick Gibson's property. It was definitely the better job of the two. She thought perhaps he might be trying to make up for blocking her questioning the Palmers. Was this his way of showing he still believed in her?

It didn't take long for the warrant to come through, and the teams coordinated to meet at Nick Gibson's residence. Karen drove there in a fleet car with Sophie in the passenger seat.

Sophie was practically buzzing with anticipation. She kept fiddling with the radio and then clutching her hands together and grinning at Karen. It was distracting.

'Thanks for letting me come along, Sarge. I really admire the way you work. I see you as my mentor.'

'You're welcome.'

'I think us women have to stick together in the force, so it's great to have a role model and someone to look up to. What level were you at when you were my age?' Sophie asked.

Feeling positively ancient, Karen replied, 'I was in uniform for a few more years than you.'

'So I'm ahead of the curve then.' Sophie smiled. 'That's good to know.' She reached for the radio to change the station yet again.

When Sophie opened the window half an inch and closed it again for the third time, Karen turned to her and snapped, 'Sophie. Do you think you could keep still for just one minute?'

The excited smile slid off Sophie's face. 'Sorry, Sarge. I'm just looking forward to my first proper search. We could find something at Nick Gibson's place that could solve the case.'

Karen felt guilty for taking the wind out of the young detective's sails. 'I hope we do. Just follow my lead and watch how things progress.'

'Do you think he'll confess when we get there?' Sophie asked. 'I mean, he'll know we're on to him.'

Sophie was acting as though they'd solved the case already and it was simply a matter of extracting a confession. That would be nice but Karen wasn't convinced.

'We don't know if he's taken the girls, Sophie.'

Sophie pulled a face. 'But . . . he took photographs of a young girl in the past. Surely that suggests he'd do it again given half the chance.'

Karen shrugged. 'Yes, and that means he's a suspect, but our missing girls are a lot younger than Phoebe was. Usually in this type of case, as sick as it sounds, they stick to a particular age range.'

Sophie's lower lip poked out in a pout. Karen glanced at her and then turned her attention back to the road. Sometimes she felt like she was babysitting these younger detectives rather than training them.

'Now you sound like DI Morgan,' Sophie said. 'Wasn't that exactly the reason he thought the Palmers couldn't be involved in the girls' disappearance? Because Amy Fisher was so much older?'

Karen nodded and conceded the point. 'Yes, and he's right.'

She was about to go on and try and explain her feelings regarding the Palmers to Sophie but although she hated to admit it, in this case, DI Morgan was justified. Her gut instinct about the Palmers relied on hunches and intuition, but they needed hard, concrete facts. There was an underlying evil lurking beneath the surface in the Palmer family, but it was hard to put her sense of foreboding into words. Instead, she went over some of the technicalities involved with a search warrant, and Sophie listened intently, absorbing every word. Karen had never known such an eager pupil.

They met the rest of the team just around the corner from Nick Gibson's residence, and when everything was synchronised, they moved in.

CHAPTER TWENTY-FIVE

The door was opened by Nick Gibson, who despite the time had clearly just woken up. His hair was sticking up and he wore a T-shirt and striped boxer shorts. 'What's going on?'

Karen handed him the warrant and showed her ID. 'We're here to search your property, Mr Gibson, and remove any items pertaining to our investigation.'

Mr Gibson stared at the piece of paper open-mouthed and then looked up at Karen and blinked a couple of times as the officers moved past him into his flat to start the search.

'I don't understand. What are you looking for? I've been up day and night searching for Sian and Emily. I've only just put my head down.'

Karen could feel the waves of dislike coming off Sophie, who stood beside her.

'Perhaps you could put some clothes on, Mr Gibson, and we can have a chat,' Karen said and assigned a male officer to accompany Nick Gibson to make sure he didn't try to hide any evidence or tamper with any electronic devices.

'If you could put your mobile phone on the kitchen counter, please, Mr Gibson,' she said as he began to walk towards his bedroom.

'You want my phone as well?' He looked crestfallen as he walked into the bedroom to get his phone and then brought it to Karen.

She nodded to one of the search officers, who put it in a plastic evidence bag and labelled it.

'You can't suspect I have anything to do with my niece's disappearance?'

'Can't we?' Sophie asked with an arched eyebrow.

Karen shot her a warning look. 'It's come to our attention you took indecent images of a young woman some years ago.'

'I was never charged! It was all a misunderstanding.' Nick looked at Karen and then at Sophie pleadingly. 'We were both young. She let me take the photographs. I didn't pressure her into it.'

Karen said nothing and Sophie glared at him.

Nick Gibson covered his face with his hands and let out a muffled sob. 'I can't believe this is happening. Does my brother know about this? He knows I would never hurt Sian. Ask him.'

'We'd like to take you to the station to answer some questions, Mr Gibson,' Karen said. 'We can do it now if that's convenient for you.'

'What if I refuse?'

Sophie folded her arms over her chest. 'Well, if you refuse that just makes you look guilty.'

His face crumpled in frustration, and he slammed a hand against the kitchen counter. 'I can't believe this is happening,' he said again. 'Why are you wasting time on me when somebody out there has got those two little girls?'

'It'll be easier for you if you come with us now and answer our questions, Mr Gibson,' Karen said. 'By the time we finish, the search should be over.'

Reluctantly, Gibson agreed, and he went to get dressed.

Sophie and Karen had a quick word with the officer overseeing the search and let him know they would be off-site. Karen signed the paperwork and then, with Sophie by her side, escorted Nick Gibson out of his flat and towards the fleet car.

All around them curtains twitched, and people walking on the street stopped to stare.

'I can't believe this is happening,' Nick muttered yet again. 'They're all going to think I had something to do with it now. I'll never live this down.'

'Mind your head, Mr Gibson,' Sophie said coldly as she opened the car door, allowing Nick to climb into the back seat.

Once he had fastened his seatbelt, she slammed the door and brushed her hands together.

'He's full of it,' she mouthed to Karen as she walked around to the passenger side.

Karen wasn't feeling as confident as Sophie. In fact, she couldn't help thinking that like Les Greenwood, this was another false lead.

They drove Nick Gibson back to Nettleham station in silence, and frankly, Karen was relieved to have some peace and quiet. Sophie's chatter and hero-worshipping tendencies could get a little much.

At the station, she left Nick Gibson in interview room three under the watchful gaze of Sophie, while she went to get the paperwork and grab them some coffee.

When she entered the open office area, she saw Rick and decided to have a quick word. She'd been abrupt with him on the phone earlier and events since then had meant she hadn't had a chance to speak to him about it.

'Did you bring Nick Gibson in, Sarge?' Rick asked as she approached his desk.

'Yes, he's in interview room three.'

Rick beamed. 'Great.' He got to his feet, grabbing his phone and tablet.

'Sophie's going to take this one, Rick. I think it'll be good for her.'

Rick's face fell, and he nodded before sitting down. 'Okay, boss, I understand.'

'Look, Rick. I know this job can be tough, especially when we get cases like this, but heavy drinking isn't the answer.'

Rick stared down at the desk.

'You know I'm always here if you want to talk about it, and if you'd prefer to talk to someone outside of the force about the situation, the police service has contacts with excellent counsellors. In fact, I could recommend one I saw on and off a few years ago. It can really help to talk things through.'

Rick shook his head. 'Thanks, Sarge, but I'll be fine. It won't happen again.'

Karen couldn't help feeling disappointed. 'Well, if you're sure . . . If you change your mind, you know I'm always here.'

Rick looked up and parted his lips. He looked at Karen as though he were about to confess something.

'What is it?'

But Rick looked away again and the moment was lost. 'Nothing, boss. I just wanted to say I really am sorry.'

Karen decided she would have to leave it for now. She couldn't force Rick into talking to a counsellor, and maybe it had just been a heavy night. He was young, and Rick had a reputation for knowing how to enjoy himself.

Reluctantly, she scooped up the paperwork and headed to the coffee machine.

◆ ◆ ◆

The interview went pretty much as Karen had anticipated. They got no new information out of Nick Gibson. He stubbornly insisted that the photographs were a private moment between him and Phoebe, who'd been his girlfriend at the time. He swore the photographs had been taken after her sixteenth birthday. Karen had her doubts, but they weren't strong enough to conclude that Nick Gibson was involved in the disappearance of his young niece and her friend.

Karen ended the interview, and after getting feedback from the search team that nothing incriminating had been found during the physical search of his home, she allowed Nick Gibson to leave.

Sophie took the lack of progress personally. 'I can't believe we're just going to let him go. Surely if we just kept him here a bit longer and put some pressure on, he'd crack.'

Karen sighed and stretched out at her desk. 'This isn't an episode of *Miami Vice*, Sophie.'

Sophie's smooth skin puckered as she frowned. 'What's *Miami Vice?*'

Sitting at the next desk over, Rick chuckled. 'It's a US police TV show. You're probably a bit too young to remember it.'

Karen scowled. 'Yes, well, it's been made into a film recently too.' Sometimes Sophie and Rick made her feel ancient.

Sophie huffed under her breath and walked back to her own desk, leaving Karen to fill in the paperwork.

'Don't look so despondent, Sophie,' Rick said. 'They didn't find anything at his property, but that doesn't mean they won't unearth something on his computer or phone.'

Sophie nodded and perked up a bit. 'True. How long do you think it'll take to hear back from the lab?'

'Depends how much they've got on, but I'm sure they're treating it as a priority.'

Karen heard footsteps and turned to see DI Morgan striding towards them. He'd been out talking to the Gibsons, and from the look on his face, Karen guessed it hadn't been a pleasant experience.

'I take it Thomas Gibson didn't take too kindly to our theory his brother could be involved in Sian's disappearance.'

DI Morgan shook his head. 'No, but that's not my current concern.'

Karen pushed her chair back from her desk, so she was facing DI Morgan. 'Why? What's happened?'

'Dennis Dean,' DI Morgan said grimly. 'Grab your jacket. You're coming with me.'

◆ ◆ ◆

A few minutes earlier, Jenny Dean had been pacing her small sitting room. It wasn't easy. With a three-piece suite, a huge television and a large dining table all squeezed into one small living room, it didn't leave much empty floor space.

Her long, dark hair was tangled because she kept tugging her fingers through it. The family liaison officer had gone to the kitchen, thank God. She was really getting on Jenny's nerves. At any other time, Jenny would have told her to leave, but she knew there was a good chance the officer would hear any news about Emily first, so Jenny couldn't risk turfing her out.

She wrapped her arms around her stomach. It was aching with a dull, burning emptiness.

She didn't understand. Emily always made her way home after school. She was a cheeky little thing, and she made Jenny want to pull her hair out on occasions, but even Emily would know this was wrong.

She should have paid more attention. Just recently, Emily had been quiet, and Jenny had put that down to things being so tense between her and Dennis. It couldn't be easy for the poor thing to be stuck in the middle.

Despite her good intentions to put her daughter first, Jenny had sometimes used Emily to spite Dennis. He just made her so angry when he let them down time after time, and she wanted to protect Emily from that. But perhaps her barbed comments about Dennis had upset Emily.

Jenny continued to pace, chewing her fingernails. It was dark outside and getting very cold.

She hated to think of Emily out there wearing only a thin anorak. She really should have bought her a winter coat by now, but there never seemed to be enough money to go around these days.

'You're gonna wear a hole in that carpet if you're not careful.' Jenny's mother, Louise Jennings, sat on one end of the sofa, quietly knitting.

She'd been so quiet that Jenny had forgotten she was even there. Outwardly, her mother showed no sign of panic. Her voice was the same as always and not softened by sympathy, but Jenny knew her mother was worried sick about Emily.

Jenny sat down beside her on the sofa. 'Do you think they just walked off and got lost? I mean, that could happen. Maybe they've found shelter somewhere. Just because they didn't come home doesn't necessarily mean they've been taken by anyone, does it?'

Her mother put her knitting down on her lap. 'It's getting late,' she said, not answering Jenny's question.

'I wish I had a time machine so I could travel back and pick the girls up from school. It's my fault. All of it. It would never have happened if I'd gone and met them.'

Her mother reached out and drew Jenny in for a hug. 'Blaming yourself isn't going to do anyone any good at this point. We need to stay strong for Emily.'

'What will I do if she doesn't come home, Mum?'

Jenny was sobbing against her mother's shoulder when there came a loud hammering at the front of the house. Thinking it was news about her daughter, Jenny sprang to her feet and rushed to the door before her mother had even managed to get up from the sofa.

Jenny flung open the front door. In the split second before the door was fully open, she pictured Emily standing on the doorstep, looking surprised at all the fuss.

But when the door opened, it wasn't Emily standing there. It was Dennis, and his face was contorted with rage.

CHAPTER TWENTY-SIX

As soon as they were heading out of the car park, DI Morgan began to fill Karen in.

'I've spoken to Becky Carpenter. She's the family liaison officer who's staying with Jenny Dean. There's a situation at the family home. Dennis turned up half an hour ago. He lost the plot after finding out Jenny's been seeing another man. Becky had no choice but to call for backup.'

Karen raised her eyebrows as they headed towards Lincoln. 'Well, she did the right thing. I know Becky and she's an excellent officer, but she shouldn't have to handle Dennis Dean alone.' Karen turned in the passenger seat. 'Is it true, though? Has Jenny Dean been seeing another man? Because if it is, she should have told us. He's a possible suspect.'

DI Morgan accelerated away from the roundabout, with a grim expression on his face. 'Yes, she should. But she didn't.'

Karen gazed out of the window as a light rain began to fall, splattering the glass with tiny droplets. Why hadn't Jenny told them about the new man in her life? Did she just forget in the stress of the situation? But then, surely the family liaison officer would have noticed if he'd visited Jenny since the girls had gone missing. If he hadn't visited to comfort Jenny at such a time, well, that raised even more questions, which made Karen suspect that Jenny was purposely keeping this from them. But why?

Karen's mobile began to ring, and she reached down to the footwell, grabbing her bag.

'It's Rick,' she said as she pulled out her phone. 'Yes, Rick, any news?'

'I thought I'd better update you, Sarge. Uniform's on the scene already but they haven't been able to get inside the house. Apparently, Dennis has wedged something heavy against the door.'

Karen put her hand against her forehead. The situation was spiralling out of control fast. 'We're still a good ten minutes away, Rick. Tell them to go around the back but to tread carefully.'

'Do you think Dennis would do anything stupid?'

Karen closed her eyes. Dennis Dean wasn't known for his intelligence, but under normal circumstances, she would say he was unlikely to be a threat to his family. But these were far from normal circumstances.

'I don't know but we need to be cautious, Rick. We don't know if he's armed. I'll try to get through to Becky.'

'Understood,' Rick said and then hung up.

'It sounds like the situation's escalating,' Karen said as she scrolled through her contact list looking for Becky Carpenter's number. 'I'm going to call Becky and see if she can tell us what's going on.'

It was a long time before Becky answered and Karen started to fear the worst.

'Sarge, Dennis is here.' Becky sounded slightly breathless.

'We're on the way, Becky. How are you holding up?'

'We're downstairs in the living room. I've got Jenny upstairs in the main bedroom, and I'm trying to stop him going upstairs, but I don't think I can keep them apart much longer. Jenny's mother is here, and she's just making him worse. He's really riled up.'

'Is anyone hurt?' Karen asked.

'Not yet,' Becky said ominously.

'All right. We'll be with you in about ten minutes. A uniformed unit is already there, but they can't get in the front door because Dennis has blocked their way. They'll attempt to come in through the back if you can keep him distracted.'

'I'll do my best.'

'Is he armed?'

'No. He hasn't got any weapons.'

'Good,' Karen said, thinking at least that was something on their side. 'If the situation gets worse, Becky, you need to get out of there.'

'I can't leave Jenny to face him, Sarge. He looks like he wants to murder her. He's convinced this bloke Jenny's been seeing has taken Emily.'

'Is there any truth to that?'

'Honestly, I have no idea. Jenny hasn't mentioned him to me at all. According to Dennis, his name's Phil Carver – that's all I know.'

'All right, Becky. We'll look into it. I'll let you get back. Try to get Dennis's mother-in-law out of the house if you can.'

After Karen hung up on Becky, she quickly dialled Sophie's number and gave her Phil Carver's name so she could do a background check.

When Karen finally hung up, they were only minutes away from Jenny Dean's house.

'Did Becky tell you why Jenny had been keeping this man a secret?' DI Morgan asked as he turned left towards Washingborough.

Karen shook her head. 'No, but it's very strange. Not only did Jenny not mention him, but Becky's never seen him. I mean if your girlfriend's child had just gone missing, wouldn't you be there offering support?'

Karen didn't think it was possible for DI Morgan's frown to get any deeper, but it did.

'It's not looking good,' he said.

Karen stared straight ahead as the fields slipped past them on either side of the road. She couldn't agree more. It didn't look good, at all.

◆ ◆ ◆

They reached Jenny Dean's house and dashed up the driveway. The front door was ajar, and DI Morgan entered first. It looked as though someone had already got rid of the barricade at the front door. A heavy oak cabinet had been shoved to one side.

DI Morgan called out, 'Police,' and announced his name and Karen's. He stepped out of the hallway into a small living room stuffed full to the brim with furniture and people.

The room felt even more cramped with DI Morgan and Karen joining two uniformed officers, Becky Carpenter and Jenny Dean's mother, all crammed into one end of the living room. The huge bulk of Dennis Dean loomed at the other end of the room. The tense way in which he stood made everyone watch him as though he were a bomb about to explode.

Becky's hair was usually neat and tidy, in a low ponytail at the base of her neck, but today strands of hair had come loose, and her fringe stuck up on end as though she'd been raking her fingers through it.

The uniformed officers were glad to see Karen and DI Morgan and introduced themselves quickly.

'We managed to remove the barricade. But unfortunately, Mr Dean refuses to leave the property,' the taller of the two officers said.

Dennis Dean turned to face DI Morgan with a sneer on his face. 'I pay the rent on this place. I've got more right to be here than all you lot.'

'Let's talk about this outside, Dennis,' DI Morgan said, keeping his voice low but firm.

'That's right. You get out of here. Otherwise, they can drag you out and lock you up, and it'll be no less than you deserve.' The small grey-haired lady strode up to Dennis and poked him in the chest.

DI Morgan winced. This was not exactly de-escalating the situation. 'Please, Becky, perhaps you could take Jenny's mother into the kitchen?'

Becky stepped forward and put her hands on the woman's shoulders. 'Why don't we make a cup of tea, Mrs Jennings?' Becky said, practically pushing the woman towards the kitchen.

'I don't want a cup of tea,' the woman insisted, twisting round in Becky's grasp and shooting evil looks at Dennis Dean.

But Becky wasn't taking no for an answer.

DI Morgan began to breathe more easily. With his mother-in-law out of the room, Dennis seemed visibly less angry.

'What's all this about, Dennis?' DI Morgan asked.

'It's that slapper upstairs,' Dennis said. 'She's been seeing someone else. She barely knows him. He could be capable of anything, and I don't think it's a coincidence that Emily went missing just after she got a new bloke.'

There was a sudden scream, and Dennis's mother-in-law ripped herself from Becky's grasp and launched herself out of the kitchen, barrelling towards Dennis with her fists flying. 'She was only looking for a bit of comfort. Who could blame her after living with you for all those years?'

DI Morgan moved quickly. They needed to remove that woman from the situation.

He put himself between her and Dennis just in time. Dennis gave a frustrated shout and, unable to take his anger out on anyone else, he reached down and grabbed one side of the dining table and flipped it over, sending the fruit bowl and phone crashing to the floor. DI Morgan braced himself, expecting the table to slam into his back, but fortunately, it stopped just short.

'Stop acting like children,' Karen said from behind them. 'This isn't helping at all. Dennis, pick up that table and pull yourself together.'

DI Morgan turned to look at Dennis, keeping himself between Louise Jennings and Dennis, just in case. But the fight seemed to have drained out of the big man and to DI Morgan's surprise, Dennis did as he was told, leaning down and righting the table, and even picking up a couple of pieces of fruit and sticking them back in the bowl – which miraculously hadn't broken. Then he picked up the phone and stared at it before setting it down next to the fruit bowl.

Karen turned her attention to Dennis's mother-in-law. 'You, come upstairs with me. We're going to talk to Jenny.'

She turned and nodded to DI Morgan, who smiled. He was enjoying working with Karen. She used her initiative and they worked well together. It made the job easier when you could trust a colleague enough to divide up the caseload on the hoof without having to worry about the details.

While Karen spoke to Jenny and her mother upstairs, DI Morgan would be able to focus on Dennis Dean.

CHAPTER TWENTY-SEVEN

When DI Morgan finally managed to persuade Dennis Dean to go out-side, he followed him out, after making sure Karen had Jenny's mother under control.

Dennis leaned against the front wall of the house and lit a ciga-rette. 'Scary lady,' he said nodding towards the house, and DI Morgan guessed he was referring to Karen. 'Is she your boss?'

DI Morgan stifled a smile. 'Believe it or not, no. I'm the boss.'

Dennis pulled a face. 'I wouldn't like to get on the wrong side of her.'

'Look, Dennis. We're trying to help you. We want to find Emily and bring her home.'

Dennis paused and flicked cigarette ash on to the grass. 'Do you think she's still alive?'

When Dennis asked the question, he was staring down at the floor, but he slowly raised his head to gaze at DI Morgan and wait for an answer. DI Morgan shifted awkwardly under those steely blue eyes. He couldn't lie.

'I really don't know. I hope so.'

Dennis slumped against the wall, looking like a broken man.

'Is there a reason you suspect the man Jenny has been seeing, Dennis?'

The big man dropped the cigarette on the floor and crushed it under his foot. 'I can't help suspecting everybody these days. This bloke, Phil Carver, is some sort of computer nerd. You hear stories about that, don't you? Sleazy websites with little kids.'

'We'll talk to him, Dennis. We'll find out if he has anything to do with Emily's disappearance.'

Dennis nodded but didn't reply.

'I have to ask you to come to us first with things like this. We'll act on any genuine information we receive. If you leave us in the dark and try to sort things yourself, it won't end well.'

Dennis gave him a twisted smile. 'You're new to these parts, aren't you?'

'Relatively.'

'I don't trust the police, and I can't say they've ever helped me.'

DI Morgan nodded. 'There's a first time for everything, Dennis.'

Dennis pushed off the wall. 'Well, what are you waiting for? Go and talk to Phil Carver and find out if he had anything to do with my daughter's disappearance.'

'I'm waiting for DS Hart. She's asking Jenny about him. We need to find out everything we can. That way, when we talk to Phil, we go in with a position of strength.'

Dennis thought for a moment and then said, 'I can understand that. Knowledge is power, right?'

DI Morgan nodded. 'Right.'

Dennis turned and stared off across the road. 'I just hope you're not too late.'

◆ ◆ ◆

Ten minutes later, DI Morgan and Karen were on their way to pay Jenny's new boyfriend a visit. Karen was driving this time.

'Why didn't Jenny mention him before?' DI Morgan asked.

Jenny's boyfriend, Phil Carver, lived in Bracebridge Heath, and it wasn't an area DI Morgan knew well.

Karen turned left at the traffic lights. 'She didn't want Dennis finding out, apparently.' \

DI Morgan huffed impatiently. 'For goodness' sake. Her daughter's missing. Why would she hold information like that back?'

Karen turned right at the Premier Inn, just behind a tractor pulling a trailer. 'For what it's worth, I think she knows she made a mistake, sir. And she's convinced he hasn't got anything to do with Emily's disappearance.'

DI Morgan didn't look mollified. 'Our job would be far easier if people didn't keep things from us.'

'You've got no argument from me on that score.'

DI Morgan called the station and spoke to Sophie, who'd been running a background check on Phil Carver. When Karen stopped at the traffic lights, she looked at DI Morgan. He shook his head.

She supposed coming up with something clear-cut like a criminal record or Phil Carver's name on the sex register was too much to hope for.

When DI Morgan hung up, he related everything Sophie had told him. 'It seems Phil Carver's a freelance computer expert. He's lived at his current address for three years. No criminal record and lives alone.'

'Ever married?'

DI Morgan shook his head.

Karen indicated and pulled in beside a small parade of shops, including a Tesco Express and a shop selling e-cigarettes. 'I think his flat must be one of these,' she said, nodding at the windows over the shops.

She parked, and they headed to the back of the shops to find the entrance to the flats.

The front of the shops had looked smart enough, but at the back, there were large, overflowing metal bins and plastic bollards, some of which had been knocked over. A wide concrete staircase rose up to the upper floors. It was open to the elements, and there were only two floors of flats above the parade of shops.

'I think this must be the way,' Karen said, beginning to climb the stairs.

Below them, there was creaking and rattling as a metal folding door opened. One of the shops must have been expecting a delivery.

'He's number twenty-one,' Karen said as they walked past two doors. 'Ah, here it is.'

The door was painted bright blue, and gold-coloured numbers were screwed in place above the rusted letterbox. There was no bell, so Karen rapped with her knuckles.

They had no reason to think either girl was here, but both DI Morgan and Karen scanned the area and the parked cars as they waited for Phil Carver to open the door.

When he finally did open up, DI Morgan was taken aback. He was Dennis Dean's complete opposite. Clearly, this time around, Jenny had chosen a very different man. The only thing they had in common was their height. But where Dennis was strong and muscular, Phil Carver was thin to the point where DI Morgan wondered if he'd been ill. His face was pale and he had dark circles under his eyes. He blinked at them initially, screwing up his face as though he were allergic to the sunlight.

'Phil Carver?' Karen asked.

Phil narrowed his eyes. 'Yes,' he said nervously. 'What's all this about?'

They showed their ID and Phil's shoulders rounded and slumped. 'I thought you'd get here eventually. It's about the girls, isn't it?'

Karen lifted an eyebrow. 'That's right.'

He led the way inside. The flat was small and dark and the air was stuffy. The windows had not been opened in a very long time. A faint smell of old fried food lingered in the air.

Phil walked in front of them. His tracksuit bottoms hung so low on his hips it looked as though they were about to slip down and expose his backside. His arms sticking out of his baggy, black T-shirt were painfully thin.

He led the way into a small living room crammed with electronic equipment. One wall was almost covered by four huge monitors. Computer equipment and games consoles were stacked below them.

In front of the equipment stood a chair. DI Morgan recognised it as one of those fancy ergonomic models – much more expensive than the ones they used back at the station.

Phil collapsed down into the chair, spun around and then nodded over to a couple of red bucket chairs. 'Take a pew,' he said.

Although the computer equipment and games consoles had green lights flashing, indicating they were on, all the monitors had been switched off, which immediately made DI Morgan suspicious.

'It's dark in here, Mr Carver,' Karen said as she sat down. 'Don't you ever open the curtains?'

Phil shook his head. 'No, the sun shines on the screens and makes them hard to see.'

'You certainly have a lot of computer monitors,' DI Morgan said, looking around the room.

'It's my job,' Phil said.

'And what is your job exactly?' Karen asked.

'I'm a champion,' Phil said proudly, surprising DI Morgan.

'Really?' Karen asked drily.

Phil nodded enthusiastically. 'Yeah, I compete professionally: online gaming. Mostly Xbox. I do very well at that, but I play some PC games as well.'

'And you earn a living from that?' DI Morgan asked.

'Yeah, I do.' He smiled. 'There aren't many people who can say they earn a living out of their favourite pastime.'

Although the computer equipment looked top of the range, the other furniture in the flat was mismatched and tatty. DI Morgan wouldn't be surprised if it had come from a charity shop or had been donated by relatives or friends. He didn't seem to be making a very good living out of these competitions.

'Does Emily like these games, Phil?' Karen asked.

'Emily?' The boastful expression left Phil's face, and now he just looked guarded.

'Yes,' DI Morgan said. 'Emily's ten years old. That's the sort of age kids love to play computer games, isn't it?'

Phil gave a sulky shrug. 'I don't really know the kid.'

'You're in a relationship with her mother?'

Phil shifted uncomfortably in his seat. His tongue slid along his lower lip. 'Kind of. I mean it's early days. But she's a good-looking woman, right?' He raised his eyebrows and looked at DI Morgan for confirmation, but DI Morgan remained silent. 'Any red-blooded male would be interested in Jenny Dean. The only problem is, her ex is a nutter.'

'Did you ever meet Emily?' Karen asked.

Phil shrugged. Again his tongue flicked across his lower lip. 'Only a few times. I mean, as I said, it's early days. We went out for a couple of meals in Lincoln and spent an evening at my local. Jenny doesn't want to rush into anything, not with her kid to think about. She just introduced me to Emily as her friend. I barely spoke to her the first time, and the second time I went to Jenny's house I didn't see her for more than five minutes.'

'And when was this?'

Phil's eyes darted between the two detectives. 'What do you mean?'

'You said you saw Emily for five minutes. When was this?'

Phil swallowed and focused his dark, dull eyes on Karen. 'It was about a fortnight ago, I suppose. A couple of months after she kicked Dennis out. She likes me because I'm nothing like him. I called round to pick Jenny up, and she hadn't finished doing her make-up, so she invited me to wait inside. There was nothing sinister about it.'

Karen nodded slowly. 'What did you talk about?'

Phil threw up his hands. 'I can't remember. I probably asked how school had been or something. I was only inside the house for a couple of minutes. To be honest, I was more scared of Jenny's mother.'

'So you met Jenny's mother too.'

'Well, of course, she was there to look after Emily. Jenny's a good mum, you know. She wouldn't just leave Emily all alone without a babysitter when we were off down the pub for the night.'

'What were you doing the day the girls disappeared?'

'Playing in an online competition. They keep records of where and when players are active, so you can check if you want.'

Karen removed a sheet of paper from the folder in her bag and balanced it on her legs. It was a printout of Sian Gibson's most recent school photo. She held it out to Phil Carver. 'Recognise her?'

Phil peered at the printout. 'Is this the other girl?'

'Yes.'

He sat back in his chair and shook his head. 'No, I've never seen her before in my life.'

CHAPTER TWENTY-EIGHT

Karen breathed in deep lungfuls of fresh air. The inside of the flat had been claustrophobic and stale. She couldn't wait to escape. The reptilian way Phil Carver ran the tip of his tongue along his lower lip before answering their questions had made her skin crawl.

'Did you notice the computers were on even though the monitors were off?' DI Morgan asked in a low voice once Phil Carver had closed the door.

Karen nodded. 'Perhaps there was something on them he didn't want visitors to see?'

DI Morgan looked back towards the flat. 'I didn't ask him about it because I didn't want to tip him off before we get a warrant. We'll need forensics to analyse all the computer gear he has up there and take a look at his internet history.'

'If he does have something to hide, I hope our visit doesn't provoke him to start deleting stuff,' Karen said.

'What did you make of him?' DI Morgan asked as they walked side by side down the concrete steps.

'My instinct tells me he's not to be trusted, but that doesn't necessarily mean he had anything to do with the girls' disappearance. What does your gut tell you?'

'My gut doesn't tell me anything. I don't believe in that mumbo jumbo.' DI Morgan shook his head and looked irritated. 'But there's no evidence that he had anything to do with it. No relevant history, and he claims to have an alibi.'

Karen was about to reply when a large lorry pulled up in front of them, its rumbling engine drowning out her voice as they walked around it. She watched DI Morgan walk a few steps ahead of her and pulled a face at him, feeling as immature as Rick and Sophie, although it was probably a better way to let off steam than start an argument.

'By the time we get the warrant, there'll probably be nothing left to look at. He's some computer whizz, so he'll know how to delete things without leaving a trace,' Karen said once they were far enough away from the lorry for him to hear her.

'I agree, but without him handing the equipment over voluntarily, our only option is a warrant. Look, do you mind waiting for a minute?' DI Morgan said, loosening his collar and handing her the car keys. 'I'm getting a headache and want to grab some paracetamol from Tesco.'

'Of course,' Karen said.

She was planning to wait by the car, but as she stood there watching people nipping into shops and queuing in traffic, she suddenly felt furious. Two little girls were still missing, and life was going on as normal.

She stomped over to the boot and removed a couple of large plastic evidence bags, along with some official forms and a marker pen, then locked the car and stalked off back towards Phil Carver's flat.

◆ ◆ ◆

When DI Morgan arrived back at the car, tablets in hand, he was surprised to find Karen had gone. He looked around the car park but still couldn't see her. Had she decided she needed something from one of the shops too?

He pulled out a strip of tablets and swallowed two. He was beginning to grow concerned and was considering going in search of Karen when suddenly she appeared. He frowned. She was carrying a big desktop computer and what looked like a laptop in large evidence bags.

He walked forward to help her and asked what was going on.

'I decided you were right,' Karen said. 'We only had two options. Wait for a warrant or get Phil Carver to hand over his computer equipment voluntarily.'

DI Morgan raised an eyebrow. 'How on earth did you manage to persuade Phil Carver to hand over his computer equipment?'

Karen smiled a little sheepishly. 'Um, could you open the boot for me?'

DI Morgan took the keys and did as she asked, helping her load the evidence. The bags were labelled, and Karen showed him that the forms had been filled in correctly.

DI Morgan shook his head in disbelief and walked to the driver's side. 'I hope this is all above board, Karen.'

'Of course. He gave me his computer equipment voluntarily and signed the forms. We'll still need a warrant for his ISP provider.'

'Those computers are his life,' DI Morgan said. 'I find it very hard to believe he'd just hand them over like that.'

Karen shrugged. 'Well, he may have had a little encouragement.'

DI Morgan frowned. 'What sort of encouragement?'

'I happened to mention how terrible it would be if Dennis Dean discovered where he was living, especially if Dennis heard Phil wasn't cooperating with our enquiries.'

'You threatened him?'

Karen shook her head. 'I wouldn't say threatened exactly, more focused his train of thought.'

DI Morgan leaned on the roof of the car and studied Karen. 'And what if this evidence is ruled inadmissible? If he's done anything to the girls, he might get away with it.'

'There's no reason it would be. And I'm sick of waiting around, sir. We don't have time to wait for the warrant. If he is involved and the girls are still alive, the clock is ticking.'

'If the superintendent finds out about this, Karen . . .'

'Then we'll cross that bridge when we come to it,' Karen said stubbornly.

'I was planning to go back via Heighington and visit Matthew Saunders, but I suppose we can't do that with the evidence in the car. We can't leave it unattended.'

Karen pulled out her mobile phone. 'That's not a problem. I'll get Rick to pick the equipment up and take it back to the tech lab at Nettleham. We just have to make sure we maintain the chain of custody.' All stages in the processing of evidence had to be recorded. If the evidence was relied upon for a conviction, every movement or transfer had to be accounted for or the case could fall apart in court.

Back in the car, Karen asked Rick to come and meet them at Heighington to collect the evidence, while DI Morgan started the engine. Karen had certainly taken a risk. There were all sorts of things that could go wrong. For one, Phil Carver might have other computers that they hadn't spotted, and without a full search, they could miss something really important. DI Morgan was caught between wanting to reprimand Karen and understanding why she'd behaved the way she had.

If they'd waited for the warrant, chances were that everything would have been wiped from the computers and they'd have nothing to go on. At least now they had a fighting chance of finding out what Phil Carver was up to. Whether his shady behaviour had anything to do with the girls' disappearance remained to be seen.

◆ ◆ ◆

Karen slid into the passenger seat and buckled her seatbelt. She'd been expecting a dressing-down from DI Morgan for acting alone when his back was turned. She should have talked this over with him first. She still believed she'd done the right thing, but it had been reckless – even she had to admit that.

She knew she and DI Morgan had a difference of opinion on certain matters. Karen very much relied on her instinct when it came to working out whether someone was telling the truth or not. DI Morgan played things by the book. That wasn't what annoyed Karen. The thing that had got under her skin was the fact that he relied on hunches but pretended he didn't. Take Matthew Saunders, for example. They were paying him another visit because DI Morgan had a hunch Matthew Saunders was hiding something.

Karen knew she was better off keeping her mouth shut. DI Morgan wasn't exactly a tyrant, but pointing out your senior officer was wrong wasn't the wisest move.

She stayed silent as he drove out of the car park and headed back to the main Lincoln road, but once he'd turned left and headed back towards Heighington, Karen couldn't keep quiet any longer.

'How do you explain Matthew Saunders?' she asked.

'What do you mean?'

'Well, you have a hunch. Your gut told you he was lying.'

'No, not at all. It had nothing to do with my gut. It was something concrete. Something about his behaviour tipped me off. I just didn't know what it was at the time.'

'Well, isn't that what hunches are? People relying on small signs and tells, body language. Being able to read people.'

'I'd like to think it's more scientific than that,' DI Morgan said mildly.

Karen clamped her mouth shut. Maybe they should just agree to disagree on this one.

'I'll park up on the High Street,' DI Morgan said. 'I think Matthew Saunders might open up to me if I talk to him alone.'

Karen was a little surprised, but she shrugged and said, 'Okay. If you think that's best. After Rick gets here, I'll pop into the Spar and grab a sandwich. I missed lunch and I'm starving. Can I get you anything?'

DI Morgan pulled into a parking space, put the handbrake on and then said, 'I'll have a chicken sandwich if they've got one.'

They got out of the car, and Karen glanced at her watch. Rick shouldn't be too long. She turned and watched DI Morgan walking towards the Saunders's house by the river. One of these days she'd get him to admit he relied on hunches.

◆ ◆ ◆

After Rick had collected the evidence bags and signed the paperwork, Karen walked across the road to the small Spar supermarket. Inside, she picked up orange juice for herself and water for DI Morgan and then headed to look at the selection of sandwiches.

She'd just rounded the corner and headed into the next aisle when she spotted someone she recognised.

Cathy Palmer.

Cathy wore an old-fashioned faded dress with a brown anorak over the top. Her hair hung limply down to her shoulders, and she'd tucked it behind her ears. She wore no make-up, which wasn't unusual. Karen had never seen Cathy wearing make-up, but she'd also rarely seen her away from the farmhouse. Somehow, here in the brightly lit shop, Cathy looked even more washed out than usual. She was stooping to examine coffee on the bottom shelf. She reached out to pick up a jar of Nescafé and the sleeve of her anorak slid back, revealing a nasty-looking bruise on her forearm.

Karen wondered how she'd got that bruise. Was Cathy's father or brother responsible? Although her father was ill and infirm now, Karen could imagine him reaching out and pinching Cathy if she'd annoyed him in some way. That was the sort of man Nigel Palmer was.

Karen clutched the bottles of juice and water to her chest and walked up to Cathy. 'Hello, I didn't expect to see you here.'

Cathy quickly straightened up and looked at Karen through wide, scared eyes like a startled rabbit. 'Oh,' she said, 'I was just leaving.'

'Wait a minute.' Karen smiled and did her best to look friendly and approachable. 'I've been hoping to have a chat with you.'

'You have?' Cathy shot a nervous glance over her shoulder and then looked back at Karen.

'Yes, I thought you might have time for a coffee.'

'What for?' Cathy looked horrified at the prospect.

'Well, I know it must be difficult for you stuck in the farmhouse all day, looking after your dad, and I thought you might need some company. With my job, I don't get much chance to chat either.'

That was clumsy. Karen knew she was making a mess of this. She should have tried to be more subtle in her attempt to befriend Cathy, but she was scared the woman was about to dart off at any moment.

'I'm sorry,' Cathy said, 'I have things to do.'

'Maybe another time,' Karen said, and then reached out carefully to push up the sleeve of the woman's anorak. 'How did that happen, Cathy?'

Her cheeks flushed pink, and she yanked down the arm of her jacket. 'I just banged it against a cupboard in the kitchen. I've always been clumsy like that.'

Karen waited to see if Cathy would say anything else but she didn't.

Finally Karen responded. 'I'd like to believe that, Cathy. But I can't help thinking your father and brother aren't treating you as well as they should.'

Cathy looked down at the jars of coffee again as though they were the most interesting thing in the world. 'Oh, they're not that bad really. They can just be a bit bad-tempered sometimes.'

Karen frowned. 'Well, I'm always here if you want to chat.'

Before she could say anything else, she heard a deep voice behind them. 'Time to go, Cathy.'

Karen turned to see Jasper Palmer towering over her.

Karen glared at him, determined not to be intimidated.

'You seem to be getting a little overfamiliar with my sister, officer,' Jasper said. 'She should put in a complaint against you.'

'What are you talking about?' Karen snapped.

'I saw you tugging at her clothing.'

'I was lifting the sleeve of her anorak because I saw a bruise. You wouldn't know anything about that, would you, Jasper?'

Cathy made a squeaking noise like a startled mouse.

Jasper moved so he stood between Karen and Cathy. He took the wire shopping basket out of Cathy's hand and set it on the floor. 'We'll get our shopping later, Cathy. There's a funny smell in here,' he said, and then walked away from Karen, heading towards the exit.

Cathy sent an apologetic look over her shoulder as she followed her brother out of the shop, and Karen watched them go.

She didn't trust Jasper Palmer. Not for one second.

Feeling angry and frustrated, she made her way back to the fresh food aisle and grabbed a couple of chicken sandwiches.

Karen had seen the woman behind the till before but couldn't remember her name. She shook her head as Karen approached. 'Did you ever see such a jumpy woman? The way Nigel Palmer treats that girl is a disgrace and the brother isn't much better.'

'Have you seen Nigel Palmer recently?' Karen put her shopping on the counter.

The woman shook her head as she scanned the barcodes on the sandwiches. 'No, he's more or less a recluse these days. Good thing, in my opinion. He's a nasty man.'

'Why do you say that?'

'You've met him, haven't you?' She furiously moved the bottle of water back over the scanner when it didn't register the first time. 'That other young girl went missing from the farm. Suspicious, if you ask me.' The machine beeped, and she placed the bottle of water beside the sandwiches. 'Do you have a loyalty card?'

Karen shook her head.

'Any news on the two little ones?'

'Not yet.'

'You should search that farmhouse. That would be the first place I'd look.'

'Have you heard or seen anything that makes you think the Palmers would know what happened to the missing girls?'

The woman hesitated. 'No, but there's something weird about them. They're just not . . . right.'

Was that what Karen sounded like to her colleagues? Ready to jump to unjustified conclusions because she thought the Palmers were odd? There was a reason people should be considered innocent until proven guilty. Circumstances like these could lead to witch-hunts, especially in small, tight-knit communities. She must remember to make that appointment with Amethyst.

After paying, Karen walked back towards the car. Only a few feet away from where they had parked was the Butcher & Beast. She should have gone in there. They did lovely sandwiches.

Sitting in the passenger seat, she munched her way through her lunch while looking at an Ordnance Survey map on her iPhone. The small screen didn't make it easy, but she managed to zoom into the Palmers' farm. It ran between Washingborough and Heighington. They had a lot of land and a large number of outbuildings.

Karen went through them slowly, counting each one. There were two grain stores, an old windmill that had lost its sails and fallen into disrepair, and a number of large barns. Some she knew were empty, others contained valuable farm machinery and were kept tightly locked up.

The orders of the search had been to inspect every outbuilding in the search perimeter. Karen had no doubt these buildings had been searched, but she wondered if there could be something they'd missed. She polished off the last of the sandwich and then phoned to check in with Sophie at the station. The search was still ongoing, and Sophie promised to check with the officers in charge regarding all the outbuildings on the Palmers' farm.

A low rumble above her made Karen look up. The grey Sentinel R1 aircraft was flying overhead. The spy plane was a familiar sight in the area and was based at RAF Waddington along with the Sentry. The RAF reconnaissance planes regularly flew low over Branston, where Karen lived. The huge Sentinel was an impressive sight. She could do with a spy herself. Ideally, one planted in the Palmer household.

As browbeaten as Cathy Palmer was, surely she wouldn't just stand by and do nothing if she knew two little girls were being held captive by her father or brother.

The more Karen thought about it, the more it became clear that Cathy could be the key to unravelling the mystery around the Palmers. If she got Cathy onside, maybe she could crack the Palmers once and for all.

CHAPTER TWENTY-NINE

Matthew Saunders's strange behaviour had been bothering DI Morgan since he and Karen had first spoken to the man. With an overwhelming number of suspects to talk to and leads to follow, he'd been forced to leave Saunders on the back burner, but something kept niggling at him. He was sure Matthew Saunders had been lying to them, and he intended to find out why.

DI Morgan walked along the pretty Heighington High Street. On the surface, it appeared to be a lovely place to live, with its old stone buildings, a narrow stream running through the centre and two pubs and a village shop. DI Morgan thought he might consider Heighington as a place to move to after this case was over. He needed something more permanent than his current draughty rental property. Not that he'd need a big place. He hadn't heard from Julia since she'd dumped him, and the way his future was looking, he'd be living alone with only his job for company. He sighed. He didn't even have the time for a dog. Dogs needed regular exercise, and it wouldn't be fair to keep one with the hours he worked. Maybe he'd get a cat. They were far less needy.

He approached the Saunders's house and rang the doorbell. On the other side of the road, the GP surgery was busy. A number two double-decker bus chugged along the narrow High Street, only just missing the parked cars. Further down the street, the spire of Heighington church towered over all the other buildings in the vicinity.

When Matthew Saunders opened the door, he looked shocked to see DI Morgan standing on his doorstep. 'What is it? Nothing's happened to Danny, has it?'

DI Morgan shook his head. 'No, sir. I just have a few follow-up questions for you.'

'Ah, I see,' Matthew Saunders said as he stepped back to let DI Morgan enter.

'I'm not sure there's much else I can tell you.' Matthew Saunders led DI Morgan into the front room. 'Can I get you a drink – tea or coffee?'

DI Morgan said, 'No, thank you, sir. I think you know why I'm here.'

Matthew Saunders's eyes opened wide, and he licked his lips before sinking down on to the sofa. DI Morgan sat opposite him in an armchair.

'Well, no. I can't imagine why you want to talk to me.'

'The last time we spoke, I got the distinct impression you were hiding something.' DI Morgan watched him closely.

Matthew Saunders shook his head rapidly. 'I've got nothing to hide.'

DI Morgan narrowed his eyes but said nothing. He waited for the silence to do the work for him.

A light sheen of sweat had appeared on Matthew Saunders's brow. He linked his fingers, inverted them and set them on his lap before wringing his hands together.

'I really can't think what gave you the impression I was hiding something. I want to cooperate fully. I want to make sure the girls are okay. I mean, I can't even imagine how I'd feel if it was Danny who'd gone missing.'

'So tell me what you're holding back.'

Matthew Saunders pulled a face. 'Really, I swear it has nothing to do with the girls' disappearance.'

'I'm afraid I can't take your word for that, sir. So you'll have to tell me.'

Matthew Saunders ran a hand over his face then glanced at the brass clock on the mantelpiece over the unlit log burner. 'My wife works at the doctor's surgery. It's only a couple of minutes' walk away and she'll be home soon.'

DI Morgan also glanced at the clock but said nothing and waited for him to continue.

'If I tell you, can you promise me my wife won't find out?'

DI Morgan resisted the urge to roll his eyes. He saw where this was heading and it infuriated him. 'I can't promise,' he said. 'But if there's no need for her to find out, then she won't find out from me. I'm not out to cause any problems in your marriage, Mr Saunders. I just want you to tell me the truth.'

Matthew Saunders stood up and began to pace back and forth in front of the fireplace. Then he looked up and glanced out of the window as though he were expecting his wife to be walking along the street.

'We're running out of time,' DI Morgan said.

'What?' Matthew Saunders looked startled.

'You said your wife will be home soon. So you're running out of time to tell me whatever it is you're hiding before she gets here.'

Matthew Saunders raised his face to the ceiling and then closed his eyes. He groaned. 'Okay, I'll tell you. But please do everything you can to make sure my wife doesn't find out.'

DI Morgan waited.

Matthew Saunders looked at him with an anxious expression. 'It was just an affair, a short-term thing. It didn't mean anything.'

DI Morgan sat and listened to the whole sordid story, trying to keep his expression blank. He'd only met Tanya Saunders once, but she'd seemed a warm, friendly woman who didn't deserve a philanderer for a husband.

It was all so predictable, DI Morgan thought, as Matthew Saunders relaxed into his story and made a little joke.

'I mean you've seen her – you can't blame me, can you?' He gave DI Morgan a wink.

DI Morgan did not respond. He'd met the woman Matthew Saunders referred to, and he was annoyed he hadn't seen it coming.

Karen sat in the car, trying to work out what was bothering her about her encounter with the Palmers. Jasper's abrasive personality and intimidating presence were enough to set Karen's teeth on edge, but there was something else bugging her. Then she remembered. Cathy hadn't asked about the two girls.

Everyone in Heighington was waiting for news, so why hadn't Cathy asked whether there had been any developments or if they were any closer to finding the girls? Unless, of course, she knew where those girls were.

She spotted DI Morgan walking back to the car with a stern look on his face, and guessed he'd achieved something.

She waited until he was sitting in the driver's seat and then handed him his sandwich. 'Well, tell me what happened.'

'He's been having an affair,' DI Morgan said, peeling back the plastic wrap.

Karen took a sip of her orange juice. 'Your hunch paid off.'

DI Morgan managed a small smile. 'It wasn't a hunch. It was a fact-based opinion. I noticed he carefully thought through his answers before he opened his mouth, and he wouldn't maintain eye contact. All of that made me think he wasn't telling us the full story. It had nothing to do with gut feelings.'

'If you say so, sir,' Karen said, screwing the lid back on her orange juice. 'So his affair has nothing to do with our case then?'

DI Morgan finished a mouthful of the chicken sandwich and then said, 'Quite the opposite. The woman he was having an affair with is Leanne Gibson.'

CHAPTER THIRTY

Jasper Palmer swung himself down from the cab of the tractor and landed with a thud. He'd parked it out behind the barn, some distance from the farmhouse so Cathy wouldn't realise he'd come back. She'd been acting very strangely recently. She was usually very meek and obedient, their father's doormat, but yesterday, Jasper had seen a glimpse of steely rebellion in her eyes. And it made him nervous. It made him wonder if Cathy was planning something.

He made his way to the back of the farmhouse. At this time of day, Cathy normally had some time to herself. Their father tended to doze by the fire most of the day. Even the simplest tasks wore him out. It was hard to remember him as he had been – an imposing, domineering man, as tall and strong as Jasper was now.

When he approached the kitchen window, he leaned on the windowsill and looked inside. Cathy was sitting at the kitchen table with her back to him.

She didn't seem to be doing anything unusual.

Maybe he was letting his imagination run wild. The police had been sniffing around again and that had made him nervous. They'd put him through hell after Amy Fisher's disappearance.

He missed having Amy around. She'd cheered the place up, and she'd been interested in him. Even though she'd played coy and hard to get, Jasper knew what she really wanted. The look on Cathy's face the day she caught him talking to Amy in the studio had made Jasper laugh out loud. Cathy had always been very prim and proper. Credit where it was due, though. His sister hadn't breathed a word of that to the police. She'd backed up his story when he insisted that he'd barely known the girl.

It was just as well. The police were bad enough without any evidence. They really would have been on his back if they'd known how much time he'd spent watching Amy.

Jasper smiled. Cathy was a good girl. The secret was safe with her.

Before he turned away, he caught sight of his father's mobile phone by Cathy's elbow.

Jasper frowned. It was an old-fashioned flip phone. His father barely used it any more but kept it for emergencies. It had been useful when he used to go out on the farm, but these days he never left the house.

Was Cathy planning to call somebody? Jasper wondered if that was why she'd been acting oddly. Perhaps she'd found herself a man. The thought made Jasper grin. Not very likely. Cathy was destined to die an old maid. She looked after the farmhouse for her father, and when the old man died, which wouldn't be long now, Cathy would stay with Jasper and earn her keep by looking after the house for him.

He didn't have to worry about Cathy. She wouldn't tell anyone. How could she? She had no one to tell.

◆ ◆ ◆

Cathy Palmer tiptoed over to the fireplace and stared in silence at her father. Was he asleep? He looked as though he was. His thin eyelids fluttered a little but other than that he remained still. There was a faint wheezing as he took in a breath, but that happened most of the time now.

Cathy shot a look at the large kitchen table. Her father's mobile phone sat on the surface, taunting her. Her fingers itched to pick it up.

She raked a hand through her hair and blinked back tears. She couldn't make up her mind. If only she could stop second-guessing herself. When she left the Spar, she'd promised herself she would do it just as soon as she was alone.

Jasper had gone to the fields to work, and her father was asleep, but still, she couldn't bring herself to do it. She was terrified they'd find out.

What if her father was only pretending to be asleep? Or what if he checked his bill and found out she had used his phone? She was already hiding his bank statements. If he knew she'd been transferring his money to her account, he'd kill her.

Cathy shivered and moved a little closer to the fire. It was starting to die down, and she would need to put some more logs on soon. They had a central heating system, which ran on oil that was delivered every four months, but her father said there was no need to have it on during the day.

Maybe that would be true if they lived in a well-insulated modern cottage, but the windows at the farmhouse weren't even double-glazed. The walls were thick stone but they didn't do much to keep out the October chill. Later winter months were even worse.

Cathy spent most of her time rushing around, attending to the household tasks as well as tending the small number of chickens they kept on the farm. She tried to keep moving so the chill didn't creep inside her bones. It wasn't so bad now, but when the cold snaps arrived in January and February, it would be unbearable.

Her father didn't mind at all. He spent his days sitting beside the fire they always kept burning, which meant she had to clean it out every morning on her hands and knees. The rest of the house could be frigid with cold, and he wouldn't care. Last winter, she'd had ice on the inside of her bedroom window.

She stared at her father with dislike. His face was gaunt, and his once tall, strong frame looked withered as he slumped in his wheelchair. *Look*, she told herself, *there's nothing to be scared of. What's he going to do to you? He wouldn't be able to catch you anyway.*

She needed to do it. It was the right thing to do, and if she didn't get it out of the way now . . .

Cathy scurried over to the kitchen table. Quietly she pulled out a chair and sat down, then slowly picked up the small black phone.

She didn't have a mobile of her own. Her father wouldn't allow it.

She'd once dreamed of getting away from here. When she was younger, she'd believed if she could just escape, she would blossom, an ugly duckling into a swan, but of course, real life wasn't like that. Cathy had no fight left in her, and even if she wanted to leave, there was no one who would take her in.

It hadn't always been so bad. When her father was fit and well, he would be out of the house for most of the day, and Cathy had enjoyed her time alone. Even Jasper was less of a tyrant back then. There was a time when he used to talk to Cathy about the girls he'd met at the pub and even asked for her advice on what clothes to wear on his dates. But gradually things changed. Now he'd started to treat her just as their father did, like a doormat. She was just somebody who waited on them, no better than a servant. Though Jasper had never hurt her, not like their father.

Cathy ran her fingers over the smooth black plastic casing. She was trembling. Why was it so hard to do the right thing? She pulled out a scrap of paper from her pocket and studied the number she'd scribbled down and then slowly began to key in the digits.

She was halfway through the number when she heard a noise outside. Who was that? Jasper was supposed to be in the fields. Flustered, she panicked and cancelled the call.

She got to her feet, scraping the chair legs on the flagstones. Looking around wildly for somewhere to put the phone so she wouldn't be suspected of using it, she dashed around the kitchen.

She heard her father groan as he awoke from his nap.

Heart pounding, she darted towards the small cabinet just behind his wheelchair. Maybe he'd think he'd left it there himself. She had taken it from his pocket but didn't dare put it back now that he was half awake.

She looked out of the window and saw Jasper walking towards the back door.

With a heavy heart, Cathy walked towards the sink and filled the kettle. She had to behave normally.

She had failed. She should have acted earlier. This had been her chance to put things right. Maybe she wouldn't get another.

CHAPTER THIRTY-ONE

Before they headed back to the station, DI Morgan and Karen called in to check up on the search. In the first few hours after the girls went missing there had been a sense of urgency, but now the girls had been missing for so long that fatigue had affected every civilian and officer involved.

The search team moved with weariness and sad resignation. Karen hated to admit it but the chances of them finding the girls alive at this point were not good.

The local residents had been amazing, coming together to join in the search as well as providing cups of tea and snacks for those combing the area. But the sense of futility and sadness now weighed heavily on them all.

As they made their way back to Nettleham headquarters, Karen tried to work out the puzzle of Leanne Gibson and Matthew Saunders. That little bombshell certainly had come as a surprise, but she supposed it made sense. At least it explained Leanne's odd reaction to Matthew when she'd rushed to the school after finding out Sian was missing.

'Do you think Thomas Gibson found out about his wife's affair and decided to take the girls to teach her a lesson . . . To scare her?'

DI Morgan pulled a face as he reversed neatly into a parking spot at Nettleham police station. 'I don't think so. It would be a pretty extreme reaction, and besides, why would he take Emily as well?'

'You're right. It makes no sense. What are we going to do about it?'

DI Morgan shrugged as he locked the car. 'I'll try to broach it with Leanne when I go to see the Gibson family this afternoon. It won't be easy. Obviously, she's consumed with worry about Sian, and quite frankly, I don't think the affair is going to have much impact on our investigation, but I have to ask.'

Karen nodded and they walked in silence back into the station.

Upstairs, the main office was a hive of activity. DI Freeman's team were now working on the case full-time as well. Instead of going straight to his own office, DI Morgan perched on the edge of Karen's desk. He called Rick and Sophie over for an impromptu briefing.

Karen could sense his frustration. There was something in this case they were missing, and they'd been distracted by too many false leads and secrets.

He brought Rick and Sophie up to date and then said, 'Right, let's have a brainstorming session. What do we have so far?'

'Jasper Palmer found the glove,' Karen said.

DI Morgan nodded slowly. 'What else?'

'We've ruled out the man seen at Washingborough Primary School,' Karen said. 'We now know that was Les Greenwood.'

'Yes, and we've discovered that Matthew Saunders was having an affair with Leanne Gibson, but we can't see any reason why that would give someone a motive to take both girls,' DI Morgan said with a sigh.

'And the preliminary results on Sian's uncle, Nick Gibson, have come back,' Sophie said. 'His computer and mobile phone are both clean. There's nothing that links him to the abduction. And his alibi checks out. He was caught on a CCTV camera just minutes after the time the girls went missing.'

'So we come back to the Palmers,' Karen said.

'What evidence do we have against them apart from the glove?' Sophie asked.

'Amy Fisher worked in one of the outbuildings on the Palmers' farm before she disappeared.'

'That isn't related to this case, though, and it could be a coincidence,' DI Morgan said.

Karen tried not to show her irritation. 'I don't believe in coincidences.'

She clenched her fists. Why couldn't she keep quiet? These outbursts weren't helping. They wouldn't persuade her colleagues to take her seriously. If anything, they'd make them wonder if she was losing the plot.

DI Morgan didn't rise to the bait. 'Obviously, we're still going to follow up with the Palmers.' He turned to Rick. 'Rick, do you have the maps handy showing the outbuildings on the Palmers' farm?'

Rick nodded and shuffled through the paperwork on his desk before passing a few sheets of paper to DI Morgan.

DI Morgan flicked through them and then handed them on to Karen. 'Rick has double-checked the outbuildings against the list of what's been searched. Everything matches. There's no sign the girls have ever been there.'

Karen looked at the various charts. There used to be an old barn close to the farmhouse, which was converted and divided into artists' studios. The Palmers had been raking it in at one point. They'd had a few small companies and artists renting the space over the years. While Amy was renting a workspace there, three others had used the studios. They all left after Amy disappeared. The tenants had all been questioned exhaustively and eliminated from the investigation early on. 'Did anyone search the studios? I think they've been empty since Amy went missing.'

Rick reached over and flicked through the papers before pulling out the third sheet and pointing at it. 'Yes, and there's somebody renting one at the moment, using it for pottery.'

'And have we looked into them?'

Rick nodded. 'Sophie has.'

Sophie shrugged and looked apologetic. 'Nothing interesting, I'm afraid. A fifty-year-old woman called Susan May. She's been there for about six months.'

Karen frowned. 'I'm surprised anyone wanted to rent from the Palmers after what happened to Amy.'

Sophie shrugged. 'Mrs May said she thought Amy had run off. She knew her from when she was young and said she was a flighty young thing.'

That annoyed Karen more than it should have done. She was convinced Amy Fisher hadn't run away. Christine knew the Fisher family well and she'd not seen anything to indicate Amy was unhappy. Besides, people didn't just run away and leave money in their bank account like that. Not when they were doing well. She'd had everything to live for. There were no signs she suffered from depression. Everything Karen had learned suggested Amy had been enjoying life just like a nineteen-year-old should. If anything, Amy was more mature than most nineteen-year-olds. She'd set up a business and was renting her own place when most nineteen-year-olds were getting drunk at university or still living with their parents.

'I suppose it's too early to have anything back from the tech lab on Phil Carver's computer?' DI Morgan asked.

'Well, I did chase the tech team earlier. Harinder has been really helpful. He knows we're anxious for the results,' Sophie said. 'The trouble is, he reckons some software's been used on both computers to wipe certain areas of the hard drive.'

'I knew he'd try something like that,' Karen said and then cursed. 'I'd hoped we'd got to him before he had a chance.'

'We might still have a chance. You know Harinder is pretty much a genius.' Sophie flushed a little, and Karen wondered if Sophie had developed a crush on the tech wizard. 'Well, he's confident he can rescue the files, but it'll take a little time.'

'You didn't mention that to me,' Rick said, clearly put out. 'I was sitting opposite you when you called him.'

'I didn't think it was important,' Sophie said. 'I could handle it, and there's nothing to report until Harinder has discovered what's in those deleted files.'

'You still should have mentioned it,' Rick said.

Sophie opened her mouth to retaliate, but Karen put up her hand. 'Enough. Sophie, keep us all updated on the content of those files. If we're lucky, Phil Carver may have screwed up, and Harinder could save this case.'

Sophie pouted, but Karen ignored her and stared down at the maps again, reading Rick's careful handwritten notes beside each outbuilding.

DI Morgan began to talk to Sophie about Leanne Gibson's extra-marital affair, and Karen turned her attention to Rick. He looked tired, and she'd never known him to be so quiet and grumpy. She'd been too harsh on him again earlier. It was a well-known fact stress could drive officers to drink.

As Rick ran a weary hand over his face, Karen felt a pang of sympathy. Perhaps when this case was done and dusted, she'd try again. Sometimes the most important step was admitting you had a problem. Maybe Rick needed some encouragement to take that step.

◆ ◆ ◆

The team were going through progress reports and planning the future direction of the investigation when the phone rang on Sophie's desk. She got up, pushed her chair back and quickly picked up the handset.

Rick was running through some background information on a couple of leads generated from members of the public calling the designated line, but Karen was only half listening. She was watching Sophie.

The young detective constable's grasp tightened on the phone and her eyes widened. She looked back at the team as she replied to whoever was calling.

Was it Harinder? His colleagues had nicknamed him Harry due to his computer wizardry, and they could really use some of his magic right now to move the case along.

Even though Sophie didn't utter a word, Karen sat forward in her chair, waiting for her to finish the call. Everything about her body language suggested this was promising information.

After a moment she put her hand over the bottom of the handset and said, 'I think we have something. I've got the tech unit on the phone and you should speak to them, sir. It's Harinder.'

Sophie held out the phone for DI Morgan.

Rick clapped his hands together. 'Good old Harry!'

Karen didn't dare celebrate yet.

As DI Morgan talked to Harinder, Sophie told Karen and Rick what the tech unit had unearthed. 'They managed to get into Phil Carver's computer and retrieve the deleted files. From his files and online browsing history, they were able to determine he's a member of various online groups and forums.'

Karen could guess where this was going. 'What sort of groups?'

'Groups where they swap photos of children, indecent images, and talk about disgusting things.' Karen knew Sophie was trying to be calm and objective, but her face betrayed her true feelings. She shuddered. 'It sounds pretty bad. They're going to send an initial report to DI Morgan, and Harinder believes the evidence could be strong enough to get a conviction even if Phil Carver has nothing to do with Emily and Sian's disappearance.'

'So Harinder hasn't found anything on the computers that relates to Emily or Sian?'

'Not yet, but it sounds like there's a lot of material for him to go through. If DI Morgan approves the request, Harinder can get more specialists assigned to help him sift through all the electronic evidence.'

'I've given him full approval,' DI Morgan said, hanging up the phone. 'If he's so much as mentioned either girl, I want to know about it. Let's bring him in.'

CHAPTER THIRTY-TWO

Karen flipped through the report on Phil Carver and felt her skin crawl. She'd been into his home and had had a relatively normal conversation with the man. She hadn't exactly warmed to him, but she hadn't suspected him of doing anything as bad as this.

It reminded her of something drummed into them during training. Criminals didn't wear signs. They didn't have 'murderer' or 'paedophile' tattooed on their foreheads.

They should have been focusing on this since the moment they'd heard the girls were missing. Why hadn't anyone mentioned Jenny Dean's new boyfriend earlier? Had they jeopardised their chances of getting Emily and Sian back, or was it already too late?

DI Morgan had gone back into his office. They'd already spent some time going over the interview plan, and now they were waiting for Phil Carver's arrival at the station. A uniformed unit was on their way to pick him up, and a search team would be going over his flat with a fine-tooth comb.

Karen had been very tempted to go and arrest Phil Carver herself, but she knew it was more sensible to spend that time planning their interview strategy. The satisfaction of seeing him in cuffs and dragged out of his home would be short-lived. Whereas a strong interview would go a long way to securing a conviction.

She stood up and stretched, trying to ease the tension growing between her shoulder blades. Pushing the paperwork to one side, she groaned.

Rick, who was sitting opposite, looked up. 'Are you all right, Sarge?'

Karen sighed. 'Yes, it's just cases like this . . . they get to you, you know?'

Rick nodded but said nothing. There wasn't much he could say. All they could do now was wait.

◆　◆　◆

A moment later, DI Morgan stuck his head out of his office and called Karen over.

She stepped into the room and tried to read his expression. He looked intense. Was that good or bad?

'Could you shut the door, please, Karen?'

She did as he asked. 'Do we have a problem?'

Panic fluttered in her chest, and she tried to swallow the lump in her throat. Had the search team already uncovered something at Phil Carver's flat? Something she and DI Morgan hadn't seen when they'd been there to question him?

DI Morgan shook his head. 'I wanted to ask your opinion on something.'

Karen was surprised. 'Okay, fire away.'

'I'd like to take the lead on this interview with Phil Carver.'

Karen hadn't expected anything less, and she shrugged. 'Of course.'

'And I was considering having Sophie in on the interview. What do you think?'

Karen couldn't hide her shock. This was an important interview and Sophie was very inexperienced.

'I'm not sure she'd be the best person for the job,' Karen said carefully.

Perhaps she was being unfair. Sophie was hard-working and enthusiastic, and she did need more high-level interview experience to progress to the next level.

'I don't want anything to go wrong in the interview, but we've planned the questions.'

Karen pulled out a chair and sat down. 'I don't want to hold her back, but Sophie can be quite idealistic. When something runs contrary to her principles, she has a hard time controlling her emotions.'

DI Morgan leaned back in his chair. 'You're right, but it's something she needs to work on. We've prepared the interview strategy. I thought perhaps we could go over it with her now. It's a good opportunity for her, but if you think she's not ready, I trust your opinion.'

Karen wasn't sure, but it was true that learning from textbooks and case studies was not enough. Nothing beat the experience of being in an interview face to face with a suspect and having to think on your feet when they surprised you. Was she being too hard on Sophie?

But any small mistake could have huge consequences. She worried that Phil Carver might slip through their fingers.

'If you think she's ready for it,' Karen said, 'we could try her out on the preliminary questions. If it looks like she's getting in over her head, then either Rick or I could take over.'

DI Morgan nodded. 'Good idea.'

'I'll watch the interview from the viewing room too, and see if I can pick up anything from his behaviour.'

At that moment, a member of DI Freeman's team, Farzana Shah, poked her head around the door. 'DI Morgan, Phil Carver has arrived at the station. He's with the custody sergeant now.'

DI Morgan thanked Farzana and then turned to Karen. 'Ready?'

Karen nodded firmly. 'Ready.'

◆ ◆ ◆

Karen left Rick in the main office and headed down to watch the interview. The viewing room was long and rectangular with a variety of audiovisual equipment set up on a desk set back against the wall. Karen would be able to watch the interview live on a video screen.

It took her a little while to set things up, and then she sat there, staring at the black screen and waiting for the interview to start.

The interview room appeared on the screen. Phil Carver was already sitting at the table and taking in his surroundings. The duty solicitor, who'd consulted with his client in private when the cameras and microphones were switched off, now remained silent. A uniformed officer stood by the door.

Phil looked a little different from the last time Karen had seen him. He was nervous, constantly biting his fingernails and rubbing a spot on the side of his nose.

DI Scott Morgan entered the room with DC Sophie Jones and introduced himself and Sophie. The officer who'd been standing beside the door left.

Karen couldn't help fretting that they'd thrown Sophie in at the deep end a little too early, but DI Morgan looked his normal impenetrable self and Sophie looked calm and controlled. Karen was pleased Sophie was reacting well under pressure. This was the most testing interview she'd taken part in during her career as a detective so far.

DI Morgan was an experienced interviewer and kicked things off by asking Phil a few routine questions, trying to get him to loosen up and even develop a bit of a rapport.

Sophie asked her questions perfectly, and Karen guessed she had practically memorised the interview strategy.

Karen leaned forward, resting her elbows on the table, and stared intently at the screen. At the start of the interview, Phil Carver had been edgy, but now his shoulders had dropped and he was leaning back in his seat. He was still on his guard but more relaxed. Karen thought DI Morgan had done well so far.

'So, Phil,' DI Morgan said, tapping his pen on the paperwork in front of him, 'we've brought you in here today because we found you in possession of illegal material on your laptop and desktop computers.'

'I don't know what you've found but it's probably been planted,' Phil said defensively. 'I've done nothing wrong.'

'You'd recently deleted files containing images on your hard drives, but our technical unit managed to recover them.'

Phil's face paled and he licked his lips. 'I don't know anything about any images.'

The solicitor shot Phil a look, and Karen wondered what they'd discussed before the interview.

'We were also able to extract all your internet browsing history, Phil,' Sophie said.

She looked calm and in control, but Karen could hear the waver in her voice. She sat back and waited for Phil to respond.

'It's not illegal if I just happen to stumble on some dodgy websites,' Phil said.

'Remember what we discussed earlier, Mr Carver,' the solicitor said.

Phil's face tightened in anger and he slapped an open hand against the table. 'It's just pictures online. What's so bad about that? I'm not doing anything wrong. I'm not hurting anyone by looking at photographs.'

'What about the poor kids in those photos?' Sophie snapped, going completely off script. 'Those children are being hurt, aren't they?'

Phil's solicitor advised him not to say anything, and DI Morgan swiftly moved on to the next planned interview question.

Sophie's cheeks burned pink, and Karen felt sorry for her. She was trying so hard to keep control and it wasn't easy. Not when she had to listen to somebody trying to defend the indefensible.

DI Morgan wrapped up the preliminary questions and the solicitor requested some time alone with his client.

They stopped the recording to take a break. Karen jumped up from her seat, left the viewing room and headed down the corridor to find them.

She caught DI Morgan walking back to the office.

'Did that look as bad as it felt inside the interview room?' DI Morgan asked.

Karen pulled a face. 'It wasn't a complete success. Still, it's early days.'

'It's bloody annoying it takes so long,' DI Morgan said with conviction.

Karen looked up at him. Of course, she knew it bothered him. A case like this would bother anyone, but DI Morgan didn't often show his feelings.

'We'll get there in the end, sir. We just have to make sure we do everything by the book.'

They walked into the main office area and DI Morgan headed straight to his office. Sophie was standing beside Rick's desk.

She looked up and saw Karen and then looked down at the floor. 'I'm sorry, Sarge.'

Karen put a hand on her shoulder. 'It's not an easy job, Sophie. It was probably a bit too soon to put you in.'

Sophie shook her head, her brown curls bouncing. 'I don't understand how DI Morgan can bear to talk to him. He makes my skin crawl.'

'It's his job,' Karen said.

'He doesn't like it either,' Rick said. 'But he doesn't have a choice. He has to talk to him to find out if he had anything to do with the missing girls.'

DI Morgan came back out of his office carrying a pile of paperwork.

'He's entitled to a break and we're on the clock,' DI Morgan said as he looked at his watch. 'We'll only be able to fit in one more interview session before we have to call it a night.'

Sophie looked horrified. 'Call it a night? How can we just stop when he might know where Emily and Sian are?'

Rick winced as though he expected DI Morgan to reprimand Sophie for being so naive.

Instead, DI Morgan patiently explained. 'Come on, Sophie. You know all about the PACE Act. We can't question him all night, even though I'd like to. He has rights.'

Sophie screwed up her face in contempt. 'Someone like that doesn't deserve any rights.'

CHAPTER THIRTY-THREE

Jenny Dean's mother, Louise Jennings, heard the news that Phil Carver had been arrested when she was in the Spar. She'd been carefully filling her shopping basket with a variety of items to tempt Jenny's appetite. The poor girl hadn't eaten anything since Emily had gone missing. So far, she'd picked up chocolate biscuits and chicken soup. She smiled as she spotted the Jammie Dodgers. They'd always been Jenny's favourite. She put a packet in her basket and turned into the next aisle. She was about to pick up some eggs when Mrs Harris, a short, round woman, approached her.

'Oh, you poor, dear soul,' Mrs Harris said, looking at Louise with pity.

Mrs Harris considered herself a Christian and attended church every Sunday without fail. She may have looked to be kindness itself, but Louise detected a gleam in the woman's eye. She was hungry for gossip.

'You must tell me if there's anything you need. I've been praying for you and your family.'

'Thank you very much,' Louise said stiffly and tried to move past the nosey woman.

'It must have been such a shock for you all.'

Louise felt a wave of dislike for Mrs Harris. Of course it was a shock. Talk about stating the obvious. She was very tempted to tell the woman to mind her own business, but she managed to bite her tongue and leaned down to pick up some salt and vinegar crisps. Jenny had always liked those. It was junk food, but at least it would be something to give her energy, and goodness knows she needed her energy at the moment.

But Mrs Harris wasn't that easily pushed aside. Determined not to be ignored, she continued, 'Of course, now Jenny's new boyfriend has been arrested, I suppose it's only a matter of time before they find the girls.'

It took a few moments for Mrs Harris's words to sink in.

Jenny's mother turned around sharply. 'Arrested? Who's been arrested?'

Mrs Harris put a hand on her chest. 'Oh, don't tell me you didn't know! Oh, now I feel just awful.'

Jenny's mother dropped the wire basket on the floor and took a step towards Mrs Harris. How did this nosey old bat know about Jenny and Phil? They'd been keeping things quiet because Jenny didn't want Dennis finding out before she was ready. They even met up at a pub in Lincoln to avoid rumours. But why would the police arrest Phil? It didn't make any sense. Mrs Harris must be mistaken.

'Who's been arrested?' She repeated her question through gritted teeth.

'I told you. Jenny's boyfriend, Phil Carver. I bumped into them in Lincoln last week. It did surprise me she'd moved on so quickly after Dennis but that's none of my business.'

Jenny's mother felt dizzy. She reached out to steady herself on a shelf full of multipack crisps. 'Are you sure about this?'

'Yes, my next-door neighbours were shopping at Tesco's, and they saw him being taken away.'

Louise's hands curled into fists. She stood there for a moment swaying on her feet, and then quickly turned and darted out of the shop. She could hear Mrs Harris calling after her, but she ignored the horrible old bat.

Huffing and puffing, she moved as fast as her old bones would carry her. Diagnosed with arthritis three years ago, Louise had become resigned to a slower pace of life. Not today, though. Today, she ran.

She didn't bother to knock on the front door of Jenny's house, but instead made her way around the side and went in through the kitchen.

'Jenny!' she yelled.

The family liaison officer was in the kitchen, bustling about making tea like she owned the place. 'What's wrong, Mrs Jennings?' she asked, eyes wide with fake concern.

Jenny's mother narrowed her eyes at the woman. She probably knew all about Phil Carver's arrest and hadn't told them. How could the police withhold information like that?

Instead of answering the woman, Jenny's mother just shouted again for her daughter.

Jenny appeared in the kitchen, her long dark hair tangled around her pale face. 'What's wrong? Have they found her?'

Jenny's mother shook her head. 'I just heard that Phil has been arrested.'

Jenny Dean's hands flew up to cover her mouth. 'Dear God.'

Jenny's mother turned to the officer, who had the decency to look a little sheepish. 'You knew about this, I suppose?'

'I've gotta go to the police station,' Jenny muttered. 'I need to know what's going on. Do they think he's hurt Emily?'

The family liaison officer reached out and put a hand on Jenny's shoulder. 'There has been an arrest but there's no other news yet. If you wait here, I'll be able to update you soon.'

'This is unbelievable,' Jenny's mother said. 'Why should we trust you to do that? You didn't even bother to tell Jenny that her boyfriend had been arrested.'

'It's only just happened,' the officer said. 'He's not even been questioned yet and—'

Jenny turned her back on the policewoman. 'Where's my coat?'

Jenny's mother marched through the kitchen and into the living room. She plucked Jenny's black padded jacket from the back of a chair and handed it to her daughter.

'God knows what will happen when Dennis finds out about this,' Jenny's mother said.

Jenny took the jacket from her mother with shaking hands. 'It's not Dennis he has to worry about. If Phil has hurt my Emily, I'll kill him myself.'

Desk Sergeant Stuart Smith had been hoping for a quiet evening shift. Sadly, it looked as though he was going to be disappointed.

He first noticed something odd was going on outside due to the sheer amount of press hanging around the station. There had been some journalists milling about ever since the poor little girls had gone missing, but tonight they seemed to have descended en masse.

Then the shouting started.

He wasn't supposed to leave his post at the desk so he couldn't go and investigate. However, curiosity got the better of him and he picked up the phone and asked a favour from PC Clive Trees.

Clive arrived at the desk, looking a little grumpy at being called away while on his break.

'I've had to leave my tea,' he grumbled.

'Never mind your tea,' the desk sergeant said. 'I want you to go out there and find out what all that racket's about, and while you're at it, try to calm things down a little.'

Muttering under his breath, PC Trees did as he was told.

When he came back in a few moments later, his face was pale. 'Sorry, Stuart. But I think we're going to need a couple more officers out there.'

Before he could explain further, Jenny and Dennis Dean entered the station's reception area together.

The duty sergeant's immediate reaction was sympathy. He had a daughter of a similar age to Emily and Sian, and his heart went out to the couple.

But Jenny and Dennis weren't interested in his pity. They were there to demand answers. Unfortunately, the desk sergeant didn't have any information to give them.

When Dennis Dean loomed over the desk with the threat of violence in his eyes, the duty sergeant took a deep breath and picked up the phone. He had a feeling it was going to be a very long night.

CHAPTER THIRTY-FOUR

Karen was bone weary. She'd spent the last half an hour trying to calm Jenny and Dennis Dean and persuade them to go home and wait for news. It hadn't been easy. The worst part was, she didn't have any news to give them, good or bad. How did you explain that to a parent out of their mind with worry?

She was walking back upstairs when her phone beeped. A message from Christine displayed on the screen.

> Have made enough lasagne to feed a small army. Shall I pop over and leave some in your fridge?

Karen smiled and typed:

> Yes! You're an angel. Thanks :)

> No problem. Someone has to make sure you eat properly!

As she walked past the cubicles in the office, Karen looked in through the glass panel on DI Morgan's office door. He was on the phone. He'd been talking to the family liaison officers, trying to fill them in on developments. But apart from telling the officers they'd made an arrest, he didn't have much more information to deliver.

It was frustrating and Karen understood Sophie's point completely. In her black-and-white view, Phil Carver was one of the bad guys and as such they should be entitled to question him all night if they wanted.

The trouble with that was they didn't know for sure that Phil Carver had abducted Sian and Emily, and any information they received after questioning a sleep-deprived Phil Carver overnight would be inadmissible. They would jeopardise the whole case and they couldn't allow that to happen.

After a further fruitless round of questions, the custody sergeant had placed Phil in a holding cell overnight and they would have to resume questioning first thing tomorrow morning.

Phoebe Goodman had called into the station after she finished work and spoken to Sophie. She reiterated what she'd said on the phone. She'd had a relationship with Nick Gibson, and there had been no coercion on his part to get her to pose for the photographs. Another dead end.

Rick and Sophie's desks were empty. DI Morgan must have persuaded them to go home while Karen was downstairs talking to the Deans.

Karen knew she should get home too. They had a busy day ahead of them tomorrow, and she'd need to be at the top of her game if they were going to get the truth out of Phil Carver.

DI Freeman's team were already at their desks, shuffling through paperwork, preparing to carry on overnight. Karen stifled a yawn, sat down at her desk and moved the mouse so her computer monitor woke up.

After Phil discovered what they'd unearthed on his computer, he'd quickly decided to dump the duty solicitor and bring in a private one. Karen hadn't seen her before, but she knew her stuff. She objected to almost every point they raised and generally made a complete nuisance of herself. Rick put it best when he'd described her as a pain in the arse.

From the state of his flat, Karen had guessed Phil Carver didn't have much money, but he clearly had enough to employ an expensive legal adviser. Maybe playing games on the internet paid better than they'd suspected.

Although Phil Carver had some incriminating evidence against him, and he was undoubtedly a sick individual, Karen was still not wholly convinced he'd snatched the girls. After their second session with Phil in the interview room, his solicitor had been very keen to point out he was playing his Xbox online, competing against others, when the girls disappeared. There were records they could check, but the solicitor was savvy enough to know not to offer that as evidence unless she thought it would provide a good alibi for her client.

Sophie had been quick to point out that it could have been anyone using the console in Phil's flat. But if Phil was as good as he said he was, he wouldn't have been able to get just anyone to cover for him. He'd have needed someone the same level as him to fill his shoes in the game. How many Xbox experts could there be in the area?

First thing tomorrow morning they would get their hands on the CCTV from the back of the Tesco Express. The camera pointed directly at the stairwell so they'd have a clear view of anyone entering or leaving the flats. He swore he hadn't left the flat for over twenty-four hours on the day the girls disappeared. Karen could tell from the smirk on Phil Carver's face he was confident that his internet records would back him up. The same records that provided evidence against him would give him an alibi. With a sigh, Karen logged on to the system and pulled up a map of the school and the surrounding area.

The girls had simply disappeared and Karen couldn't understand how that was possible.

If they'd walked straight through the small area of woodland, they'd have come out on Longwater Lane, which was full of houses and at that time of the day would have been busy with parents arriving to pick up their children as they left school.

Two mothers had been helping with the costumes for the play, and both women had parked in Longwater Lane but neither had seen Sian or Emily. The girls had been seen at the end of the dress rehearsal, and according to young Danny Saunders, they had entered the woods shortly afterwards.

If the girls had walked on to Longwater Lane, they would have been seen. But no one saw them. Karen frowned at the screen. She could rule out Longwater Lane, which only left one option. The girls must have left the narrow strip of woodland and crossed on to Palmer land.

She picked up a blue file that DI Morgan had given her. It contained the details of all the outbuildings on the Palmer farm. Karen had lost count of how many times she'd looked at the list, each time hoping to stumble across something they'd missed. Her eyes skimmed the notes until they fell on the disused windmill. It was listed as a grain store and was located roughly midway between the farmhouse and the school. There was a handwritten note beside the listing. The door at the base of the old fire-damaged windmill had been padlocked, and the search team had to request the key. The Palmers had provided it promptly, though. There were four floors, each linked with a ladder rather than a set of stairs, so it wasn't the easiest place to search and definitely not for someone afraid of heights. But each of the four floors had been searched.

There were a number of historic windmills in Lincolnshire and most had fallen into disrepair like the one on the Palmer farm. She seemed to recall it had lost its sails a long time ago in a storm. There was no getting around it. The search team had done a good job and they'd found nothing on the Palmer farm.

Karen pushed the file across her desk in frustration.

She drummed her fingers on the desk. The outbuildings had been searched, but would the Palmers keep the girls in the farmhouse? Was it possible that the farmhouse had a secret cellar room or a hidden space in the loft? Perhaps somewhere they could keep the girls hidden? Karen shook her head. Tiredness was really getting to her.

Karen pulled up the case file on her computer. She did a quick search of the reports. She skimmed the lists and then got up from her seat and walked over to DC Farzana Shah's desk.

'Hey, Farzana, how are things going?'

Farzana looked up from the computer and sighed. 'Slowly,' she said. 'But everything seems to go slowly on the night shift.'

'You were one of the officers responsible for coordinating the search of the farmland around Moore Lane Primary School, weren't you?'

Farzana nodded. 'Yes, we searched every inch of that place, and all we got for our troubles was a glove, and even that was found by Jasper Palmer.'

'What about the farmhouse itself?' Karen asked.

'Yes, that was searched too. Nigel Palmer was perfectly happy to accommodate our request, believe it or not.'

Karen frowned. 'Really? That doesn't sound like him.'

Farzana picked up the cup of coffee on her desk and took a sip. 'I know. He's not a pleasant man. I was there when DC Lyndon asked his permission to start searching the house. He smiled.' She shivered. 'It was a creepy, smug smile, like he knew we wouldn't find anything and enjoyed watching us waste our time.'

'And it was a comprehensive search?'

'Yes, all the rooms, cupboards, even the loft. We looked all over the farmhouse.'

Karen nodded thoughtfully. 'What about a cellar? An old building like that might have a cellar?'

'We looked for a door to a basement or cellar but didn't find one. Nigel Palmer swore blind that the property didn't have one.'

'Right, thanks.'

Farzana looked at her watch. 'Isn't it time for you to go home? You'll be shattered tomorrow.'

'Yes, I'm going to leave soon. I just have to check something out then I'm off.'

Back at her desk, Karen did a quick search using the land registry records. But the search came up blank for the farmhouse, which was not surprising really. The property had always been in the Palmer family. But there had to be plans somewhere. She did another online search, hoping the Palmers had applied for planning permission recently.

This could take longer than five minutes, Karen thought, and reached for the empty mug on her desk. As she got up to recaffeinate, the screen filled with the search results.

The Palmers hadn't applied for planning permission for the farmhouse, but they had applied to restore the old windmill and to convert the barn into artist studios. Karen vaguely remembered a campaign launched a couple of years ago by a local historian who was interested in restoring the windmill to its former glory. As the campaign had begun to gather steam, Nigel Palmer had stubbornly resisted. She wasn't sure anything had come of it.

Was there a reason he was so resistant? He was an insular man, but he was also penny-pinching and miserly. One of the main ideas behind the campaign had been to use the windmill as a tourist attraction. That would have generated income, and Karen couldn't see Nigel Palmer turning down the opportunity to make money. Unless there was a reason he didn't want anyone poking around. Did he treasure his privacy to the extent he'd turn down converting the windmill into a revenue generator?

Karen couldn't remember anything else so decided to google the Palmer windmill. There was a fair amount of information detailing the campaign online, even though it since had fallen by the wayside. She found contact details for Terry Masters, the local historian who'd spearheaded the campaign, in an article from *The Sheepwash Times*. Karen made a note of his name on the pad beside her computer before beginning to read.

CHAPTER THIRTY-FIVE

After a little more digging, Karen found a website dedicated to the campaign, which had been set up by Terry Masters and provided plenty of information. The windmill dated back to the nineteenth century. There was a brief description of the construction materials that would have been used, and a picture of the type of sails it would most likely have been fitted with in those days. There was also a short section describing the fire that had devastated the windmill. At the bottom of the page, the historian's email address and contact phone number were listed.

Karen was tempted to call, but it was late, almost eleven p.m. She hesitated for a moment before reaching for the phone and dialling the historian's number.

When he answered, his voice sounded thick with sleep.

'I'm sorry to call so late, Mr Masters,' she said, and introduced herself before explaining the purpose of her call.

'Not at all, DS Hart. You did me a favour. I'd dozed off in front of the fire.'

She asked him about the windmill and his voice brightened immediately, becoming far more animated. He didn't seem in the least bit perturbed at being questioned about the building so late at night, and Karen guessed it was one of his pet topics. He enthusiastically

explained the layout and told her why it was such a remarkable historical specimen.

'We actually believe there were eight sails at one point,' the historian explained. 'That's highly unusual and of important historical
interest.'

'But Nigel Palmer wasn't interested in the restoration project?'
Karen asked.

'No, unfortunately not. He was a funny man. At first, he seemed
very eager to renovate, but then he reneged on various surveys and the
process was very drawn out. I heard whispers that he was planning to
restore it himself and then charge a fee for entry. I doubt he got very far.
It's a specialist project and requires workmen with expert knowledge.'

'How extensive was the fire damage?'

'That was a long time ago. The windmill has endured years of mis-
fortune. Some superstitious locals believe it's unlucky. It lost its sails in a
gale back in the late 1800s, and the fire in the fifties wiped out most of
the inside floors. They were made of wood, you see. The brick surrounds
were undamaged but the inside needed a complete refit.'

Karen frowned. 'Do you think it's possible Nigel Palmer attempted
the restoration on his own? Because we searched the building and our
officers have reported four floors, each linked by a ladder. If there was
fire damage or it looked unsafe, a risk report would have been carried
out and I can't find anything mentioning one.'

'How interesting,' the historian said. 'Can you leave it with me?
There are a few people I can ring around and ask. I'll find out if anyone
took this project on for Nigel Palmer. It's not something he could do
himself . . .'

'No, definitely not. I don't know when you last saw Nigel Palmer,
but he's become quite ill with emphysema. His son Jasper's fit and
healthy, though. He could have carried out some of the work.'

'Perhaps, but I really think they'd have needed expert advice.'

'Right, I'll give you my mobile number and if you manage to find out who helped him with the internal refit, I'd be very grateful.'

'Leave it with me,' the historian said cheerfully.

Karen hung up. Why was she wasting her time with this? Even if the windmill had been restored, how would that make any difference to the case? The old windmill had been searched and the girls weren't there.

She yawned again and knew she'd better head home otherwise she'd suffer for it tomorrow. She switched off the computer, grabbed her bag and coat, and on her way out stuck her head around DI Morgan's door to say goodnight.

'I'm just finishing up a bit of paperwork,' he said. 'But I'll be leaving soon too. I'll see you tomorrow.'

Karen left the building, threw her bag on the passenger seat and had just slid behind the wheel when her mobile rang.

'Hello?'

'DS Hart? This is Terry Masters. We just spoke about the Palmer windmill.'

'Oh, yes, of course. Don't tell me you've already found out who carried out the restoration work?'

She was expecting him to laugh and explain he'd forgotten to ask some question about the windmill. She didn't dare hope he had any information that might help.

'Yes, I found the chap who did the work. A contractor based in Kent called Reggie Furrows. He has a fair amount of experience.'

'Excellent. Thank you, Terry. I'm impressed you managed that at this time of night. I hope he wasn't too upset at the late phone call. Would you be able to give me his contact details? I'd like to have a chat with him at some point.'

'I can do that, of course. But I called you back because he told me some information that might interest you.'

Karen was intrigued. 'Yes?'

'He did refit the four floors as expected. But Reggie said he also blocked off the ground floor. You see, beneath the ground floor there's a small sack room. It was heavily damaged by the fire, and wouldn't be of much interest to visitors. The money to make it presentable and safe would have increased the price of the refit considerably. Nigel Palmer said he wasn't going to pay to have the sack room renovated, so the contractor blocked it off for safety reasons.'

Karen was stunned. 'So there's another floor? A basement?'

'That's right.'

'But if there'd been a way to access this sack room, then the officers searching the building would have seen it . . . They wouldn't have missed a doorway.'

'No, but they could have missed a hatch,' Terry said. 'According to Reggie, he put a small hatch in the floor so they could access the sack room for future maintenance. It would be hard to hide a doorway, but if something heavy had been laid over the hatch, it's possible the officers may have missed it.'

Karen's weariness evaporated. There was a room beneath the Palmer windmill that hadn't been searched yet. 'Thank you very much, Terry. That's really helpful.'

Karen felt a flutter of excitement. After she hung up, she quickly dialled DI Morgan's number and filled him in.

'I could go to the Palmers now and ask them for the key. I can search the place myself,' Karen suggested.

DI Morgan hesitated before saying, 'No, that's not a good idea. There's no way you're going into a fire-damaged building on your own at this time of night. My instinct is to search at first light.'

Karen clenched her fist and hit the steering wheel. 'I don't want to wait, sir. I really feel this could be it. The girls could be down there.'

DI Morgan sighed heavily. 'You're relying on a hunch.'

'No, sir, I'm relying on evidence. The girls didn't exit the wood via Longwater Lane. If they had, someone would have seen them, which means they must have ventured on to Palmer farmland. Sian's glove was found two fields away from the windmill. This basement room is the only place on the Palmer property that hasn't been searched.'

DI Morgan was silent.

'The girls can't have vanished into thin air, sir.'

'I'll get a team together and get over there as soon as possible. You go to the Palmers and see if they'll let you have the key. Otherwise, we'll have to wait for a warrant.'

Karen grinned. 'Right. I'll head over there now.'

Karen drove through Lincoln. The roads were quiet, and she cruised down Lindum Hill. She pressed a button to lower the window. The cold night air was bracing. Not that she needed it to wake her up tonight. The adrenaline coursing through her body had already done that job. But when dealing with the Palmers, she wanted to be fully alert.

She'd spoken to DC Farzana Shah again, calling the station before she'd left the car park, and learned that the officers searching the windmill hadn't mentioned a hatch on the ground floor. She told Karen there had been some large wooden cogs stored on that level which could have obscured the hatch.

At the bottom of Canwick Hill, she turned left, heading for the Palmer farm. She passed the woods by the school and the old windmill came into view. She shivered, unsure if it was simply the cold night air or the dark building that loomed menacingly over the fields. She'd never considered it creepy before, but tonight it looked sinister. It was odd how feelings could be projected on to buildings.

In the distance, she could make out the Palmer farmhouse. The lights were on, so someone was still awake. There were no streetlights, so she needed to pay close attention to spot the single track that ran up to the farmhouse.

Karen slowed the car, determined not to miss the turning. But then she saw something that made her press hard on the brakes.

There was a light coming from the old windmill.

How was that possible?

Karen pulled to the side of the road, leaving her hazards on. She got out of the car to take a better look and peered over the hedgerows. She hadn't been mistaken. In one of the small, narrow windows near the top of the windmill, there was a warm chink of light.

CHAPTER THIRTY-SIX

Jasper Palmer was pleasantly drunk. He'd spent the evening at the pub with some of the local lads, and he'd enjoyed his time there until somebody brought up the subject of those missing girls. He wasn't stupid. He saw the way people looked at him around here. The Palmer family, tucked away in their isolated farmhouse, well away from the rest of the village, were viewed with suspicion. Some of the women looked at him with open hostility.

He knew how to turn on the charm, though. He could have had those stupid women eating out of the palm of his hand if he'd spared the time, but tonight he hadn't felt like making the effort.

Jasper trudged up the single-track road, expertly avoiding the dips and muddy puddles even though he was worse for wear. He'd have to get up early tomorrow and once again he'd have a terrible hangover. He wasn't cut out for farm work. Sure, he was strong enough, healthy and fit, but he didn't like the early mornings. Never had. Not that he'd ever had any choice in the matter. It was expected of him. He was a Palmer, and the Palmer family had farmed the same land for generations.

As he got closer to the farmhouse, he was surprised to see one of the lights was still on in Cathy's bedroom. She normally went to bed early because she had to be up to attend to their father. Cathy, the paragon of virtue.

He snorted with contempt and thrust his hands into his pockets. He was almost at the farmhouse when another light caught his attention.

At first, he assumed he was seeing things. That wasn't unheard of, and he had knocked back seven pints this evening.

He turned, swaying slightly as he stared at the old windmill.

There was a glowing light coming from near the top. His initial thought was that the building must be on fire, but there was no visible smoke. He took a deep breath. The night air was clear and there was no smell of burning either. He narrowed his eyes. No doubt some local kids had broken in and decided to use it for shelter while they smoked pot or something. Bloody kids. Jasper would give them the fright of their lives. He jogged the rest of the way to the farmhouse.

Whenever he visited the pub, he took only his front door key in his wallet. Around the farm, he carried a heavy ring weighed down with keys for various outbuildings, tractors and machinery. His father had a similar set. Jasper didn't want to cart them around with him all night but he needed his main keyring now to get into the windmill. He frowned, wondering how the kids had managed to get inside. A window? They were very narrow and too high up to access, surely? Maybe they'd jimmied the lock?

His keys hung on a rack in the kitchen, and Jasper reached for them without bothering to turn on the light. He slipped into the boot room and picked up his cricket bat. He hadn't used it since the villagers had closed ranks against him when Amy Fisher disappeared. Bunch of feeble-minded gossips. He'd played for the village team for years before that, and he was the best bowler they'd had in decades. They hadn't openly told him to leave, of course. They'd just driven him out with their sly comments and dirty looks. It was Amy's mother's fault. She went around telling anyone who'd listen the Palmers were responsible for what happened to her daughter. They all believed her too. Jasper could see it in their eyes. Things had been a little better after Amy's parents went back to Scotland, but he was never invited to rejoin the team.

Jasper gripped the handle and tested the weight of the bat. Those kids would soon learn not to trespass on Palmer property. He grinned. He'd enjoy teaching them a lesson.

He shut the front door behind him and set out at a jog towards the old windmill, the keys jingling in his pocket. But when he reached the entrance, he saw he didn't need them. The door to the windmill was slightly ajar. He examined the lock, expecting to see it bent and battered, but there was no sign of any damage.

When he stepped inside and heard voices, he frowned, wishing he hadn't had so much to drink. Then he headed for the spindly ladder that led to the next floor. Tightly gripping the rungs, he began to climb up.

Karen called DI Morgan as she headed across the field towards the windmill. The mobile signal was patchy, but she managed to convey her point after repeating herself a couple of times.

DI Morgan was adamant in his reply. 'Do not go in there alone, Karen. I'll direct backup units to go straight to the windmill, but wait for us to get there.'

'Of course,' Karen said. 'I just want to get a bit closer so I can see what's going on.'

'Just don't go inside alone. The place could be on fire. Maybe somebody's up there trying to destroy evidence.'

'It doesn't look like a fire to me. There's no smoke and the light isn't flickering as you would expect from a fire.'

'Just be careful. I'm on my way,' DI Morgan said and then hung up.

Karen hesitated when she reached the base of the windmill and saw the door was open. She was sure someone was inside. The light filtered out from the narrow windows on to the field. Karen's shoes were muddy and damp, and the long, wet grass had soaked the bottom of her trousers.

She looked back over her shoulder towards the car. She was a long way from the road now. Why was backup taking so long? The logical thing to do was remain outside and keep a close watch in case anyone left the building. She needed to keep out of sight and keep her eyes and ears open.

But as the door was already unlocked, surely it couldn't hurt to take a quick look?

She moved silently towards the door and carefully pulled it wide open. She held her breath, waiting for the hinges to creak.

But the door moved smoothly, and Karen slipped inside. The light was coming from one of the upper levels, but it filtered through to the ground floor so that Karen could see the boarding. There were no scorch marks or dark wood. The only signs there'd been a fire here, decades ago, were the dark sooty scars on the bricks. The wood looked new and fresh, recently replaced.

She heard a sound above her and took a step back, pushing herself against the curved brick wall. Someone was in the windmill, and they were moving fast.

She remained in that position, pushed back against the wall in the shadows, and tried to get her bearings. Karen couldn't see any hatches in the wooden floor or visible openings that could lead to a basement room, although the light wasn't great. Above her, the gearing system for the windmill mechanism was partially assembled. There was a round grinding stone and large wooden cogs beside it on the floor. She guessed they were replicas.

Was it possible that the stone or cogs concealed the hatch? It was the only way the search team could have missed it. The grinding stone would be too heavy to shift, but a wooden cog could be shoved across the floor with some effort, although it would be virtually impossible to force the hatch open from below with the weight of the cog sitting on top.

Deciding to test her theory, Karen crept forward, looking for scratch marks to indicate the cogs had been moved recently. To her surprise, not only was there a hatch clearly visible behind the wooden cog closest to her, but it was propped open.

She stared down into the darkness. She could just about make out the first two rungs of a ladder, and beyond there was just black. Karen shuddered. She was about to get down on her hands and knees and try to get a better look into the basement when she heard something from one of the higher levels. She froze.

She could hear a low rumbling voice, but it wasn't clear enough for her to identify. One thing she knew for sure. It wasn't a child's voice. Were the children here? Or was something else going on here tonight, completely unrelated to the missing girls?

The last thing she needed was to be caught trespassing by Jasper Palmer.

'You're an idiot,' the voice shouted.

Karen held her breath. Now, that was definitely a male voice and it sounded a lot like Jasper Palmer. But who was he talking to?

She moved away from the hatch to the basement room and tiptoed across the floorboards towards the ladder. But she didn't dare go any closer. Instead, she waited and listened.

'What the hell have you done?' the male voice demanded.

Karen heard a murmured response – the voice of a woman or maybe a child? She put her foot on the first rung of the ladder, straining to hear more.

'I had to do it. She was hurt and I couldn't see properly in the dark,' the female voice said.

'You're a fool,' the man growled. 'You may as well have lit a beacon. I could see the light from the farmhouse.'

Karen felt her pulse spike and heard the blood rush in her ears. That was definitely Jasper Palmer. But who was the woman? Cathy?

'The girls were freezing,' the woman said. 'I was worried because it's damp down there, and it's so cold tonight.'

'Well, they're not going to have to worry about the cold for much longer. There's nothing else for it. We have to get rid of the evidence, including the children.'

CHAPTER THIRTY-SEVEN

Karen had been holding her breath. But adrenaline flooded her system on hearing Jasper's words. She couldn't hide down here if the children's lives were in danger. But where were they? Karen hadn't heard a peep out of them.

'No! You mustn't touch them,' the woman pleaded.

'Get out of my way, Cathy. It doesn't look like it's going to be difficult. They're out of it. What did you give them?'

Karen tightened her grip on the ladder and began to climb. It was no good. She couldn't just wait down there. She needed to see if the children were up there. She had to.

Cathy said, 'Medicine. I just gave them medicine.'

Karen paused at the top of the ladder. There was a hole in the boards, and from her position she could see straight up to the next level. The windmill went on for another two floors, but it looked as though both Jasper and Cathy were on the floor above her. She strained forward a little and saw two small figures huddled together on the floor. Emily and Sian?

They weren't moving.

'I can't believe after all this time *you* were the one who did it,' Jasper said. He laughed, tottered a little and then leaned heavily on the wall. 'I would never have thought you had it in you.'

'Please don't hurt them, Jasper,' Cathy whispered.

Karen took one more step, trying desperately to see if the girls were okay. She had a better view, but unfortunately she was more exposed.

Jasper turned and saw her before Karen could duck back down out of sight.

'What the . . .' Jasper strode over to the ladder, and before Karen could scramble to safety, he grabbed hold of her.

She fought him as he pulled her from the ladder and dumped her on to the wooden floorboards.

She got to her feet quickly.

'Police!' Karen said, not for Jasper's benefit because it was clear he'd recognised her, but for the little girls if they could hear her. 'Backup is on the way. I suggest you leave the building and wait outside.'

Karen tried to sound confident and in control, but the look on Jasper's face sent a chill up her spine.

Hardly daring to take her eyes off Jasper, her gaze flickered over to Cathy briefly. 'You were involved in this, Cathy?'

'No, I was trying to help them, to save them.'

'She's lost it. She needs to go to the funny farm,' Jasper shouted.

Karen ignored Jasper's outburst. 'Who are you saving them from?'

Cathy shook her head and her eyes filled with tears. 'They needed my help.'

'How could you be so stupid?' Jasper leaned towards Cathy and muttered something in her ear.

Cathy paled and shook her head. 'No, I won't let you hurt them.' She turned to Karen. 'Quick, get out of here.'

But Karen couldn't do that. Not when there were two helpless children lying on the floor only a few feet away.

Jasper lifted an object from the floor and swung it from hand to hand. He had a cricket bat. Karen backed away. Where on earth had that come from? She didn't have time to dwell on that for long because he took another step towards her.

'What are you planning to do?' Karen asked, trying to keep the fear from her voice. 'Are you hoping to get rid of us all before the police get here? It's not going to work, Jasper. You may as well give up now before anyone gets seriously hurt.'

She shot a glance at the children, wondering if they were still alive. Jasper didn't reply. He merely gave her a wolf-like smile.

'Police backup will be here at any moment. You're never going to get away with it.'

His smile widened and he took another step forward. 'Oh, I don't know about that. They say fire can hide a multitude of sins, don't they? This place went up in flames once.' He shrugged. 'Maybe it'll happen again.'

He raised the cricket bat, ready to take a swing at Karen.

Karen crouched, ready to dart in the opposite direction, but out of nowhere, Cathy flung herself towards her brother, pushing him hard so he lost his footing and stumbled.

As Jasper fell, his head hit the side of the hatch with a sickening crack, then his body fell like a sack of flour, missing the ladder and falling on to the floor below. He landed with a thud.

Karen rushed to the hatch. He wasn't moving – and his neck was bent at an unnatural angle.

Cathy let out a high-pitched wail and put her hands over her face. Karen rushed past her to the children huddled beside the wall.

They were unresponsive and their skin was cold. But both girls had a pulse. She lifted Emily's eyelid and saw the pupil retract.

'They're alive. She's kept them drugged up. Some weird combination of cough medicine and something else . . . crushed-up tablets. I'm not sure what they were, though,' a raspy female voice said.

Karen turned around and was shocked to see a woman crouched on the floor beside her. She must have been hiding behind the large cogs and grinding machinery that rose up between the floors.

It took Karen a moment to process what she was seeing. 'Amy?'

The girl nodded. 'Yes. Are the police really on their way?'

Karen couldn't believe her eyes. It was Amy Fisher, the girl who'd disappeared from Heighington eighteen months ago. Her face was streaked with dirt and her hair was matted, but she was alive.

Karen looked back at Cathy to make sure she hadn't moved.

She was rocking backwards and forwards making an unearthly keening sound.

'Have you been here all this time?' Karen asked.

Amy's eyes were like pinpricks and she was far too relaxed considering the circumstances. Karen suspected she'd been drugged as well.

'She kept me in the basement. She kept saying she was going to let me out when it was safe. But she never did. She only let us out today so she could take a look at one of the girls' legs. Sian cut herself and it got infected, I think.'

'Okay, stay calm,' Karen said, although she needed to keep calm more than Amy did. She seemed strangely detached from everything.

Karen's heart was thundering as she tried to process what was happening. She dialled dispatch and quickly explained the situation, telling them they'd need more than one ambulance. She guessed that Jasper was beyond help, but all three girls needed attention as soon as possible. God only knew what drugs were in their systems.

Sian was burning up, and Karen pressed the back of her hand against the girl's forehead.

'She gave them crushed-up tablets in their orange juice,' Amy said, crossing her arms over her chest. 'But I think the girls were too small to cope with whatever was in them. They've been out of it most of the time.'

'What did she give you, Amy?'

Amy let her arms drop to her sides then pulled up one of her sleeves, displaying puncture marks. 'She let me have something a little stronger.'

Karen winced, wondering where the drugs had come from.

After putting both girls in the recovery position, Karen called out to Cathy, 'Can you check on your brother and see if he's still breathing?'

Cathy turned to Karen, looking horrified. Her eyes widened as she shook her head.

'I don't think I can,' Cathy said. 'I'm sorry. I only wanted to help.'

'That's what she always said,' Amy whispered. 'Every time I begged to leave, she said she was helping me.'

Karen stared at Amy as the young woman's eyes struggled to focus. Amy put her hands flat on the floor and took a deep breath as though talking had worn her out.

'It wasn't Jasper who took you?' Karen asked.

Amy shook her head. 'No, I never saw Jasper here until tonight. I think he just found us the same way you did. I only ever saw her.' Amy pointed at Cathy, who was starting to enter the hatch and climb down to the next level.

'Cathy,' Karen said sharply. 'Did you take the girls? Or were you helping Jasper?'

'I was saving the girls like I saved Amy from Jasper.'

Karen's mind was racing. All this time she'd thought it was Nigel or Jasper behind it all. 'Did your father know about this?'

Cathy shook her head. 'No, I would never have told him. The girls wouldn't have been safe if I'd told him.'

'Cathy, you're going to have to explain. Tell me why you were keeping them safe.'

'Emily was scared. She needed my help. She liked the horses and she trusted me. Her mother had a new boyfriend . . .'

'Did Emily tell you about him?'

Cathy nodded solemnly. 'He was a bad man.'

'Did he do anything to Emily?'

'He scared her. She didn't like him.'

'Is that why you brought her here?'

'I wanted her to be safe.'

'What about Sian?'

Cathy's face crumpled and she leaned heavily on the ladder. 'I didn't mean to take Sian, but she came with Emily and I didn't have a choice. If I'd left her behind, she'd have told people and then Emily wouldn't be safe.'

'Why did you take Amy Fisher? I asked you about her when she went missing, Cathy, and you lied to me.'

Cathy started to cry.

Karen wanted answers, but the harder she tried to get Cathy to talk, the harder the woman cried.

CHAPTER THIRTY-EIGHT

The accident and emergency department at the hospital was packed as Karen made her way through to reception. Emily Dean, Sian Gibson and Amy Fisher had been brought to the hospital by ambulance, and Karen desperately hoped they had got there in time for the antibiotics to clear Sian's infection.

The paramedics couldn't do anything for Jasper Palmer. He was dead by the time they arrived, and Karen suspected he'd died soon after he'd hit the floor. The paramedics said it looked as though he'd broken his neck in the fall.

Karen was unhurt but had decided to travel to the hospital with DI Morgan rather than drive herself. She was still shivering.

'It's ridiculous,' she muttered, shoving her hands in her pockets.

'What is?' DI Morgan asked as they waited in line at the reception desk.

Karen held out a trembling hand. 'I'm still shaking.'

'It's hardly surprising. You've been through a very traumatic event.'

Karen put her hand back in her pocket and they shuffled a little closer to the desk as one person in the queue ahead of them left to sit down on a plastic chair in the waiting area. A drunk young man was singing to himself on the opposite side of the room.

The large double doors at the entrance slid open, letting in a rush of cold air from outside, and a worried-looking couple holding a toddler with red cheeks joined the queue behind Karen and DI Morgan.

The hospital reception staff dealt with new arrivals from behind a Perspex screen. When a member of staff opened another window to deal with the queue, Karen waved the couple with the toddler ahead of them. She could see the fear on the couple's faces, and it wasn't as though she and DI Morgan were in a rush.

A uniformed officer had travelled with Cathy in the ambulance.

'I think Cathy found out about Jenny Dean's new boyfriend and the risk he posed to Emily,' Karen said.

DI Morgan nodded. 'That would make sense, but how did she find out? Cathy Palmer was known to keep to herself. I can't imagine her cosying up to Jenny Dean for a chat over coffee.'

'I have a feeling we might find out the truth from Emily.'

DI Morgan raised an eyebrow. 'You do?'

'Yes, I think Cathy befriended Emily and the little girl confided in her.'

'But Jenny swore that Phil Carver had never been alone with Emily.'

'Let's hope Jenny's right. But if she left the room when he visited, even just to make a cup of tea, that could have been enough time to make Emily uncomfortable or scared.'

The window ahead of them became free, and DI Morgan introduced them both and gave the names of the patients they were waiting to speak to. They wanted to see how Cathy was getting on and find out how long they'd have to wait until she was fit enough for her psychiatric evaluation, but they also wanted to check on the girls.

Amy Fisher had been drugged for a long period of time. Karen could only presume that was how Cathy was able to keep her presence in the windmill secret for so long. The property had been searched on two occasions and there was no soundproofing – so if Amy had been conscious, she'd have been able to call for help. Karen could only guess that Cathy had decided also to drug Emily and Sian after she had taken them.

The reception staff were able to give them the locations of the four patients. Sian Gibson was in ICU, Emily was on a paediatric ward, and both Amy Fisher and Cathy Palmer had been given separate rooms on Lister ward. Following the directions, DI Morgan and Karen set off to find them all.

DC Farzana Shah had been assigned the unenviable task of informing Nigel Palmer that his daughter had pushed his son to his death. Emily and Sian's parents were on their way to the hospital after Rick had phoned and told them the girls had been found.

Amy Fisher's parents had moved back to the Scottish Highlands, so it would be some hours before they made it down to Lincoln. Sophie had called to give them the extraordinary news – perhaps one of the few instances when a late-night phone call would be gratefully received. Karen could only imagine the joy they must have felt at hearing their daughter was still alive. After eighteen months, had they given up hope? Or had they somehow known, deep down, that she was still alive?

◆ ◆ ◆

Karen and DI Morgan decided to talk to Amy Fisher first. Sian was in intensive care and Emily was still heavily sedated. It would be a while until they could speak to the children.

The doctors were not happy with them talking to Cathy Palmer until after she had had her psychiatric evaluation. Under other circumstances, DI Morgan would have pushed this, but on this occasion, now that the girls were safe, there was no immediate sense of urgency and he knew that any information they got from Cathy Palmer now would be inadmissible.

Amy was in a private room, and they managed to locate her doctor to have a quick chat before they spoke to her.

He was a tall man in his mid-fifties with grey hair and a kind face.

'I'm Doctor Johnson,' he said, introducing himself. 'I think Amy should be able to talk to you now. We've done some preliminary tests and are awaiting the results, but I'd guess she's been taking heroin.'

Karen had suspected as much but the news still left a bitter taste. She wondered where on earth Cathy had been getting the heroin. They'd thought she'd led a very sheltered life.

'Amy will be in some pain and discomfort. Her other withdrawal symptoms haven't yet kicked in, but they will very soon. We'll have to manage her detox programme carefully.'

Poor kid, Karen thought. As though she hadn't been through enough over the past eighteen months. Her blood would now need to be screened for HIV and Hep C, and she'd go through hell during heroin withdrawal. Karen had spoken to addicts in the past and they'd all told her the same thing. After being hooked on the drug for a while, it wasn't about getting a high. They'd need to take a hit to feel well.

She exchanged a look with DI Morgan and wondered whether his thoughts were running along the same lines. Had Amy been hooked before she went missing, or was this all down to Cathy?

The doctor led them into a small room. Despite only seeing Amy less than an hour ago, Karen was shocked. Her eyes were bloodshot, and her skin had a grey tinge. At least someone had made an effort to clean her up and her face had been sponged clean. Her hair was still matted, though, and she looked thin, almost lost in the big hospital bed.

Amy hadn't been suffering from withdrawal symptoms when Karen found her at the windmill, but now her last hit was wearing off and she was suffering.

'Amy,' Karen said, moving forward. 'Do you remember me?'

Amy's eyes fluttered open and she struggled to focus on Karen.

'I thought I was dreaming,' she said. 'Am I really out?'

DI Morgan nodded and said, 'Yes, you're safe now, Amy.'

He didn't mention the fact that her captor was in an almost identical room just along the same corridor.

'We'd like you to tell us as much as you can remember,' Karen said. 'I know it's difficult, especially as you still have drugs in your system and you might not remember everything right now, but anything you can tell us will help.'

Amy flopped back against her pillows listlessly. 'The doctor mentioned something about giving me methadone. Do you think he's going to let me have it soon?'

There was a light sheen of sweat on Amy's pale face.

'I think they're going to prescribe methadone to help you through the withdrawal, Amy,' DI Morgan said. 'Were you taking heroin before all this happened?'

Amy looked guarded and her gaze flickered between DI Morgan and Karen.

'It's okay, Amy,' DI Morgan said. 'You're not in any trouble.'

Amy's body seemed to sag. Either with relief or weariness, Karen wasn't sure.

'Not heroin. I dabbled in some stuff, took some coke at weekends, but I wasn't an addict or anything.'

If Karen had a pound for every time she'd heard that, she'd be a very rich woman. She waited for Amy to continue.

'I shouldn't have ever started but I just wanted to try it, you know?'

'Who was your supplier?' DI Morgan asked, and Karen was surprised. As nice as it would be to put away a drug dealer, surely other questions were more important at this point.

'I'm not sure. I'd call and ask for what I needed, and he'd tell me to meet one of his runners somewhere in the city centre. Sometimes it was behind the bingo hall, sometimes near the bus station. The day it happened, I was shattered. I'd stayed up all night because I had an order I needed to get out. I wanted something to pep me up, to give me some energy. Cathy came to see me and overheard me on the phone to my dealer. At first, I panicked. I thought she was going to run and tell her father and I'd lose the studio, but she was really understanding. She offered to take the first batch of orders to the post office. When she got back, she brought me a cup of tea. The next thing I knew, I woke up in that horrible basement. I begged Cathy to let me go but she wouldn't. She kept saying I was in danger and she was helping me. She'd drugged me using her father's sleeping pills, but when the effects wore off I screamed for help. I think she took my mobile and used it to contact the dealer because the next time she came down to the basement she said she had to give me something to keep me quiet. I panicked when I saw the syringe.'

'Do you have any idea where Cathy got the money to pay for the drugs?' Karen asked. Heroin was not cheap and as far as they knew, Cathy had no income.

Amy shook her head.

'Why did Cathy think you were in danger, Amy?' DI Morgan asked gently.

'It was Jasper. He'd taken to hanging around the studio, trying to chat me up. Cathy warned me about him but he wouldn't stop coming by. I should have known something wasn't right. I tried to avoid Jasper, but I never even considered I had any reason to be afraid of Cathy.'

'Do you think Jasper or his father knew you were locked up in the basement room?' Karen asked.

'No. Cathy said she was keeping me down there so that Jasper couldn't get to me. She thought he was going to hurt me. I tried to talk to her at first and make her see sense. I didn't think it would go on for so long. She wasn't violent, but she kept me tied up down there. She wouldn't listen to reason, and when the two little girls were brought in, I knew I had to do something.' She took a long, shaky breath.

'She said she had to take the girls because Emily was in danger.' Amy paused. 'She said she was saving her from her mother's new boy-friend. I don't know if it's true . . . Emily and Sian were pretty out of it the whole time they were there. They did manage to help me get the cable ties off my wrists, though, and we tried to get out, but Sian fell from the ladder when we tried to force open the hatch. That's when she cut her leg.' Amy's eyes filled with tears. 'I was trying to help them, but it was my fault Sian got hurt.'

Karen reached out and put her hand on Amy's, careful to avoid the welts and bruises on her wrist from the cable ties and the cannula attached to the IV fluid.

'You were trying to escape. No one can blame you for that, Amy.' Trying to make her feel better, Karen told her that her parents were on their way. 'It could take them some time to get here, but they're over the moon to have you back after so long, Amy.'

For the first time, a trace of a smile appeared on Amy's face. 'How long was I missing?'

As Karen explained she'd been missing for over eighteen months, Amy started to cry. 'I didn't know it had been that long. I knew it had been at least a couple of months but . . .'

'It's okay now, Amy,' DI Morgan said. 'We're going to let you get some rest, and we can talk again later.'

DI Morgan left the room, but Karen sat next to Amy's bed until the young woman had worn herself out from crying, waiting until she was sure Amy was asleep before she got up to leave the room.

CHAPTER THIRTY-NINE

When Karen left Amy's bedside, there was no sign of DI Morgan in the corridor, so she guessed he must have gone to phone the station for an update.

She checked her watch. It was after one a.m. They'd been at the hospital for over an hour, and Karen wondered whether there'd been any improvements in Sian's condition. She hoped they hadn't been too late.

She made her way to ICU, used the alcohol sanitiser by the door and then pressed the green button and waited.

A moment later, a nurse appeared and let her in.

Over the sound of the beeping machinery, Karen explained who she was before asking for a quick report on Sian's condition. Beyond the nurse, Karen saw the Gibsons crowded around the bed. Sian looked tiny in the adult-sized ICU bed.

'We didn't have any space in the children's unit,' the nurse explained. 'But she's in good hands here. The infection is raging through her body and it's taken hold quickly, but her organs seem to be coping, which is the important thing. She's on IV antibiotics and will be for the next few days. There's not much to do now but wait and hope the antibiotics do their job and get rid of the infection.'

Karen's throat felt dry. 'Will she lose her leg?'

'The doctors haven't made a decision on that yet. They want to see how she responds to treatment over the next few hours. If the antibiotics don't do the trick, it could be the only way to save her life. In which case, she'll need an operation to amputate her leg below the knee.'

'I see. Thank you.'

'Do you need to speak to her parents?' the nurse asked, turning and gesturing to them.

Karen shook her head. The last thing the Gibsons needed at the moment was her invading their anguish.

Thomas Gibson stood close to his wife, his arm around her shoulder, and Leanne leaned into him for comfort. She wondered whether Leanne had come clean about her fling with Matthew Saunders. She hoped the couple would be able to put it behind them. They looked so close and they'd need to support each other now more than ever.

Karen left the ICU with a lump in her throat and headed towards the children's ward. She bumped into DI Morgan on the way.

'I've just taken a call from the superintendent,' he said. 'She's full of praise for you.'

Karen shrugged and felt uncomfortable. 'If only we'd tracked them down a little earlier. I just spoke to the nurse in the ICU and she said Sian could lose her leg.'

DI Morgan closed his eyes. 'Poor little mite. It's not bloody fair.'

'Let's just hope the antibiotics kick in in time. Do you want to go and speak to the Deans? I'm not sure whether Emily will be fully awake yet but we could try.'

DI Morgan agreed, and they made their way to the children's ward in silence.

Pausing before he pushed the green button to request entry, DI Morgan stopped and turned to Karen. 'Looks like you were right about that hunch.'

His face was deadpan but his eyes twinkled, and she knew he was teasing.

'Yes, you'll come to realise I'm usually right once you've worked with me a little longer,' she said.

DI Morgan smiled. 'I should have guessed you'd say that.'

They were pleased to see that Emily was already sitting up in bed, taking sips from a paper cup filled with water. Her parents stood over her bedside, and Jenny was stroking Emily's dark tangled hair back from her face. Dennis stood ramrod straight beside his daughter's bed, like a man on guard.

All three looked up as DI Morgan and Karen approached.

'I know this probably isn't the best time, but we were hoping Emily could tell us what she remembers,' Karen said, and her gaze drifted to Dennis Dean.

He towered over the bed, glowering at everyone and everything. But when Karen glanced down, she saw he was holding Emily's small hand in his huge one.

'She's still a bit tired,' Jenny said. 'She was given some sort of tranquilliser and it knocked her out.'

'Is Sian all right?' Emily asked, and from the look of stricken panic on both Dennis and Jenny's faces, Karen quickly surmised that they hadn't yet told her quite how ill Sian was.

'The doctors are treating her now, Emily,' Karen said. 'They're giving her some special antibiotics. They're very strong, and hopefully they'll get rid of the infection.'

Emily nodded but still looked anxious.

'Can you tell me what happened the day you disappeared?' Karen asked, moving a little closer to the bed.

They had most of the answers – at least, she thought that they did. They knew Cathy had been behind the abduction and it appeared she'd acted alone.

It was just so hard to imagine why Cathy, such a seemingly placid, meek person, could do something so out of character.

Emily handed her cup of water to her mother, who put it on the nightstand. 'I wanted to see the ponies. I'd gone a couple of times to the field just to watch them. I wasn't doing anything wrong.' She shot a nervous glance at her father, who nodded encouragingly.

'I saw a lady there one day, and she said her name was Cathy and that she owned a couple of horses. She seemed nice and I spoke to her a couple of times. Once I was quite upset and I went to visit the horses to see if it would cheer me up. She was there and told me not to worry and that she could help me. She said she'd helped somebody in the past who was just like me. She promised everything would be all right.'

Even though Karen stood on the opposite side of the bed to Jenny Dean, she could hear the woman's harsh breathing. This had to be extremely difficult for her to hear.

'Were you going to meet her when you left school?' Karen asked.

Emily nodded. 'She said she'd let me ride one of the ponies and I was really excited. I told Sian about it and she wanted to come too, and then we met Cathy in the woods like she told me. But Cathy seemed different. She was angry with me for bringing Sian, and then she took us into one of the fields and told us we were having a picnic before we went riding. She gave us a bottle of juice to share and sandwiches and crisps. And I thought she was being nice again. I don't remember what happened after that, but when we woke up, it was all dark and cold. She left us juice and food. There was another lady there called Amy and she tried to help us. We tried to escape, and that's when Sian fell down the ladder and cut her leg.' Emily's eyes filled with tears.

'I know it's really difficult, Emily. But you're safe now. Can you tell me why you were upset that day?' Karen asked. 'Why did you need Cathy to help you?'

Emily's whole body tensed, and she turned a fraction to look at her mother before quickly looking back down at the bed sheet covering her legs. She shook her head.

'We know all about Phil,' Jenny said in a strangled voice. 'He won't be coming anywhere near you ever again.'

Through all this, Dennis Dean had been silent but Karen could feel the fury and rage vibrating from him.

'What did Phil do to you, Emily?' Jenny asked.

Emily shrugged. 'I just didn't like him. I didn't want him in our house. It was his fault Dad didn't come back.'

The words left Emily's mouth in a rush as she explained. It seemed that Phil had never gone any further than making Emily feel uncomfortable. She told them he'd given her chocolates and other small gifts, but she still didn't like him. To Karen, it sounded very much as though Phil had been grooming Emily, but she hadn't been molested. She was thankful Emily hadn't been exposed to Phil Carver long enough for him to begin a campaign of abuse, but Karen found listening to Emily describe his little gifts and grooming tricks difficult. It must have been torture for her parents.

When Emily had finished talking, Jenny said, 'Can you believe she gave them an adult dose of tranquillisers? She could have killed them. The doctor says Emily shouldn't have any long-term damage, but how could she do that to children?'

Karen couldn't answer that.

DI Morgan moved away from Emily's bedside and said, 'Excuse me, I need to take a call. Thank you, Emily. You've been very brave.'

Karen spoke to the Deans for a little while, trying to gather as much information as she could, but didn't keep them long, knowing they needed time alone as a family.

When she left them and had almost exited the ward, she heard heavy footsteps behind her and turned to see Dennis Dean's tense and angry face.

Karen braced herself. After everything that had happened, the idea of another confrontation with Dennis Dean made her want to curl up into a ball.

Dennis reached for her and Karen stepped back so fast she stumbled. She was surprised when he grabbed her hand and squeezed it tightly.

'Thank you,' he said gruffly. 'I mean it. Thank you for bringing my little girl back. If there's ever anything I can do to repay the favour, you only have to ask.'

Karen extracted her hand but managed a smile. 'You don't owe me anything, Dennis. I'm just glad Emily's safe.'

CHAPTER FORTY

Outside the ward, she found DI Morgan. He ended the call on his mobile and said, 'I think it's time to go home, don't you?'

Karen nodded. She didn't even want to think about the amount of paperwork they'd have to get through in the coming days.

'I've just spoken to Rick and Sophie,' DI Morgan said. 'They're both pleased with the outcome and relieved you're okay. If Sian Gibson pulls through, it's going to be a better result than I dared hope for.'

'Yes, I wonder how the Gibsons are coping,' Karen said. 'Has Thomas found out about his wife's affair with Matthew Saunders? I suppose it pales into insignificance after what's happened to Sian.'

'I don't think Leanne has told her husband and it's the least of their worries right now. It has no relevance to the case so there's no reason for it to come out, but that kind of thing has a way of bubbling to the surface eventually.'

'I wish we could talk to Cathy tonight,' Karen said, smothering a yawn. 'There's so much I want to ask.'

DI Morgan walked ahead, pushing open a blue swing door and holding it to allow Karen to pass through first. 'I don't think we're going to get all the answers on this case. I think we might have to come to terms with the fact that we'll never know what made Cathy act the way she did.'

'Maybe the way she was treated by her father and brother triggered her behaviour. Perhaps she wanted to save Amy, Sian and Emily from going through what she did.'

'Well, from what you've told me, it sounds like Sian was an accidental victim. If Emily told Cathy she was unhappy with her mother's new boyfriend, then Cathy may have thought she was saving the child in some strange way. And she was obviously concerned about her brother's interest in Amy Fisher.'

'True. I can't help thinking there was something else driving Cathy. Something she hasn't told us yet.'

They stepped outside the hospital's main entrance, passed a man in a dressing gown puffing on a cigarette, and were immediately subjected to shouting and camera flashes from press photographers. 'Are you police? Have the girls from Moore Lane been found? Can you tell us about it?' someone called out.

How did they know they were detectives? It wasn't as though they were well known locally. Perhaps she and DI Morgan just looked like police officers. Maybe it was the clothes, Karen thought drily, looking down at her crumpled shirt, creased jacket and grey trousers, which were still muddy around the hems. It was time for a new look.

'Is it true?' another of the reporters called out as a flash from a camera went off in Karen's face. She put her hand up to shade her eyes.

'Has Amy Fisher been found with the two missing girls from Heighington?'

DI Morgan put an arm around Karen, leading her away from the barrage of press, and called over his shoulder, 'An official police statement will be presented soon by Superintendent Michelle Murray. That's all we've got to say at the moment.'

They sped up, running away from the journalists and heading towards the car park on the opposite side of the road.

'I think we lost them,' Karen said laughing, as they made it to DI Morgan's car.

DI Morgan rubbed his side. 'I need to get to the gym more often. I think I've got a stitch.'

'Blame it on the cold night air. I would.'

They got into the car and DI Morgan turned the heater up. Karen felt herself relax.

'All things considered, today's result was a good one, don't you think?' Karen asked as she fastened her seatbelt.

'I do. You did well today,' he said as he reversed out of the parking space. 'Although, I can't say I was too happy when I arrived at the windmill to find you were already inside. That was a big risk.'

'Well, I know I said I'd wait, but when I heard Jasper threatening the children, I just couldn't hold on,' Karen said.

DI Morgan was right. It had been a huge risk to her own safety to go into the windmill alone without backup, but in her opinion, some risks were worth taking.

◆ ◆ ◆

DI Morgan pulled in, parking at the entrance to Karen's drive.

'Are you sure you'll be all right?' DI Morgan asked.

'Of course,' Karen said. 'I'll see you first thing tomorrow.'

She shut the car door, waved and walked down the driveway. The security light above the garage turned on as she walked past.

She turned to see that DI Morgan hadn't driven off. He was waiting until she got safely inside. When she turned back, she was face to face with a woman.

'Christ!' Karen exclaimed and put her hand on her chest. 'Where did you spring from?'

It was Mary.

Karen's stomach tightened when she saw fresh bruises on Mary's face.

'Is everything all right, Karen?' DI Morgan called out. He'd got out of the car after seeing someone else in the driveway.

She turned and waved him off. 'Everything's fine. It's just a friend.'

She bustled Mary towards the front door as DI Morgan finally drove away.

Once inside, Mary stood sheepishly at the foot of the stairs. She looked even worse when Karen switched on the light. Her lip was cut, and although it was no longer bleeding, crusted blood had dried along Mary's chin.

Karen opened her mouth to once again tell Mary she was a fool to stay with a man who did this to her, but at the last moment she remembered the advice her neighbour, Christine, had given her. *Sometimes things can't be fixed. Sometimes all you can do is listen.*

'Come into the kitchen, Mary,' Karen said, and locked the front door behind them.

She switched on the kettle and noticed a note stuck to the front of the refrigerator. She peeled it off. It was from Christine, telling her she'd left the homemade lasagne in the fridge with a bag of mixed salad. She'd even left reheating instructions. Karen smiled. She was lucky to have such a good friend.

She turned on the oven, set it at the appropriate temperature and then turned to Mary. 'You're in luck. We've got a proper meal tonight. How long have you been waiting out there?'

Mary dropped her bag on the floor and wrapped her arms around her midsection, wincing slightly.

'A while. It's all right, though. This coat's quite warm.'

Karen removed the lasagne from the fridge and popped it in the oven.

'Do you want a cup of tea?'

A look of confusion crossed Mary's face. She was wondering when the lecture would start. 'A cuppa would be nice – thanks.'

Karen made the tea in silence and then carried it over to the kitchen table. 'So what happened?'

Mary shrugged. 'Same old thing.'

Karen pushed the steaming mug across the table towards Mary. 'That should warm you up a bit. Actually, I think I've got a bottle of brandy about somewhere if you fancy a proper drink.'

'Tea's fine for me, thanks.' Mary took a sip and then looked up at Karen. 'Are you not going to tell me what an idiot I am? I've been here at least five minutes and you've not mentioned the women's shelter once.'

Karen smiled. 'You know what I think, Mary?'

'No, what?'

'I think you know you need to make some changes, but you're not ready to make them yet. So, in that case, I'm not going to judge you. I'm not going to tell you what to do again. I'm just going to listen.'

Mary looked at Karen suspiciously but started to talk. Haltingly at first, then she began to open up.

She carried on talking as they ate the lasagne and finally Mary narrowed her eyes. 'I know what you're doing.'

'Oh, yes, what's that?'

'It's that reverse psychology thing. You think if you don't tell me to go to the shelter, then I'll go on my own.'

Karen laughed. 'I really am trying to help, Mary. If you just need someone to listen, then that's what I'll do.'

Mary sighed heavily. 'I know I'm not supposed to come to your home. You're someone who's tried to help me and I'm taking advantage. I just don't feel safe anywhere else.'

Karen reached out and patted Mary's hand. 'Well, you're safe here, Mary. But it's late and I'm shattered. So I'm going to have a nice hot shower and then get into bed.' Karen stood up and gathered their empty plates. 'You know where everything is, don't you?'

CHAPTER FORTY-ONE

A week passed before Cathy Palmer was ready to talk to the police. Her solicitor would plead diminished responsibility if Cathy was prosecuted for Jasper's murder, and it was unlikely a murder charge would stick. Cathy may have intended to harm or injure her brother, but she couldn't have predicted he'd fall and break his neck. The best they could hope for was a charge of manslaughter.

Charges of abduction and child endangerment would be brought against her, but Cathy would likely end up in a mental health facility.

It was hard not to feel a sense of futility as they wrapped up the investigation and ploughed through the mountain of paperwork. Whatever role Jasper had played, he was dead and would never see the inside of a courtroom. There was nothing to indicate Nigel Palmer had been involved in the abductions. He may have been the catalyst that sparked Cathy's actions, but in the eyes of the law, he was not responsible. He was in the clear, with no ties to Amy Fisher's abduction and no links to the two girls from Moore Lane Primary School. The only person left to answer for the crimes was Cathy Palmer.

Cathy sat opposite Karen and DI Morgan in interview room three, looking like a whipped puppy and shooting nervous glances towards her solicitor.

'Cathy wanted to talk to you,' the solicitor said. 'I did advise her against it, but she's been quite insistent. I will, however, stop the interview if I feel the proceedings are detrimental to my client.'

Karen nodded. Cathy Palmer was a tall woman, but she hunched over the desk, trying to take up as little space as possible.

'I'm glad you're here, Cathy,' Karen said. 'Are you ready to talk now?'

Cathy straightened, tucked her hair behind her ears and nodded meekly. 'Yes,' she said in a voice barely above a whisper. 'I'm ready to tell you everything.'

The solicitor shifted uncomfortably in her seat, and Karen suspected that statement was probably one she didn't like to hear from a client. But if the courts ever did hear the case against Cathy, they could be more lenient if she was repentant and cooperative.

'How are the girls?' she asked.

'Good. Sian is recovering well. All three should recover full fitness in time,' Karen said.

The fact that it looked as though Sian would recover without any permanent injuries seemed to comfort Cathy. Her charges would have been a lot more serious if one of the girls had died.

Cathy's eyes filled with tears. 'I'm so glad she's going to be okay. I don't think I could cope with any more death. Are you going to charge me with the murder?'

'We've discussed this, Cathy,' the solicitor said with thinly disguised irritation.

'You won't be charged with Jasper's murder, Cathy, but it's likely you'll be charged with abducting the girls,' Karen explained.

'But what about the other murder?'

'What other murder, Cathy? The girls are home and recovering. No one else died. Only Jasper.'

Cathy looked up, glancing at DI Morgan and then looking back at Karen. 'But someone else did die.'

It seemed like all the air had been sucked out of the room, and for a moment, no one said a word. DI Morgan seemed just as taken aback as Karen, and the solicitor's jaw dropped open.

The solicitor recovered her wits first. 'Just a minute,' she said, turning to Cathy. 'This is a new development and I think I need to confer further with my client.'

Karen ignored her. 'No one else died, Cathy. Amy's doing well. She's going to be moving back to Scotland with her parents. Sian will be going home soon, and Emily's safely back with her parents.'

Karen met Cathy's gaze, and it hit her. Of course. Why hadn't she guessed?

She turned to DI Morgan as the final piece of the puzzle fell into place. 'I think Cathy should tell us the story from the beginning.'

Autumn had been especially cold this year, DI Morgan thought as he braced himself against the bitter October wind. Karen stood beside him on a patch of windblown grass close to the hedgerow that ran the length of the field. They were less than five hundred metres from the Palmer farmhouse.

Karen's face was set in grim determination as she stared at the spot in front of her, and the team continued to dig. They'd cut away a section of earth, digging down two feet but had found nothing so far.

DI Morgan was confident they would, though. Cathy had told her story with conviction, and she had nothing to gain by lying. They had no reason to doubt her.

When he'd asked if she was sure about the exact location, she looked at him in disbelief and said the place was burned into her memory.

They'd listened in silent horror as Cathy told them her story.

She'd been only twelve years old when her father had bludgeoned her mother to death in front of her. She and Jasper had been forced to scrub her blood from the kitchen tiles, and then help dig the grave to bury their mother.

Helpless and unable to stand up to her father, she'd done as she was told and covered up for him. Keeping the dark secret meant she slowly withdrew from public life because she hated having to repeat the well-rehearsed lie that their mother had left them and she and Jasper still went to visit her occasionally.

Nigel Palmer certainly seemed to have thought of everything.

When he killed his wife Gwendolyn, ten years his junior, back in 1987, he'd told the whole village she'd run off with another man to live on a boat in Norfolk.

He'd hidden the children away for a couple of weeks during the Easter and summer holidays. When they returned to school, they'd been instructed to tell their teachers and friends they'd spent time with their mother on the boat and learned to sail.

Nigel Palmer's plan worked well. Gwendolyn's parents had passed away before she'd married him, and there was no one else who cared enough to report her missing. Acquaintances, neighbours and Cathy and Jasper's school friends and teachers fell for the story hook, line and sinker.

Her disappearance was never reported to the police or considered suspicious, but her death had scarred Jasper and Cathy deeply.

Knowing this history, it was easy to understand Cathy's motivations. She saw Jasper morphing into the image of their father, and noticing his interest in Amy Fisher, she'd wanted to protect the young woman she viewed as a friend.

Cathy was terrified she'd end up in a shallow grave just like her mother.

She'd believed she was protecting Emily too. The girl was unhappy at home and neglected. She told Cathy her mother's new boyfriend scared her. In Cathy's twisted mind, she'd saved Amy and could do it again with Emily.

DI Morgan thought that perhaps in some strange way Cathy *had* saved Emily. If the child hadn't been abducted, would Phil Carver have continued to groom her right under her mother's nose?

A call from the digging team pulled DI Morgan back to the present. From where he stood, he could see material and a pattern of what looked like an old carpet. He heard Karen's sharp intake of breath as the team worked to clear the dirt away.

A short time later, Gwendolyn Palmer's body was removed from the soil.

◆ ◆ ◆

Seated at her desk at Nettleham station, Karen stifled a yawn. It had been a long, tiring and very sad day. Watching the exhumation of Gwendolyn Palmer's body had been more emotional than Karen had expected. She felt desperately sorry for the woman. She'd died in such a violent manner, and then to add salt to the wound, nobody had ever reported her missing.

Karen stretched, trying to release the ache between her shoulder blades. 'What do you say to an evening at the pub?' She turned to face Sophie and Rick, who were busily typing away on their computers.

'That sounds like a great idea to me,' Sophie said.

Rick looked up but didn't reply, and then DI Morgan strolled up to Karen's desk. 'How are things going?'

'Slowly,' Karen said. 'It's always the way with paperwork. I thought we could all do with a night out. What do you say?'

DI Morgan looked a little surprised at the invitation but nodded. 'I think that's a good idea.'

Karen logged off her computer and grinned at DI Morgan. 'It's pie night at the Waggon and Horses in Branston,' she said. 'They make a fantastic steak pie.'

'Is it really that good?' he asked.

'The best I've ever tasted.'

He returned her smile. 'All right, sold. Sophie?'

'Absolutely,' Sophie said, getting to her feet and turning off the monitor. 'I'll just put some lipstick on and get my coat.'

DI Morgan turned to Rick. 'Fancy a night out at Karen's local?'

Rick flushed pink, which was unusual for him. His tanned skin didn't blush easily. 'Er, not tonight. Sorry, but I've already made plans.'

Karen turned to look at Rick with a teasing grin. 'Another date is it, Rick? I don't know where you find the energy.'

Rick gave a sheepish grin. 'Oh, you know me, Sarge. I'm known for my boundless energy.' He checked his watch. 'In fact, I'd better get a move on. I'm going to be late.'

Karen smothered another yawn as they waited for Sophie to come back from the ladies' toilets.

'I can see I'm going to have to make an extra effort with my conversation tonight,' DI Morgan said drily. 'If I'm not careful, you'll be falling asleep on us.'

'Sorry,' Karen said. 'I'll be fine once I get some air.'

Sophie walked towards them, beaming and more chirpy now that she'd applied fresh lipstick and brushed her hair.

Karen was pretty sure the only cosmetic she had in her bag was a tube of Carmex lip salve. She was happy to leave the preening to Sophie, who was still young enough to care.

Sophie pointed to Rick's desk where an iPhone sat beside his keyboard. 'That's Rick's phone,' she said. 'Has he already left?'

Karen nodded and reached for the mobile. 'Yes, it's unlike him to leave his phone. He's normally glued to the thing. He must be really preoccupied with his date this evening.'

Sophie held out her hand to take the phone. 'I'll drop it off on the way to Branston and meet you at the pub.'

CHAPTER FORTY-TWO

DC Sophie Jones tucked Rick's phone in her bag and walked out of Nettleham station. She'd picked him up a few weeks ago when his car refused to start, so she knew his address. It had been light the last time she'd visited, but now it was dark and she had to slow to a crawl as she pulled into his road.

Large houses lined the street, mostly four- and five-bed places, Sophie guessed. They weren't the type of house a young DC could afford, but she knew Rick had moved back in with his mum a little while ago. A lot of young people were doing that these days, Sophie included. It was so hard to get on the property ladder without a decent deposit, and with the high rental prices it was very difficult to save. Lincolnshire was cheaper than many counties, and Sophie hoped to buy her own place soon.

She wondered if the housing market had played into DI Morgan's decision to transfer to Lincolnshire. He had moved recently, but Sophie didn't have the nerve to ask him the reason behind the transfer. There was plenty of station gossip, of course, but Sophie tried not to listen. She could just come straight out and ask him – it wasn't an unreasonable question but she didn't want him to think she was nosey.

She glanced at the dashboard clock and hoped Rick hadn't already left for his date. After parking between a Mini and a large Transit van, she reached for her bag. Dropping off the phone wouldn't take long. She'd only had a salad for lunch and was really looking forward to this famous steak pie.

But as she reached for the phone, it beeped, displaying a message on the screen. Sophie grinned, thinking it would be from Rick's hot date. But it wasn't. It was from someone called Lauren.

I'm sorry. I can't cope with it any more, Rick. We can put Mum into Woodview or you can cope with her at home on your own.

The message disappeared as the screen went black.

Sophie frowned. She knew Woodview was a local care home. Her sister worked for an agency that recruited nursing staff and carers for residential homes around Lincolnshire.

She put her hand on the door and stared at Rick's house. The lights were on downstairs. She thought back over the last few weeks. Rick liked to boast about his love life and social exploits as though he were some kind of party animal, but it sounded like he was having a really tough time at home.

Sophie flushed. She felt guilty. Over the past few weeks, she'd been at loggerheads with Rick on more than one occasion and she'd given him a hard time. It was easy for her. She lived with her parents, who were only in their fifties, and her mum still did her washing and prepared her meals.

With a sigh, Sophie walked over to knock on the front door. It took a while for Rick to answer, and when he did, Sophie was surprised. He didn't look like the same smooth, confident Rick she saw at work. His cheeks were flushed, and his tie was askew. He hadn't bothered to change yet, and an ugly orange stain covered a patch on his usually pristine white shirt.

'Hi,' Sophie said. 'Can I come in?'

'Er, well, it's not really a great time. I'm just about to get changed and go out. I don't like to keep the ladies waiting,' he said with a grin, but the smile didn't quite reach his eyes and quickly died away.

Sophie completely ignored him and stepped inside, leaving Rick to stare after her in confusion before closing the door.

'I won't stay long,' Sophie said cheerfully. 'Just a few minutes to have a cup of tea. You owe me,' she said, pulling the phone out of her pocket and holding it out to Rick.

'Where did you get that?'

'You left it at work, dummy. I can't believe you haven't missed it yet.'

Rick glanced nervously over his shoulder and then turned back to Sophie. 'Oh, thanks. Things have been a bit hectic since I got home.'

'Rick, who's that?' a woman's voice called from further inside the house.

'Is that your mum?' Sophie asked. 'I'd love to meet her.'

She stepped around Rick and walked along the hallway, glancing into the rooms she passed until she found Rick's mother in the kitchen.

Rick followed, offering up reasons why it wasn't the best time for a social call.

Sophie stared at the kitchen table, which was smeared with baked beans.

The small woman sitting at the table looked up at her with fierce eyes. 'I don't like beans,' she said.

Rick stood in the doorway, looking uncomfortable.

'I don't like them much either. Here, let's get rid of them,' Sophie said, reaching for the kitchen roll and grabbing the plate.

She wiped the beans off the table, dumped the stained sheets of kitchen roll in the bin, washed the plate, left it to drain and then sat down.

Rick watched with a bemused expression on his face.

'If you're late for your date, Rick, I can make the tea. I'll keep your mum company while you get ready.'

Rick frowned, hesitating in the doorway, and then finally he sighed and pulled out one of the kitchen chairs and sat down opposite Sophie. 'As it happens, I cancelled the date. I'm planning a night in, keeping Mum company.'

Rick's mother gave a wide smile. 'Oh, you are a good boy, Ricky.'

Sophie saw a flicker of emotion pass over Rick's face.

It was clear to Sophie that Rick's mother had some medical problems and he was struggling to cope.

'Is Lauren your sister?' Sophie asked.

Rick looked confused. 'Yes, why? Do you know her?'

Sophie shook her head. 'No, but she sent you a message.'

Rick flicked his finger across the screen to unlock the phone and quickly read the message. His face fell.

'You could talk about it,' Sophie said. 'Maybe I could help.'

Rick put the phone down on the table and shook his head. 'I appreciate the offer but I'm fine.'

Sophie wasn't going to be brushed off that easily. She turned her attention to Rick's mother and spent the next few minutes asking her questions about Rick's childhood. When his mum launched into an embarrassing yarn about Rick getting his head caught in the railings at a local park when he was seven, Rick finally had enough.

'I just need to have a quick word with Sophie about work, Mum. We won't be long.'

He hurried Sophie out of the room. In the living room, he turned to her. 'I don't know how she remembers stories like that from twenty years ago yet can't remember what she did this morning!'

Sophie smiled. 'I think she was just getting to the good part.'

Rick folded his arms across his chest. 'Maybe she was, but you're not going to hear the rest of that particular little tale.'

'Spoilsport. Now I'm really intrigued.'

Rick sat down on the sofa and Sophie took the chair opposite.

'It's clear you're struggling, Rick, and I want to help. My sister works for an agency. She handles home help placements as well as staff for care homes and social services. You don't have to cope with this alone, Rick.'

Rick exhaled a long breath and looked away, staring at the wall.

Sophie figured she was close to cracking the front he'd been putting on ever since she met him. 'There's nothing to be ashamed of. And admitting you need help isn't a sign of weakness.'

'I'm not putting her in a home,' Rick whispered, his voice shaking with emotion.

Sophie shook her head. 'You don't have to, but you can get help. Perhaps someone to come in during the day. It'll be expensive to get someone qualified, but there are grants you can get from the local council – schemes and plans designed to help people in your position.'

Rick looked at her. 'You really think it's an option?'

Sophie nodded. 'Absolutely. I'll have a word with my sister for you and we'll see what we can figure out.' She reached over and patted Rick on the hand. 'You're not alone, you know. When things get difficult, you can mouth off to me. I'm a good listener.'

Rick smiled and it looked as though a weight had been lifted from his shoulders.

'I'm hungry. Can I have a chocolate biscuit?' Rick's mother called from the kitchen, breaking the tension.

Rick grinned as he got up and they walked into the kitchen. 'I don't see why not, Mum. Let's all have one.'

He made a pot of tea as Sophie chatted to his mum about *EastEnders*. She muddled up a few of the characters, but Sophie avidly watched the soaps and enjoyed the conversation.

Rick put three mugs of tea on the table and sat down.

'So, the Jack-the-lad act is all a front, isn't it?' Sophie teased. 'I should have guessed.'

Rick looked aghast. 'It's not an act.' He grinned. 'I can't help it if the ladies find me irresistible, Sophie.'

'If you say so, mate,' Sophie said laughing, pleased to see that Rick was almost back to his normal assured self.

◆　◆　◆

DI Morgan and Karen sat at a table in the Waggon and Horses next to the large log burner, which was flaming furiously. Karen stretched out in her chair, feeling sleepy and relaxed.

DI Morgan took a sip of his pint of Timmy Taylor Landlord and closed his eyes. 'That's perfect,' he said. 'I needed that.'

Karen raised her gin and tonic and was about to take a sip when her phone rang. She delved into her bag and pulled out her mobile.

It was Sophie.

'She said she'd be along later but she needs to help Rick with a few things first.'

DI Morgan took another sip of his pint. 'I hope that means they're getting along better.'

'So do I.' Karen got to her feet. 'I'll go and order. Steak pie?'

DI Morgan shook his head and pulled out his wallet. 'I'll get it.'

'No, you won't. Detective sergeants' salaries aren't as high as I might like but I can afford to treat you to a steak pie.'

She made her way to the bar. The way the Waggon and Horses was set out meant one side of the pub was a dedicated dining area, and the other half of the pub was fitted out as a traditional bar. They were sitting in the cosy dining area, as Karen usually did. She often walked down to the pub alone, or sometimes with Christine, to have a chat and good-natured gossip with some of the locals. She placed the order and then went to sit back at the table.

'It's not a bad result, is it? We got three girls home safe, and we were only expecting two,' Karen said.

DI Morgan nodded. 'All things considered, it's an excellent result. I'd started to think we would never find them.'

'I still find it hard to believe Nigel Palmer managed to hide his wife's murder for so long. Poor Gwendolyn,' Karen said, feeling melancholy as she took another sip of her gin and tonic.

'She's finally about to get justice,' DI Morgan said. 'I'll see Nigel Palmer is punished for her murder if it's the last thing I do.'

Karen gave a half-hearted smile. She appreciated the sentiment, but due to his advanced emphysema, doctors had advised them that Nigel Palmer would probably not make it to his own trial. Any time he had left would be spent in prison, though, so she supposed that must be some consolation.

Plus, finding the money to pay for his legal defence wouldn't have been easy. They'd found out where Cathy got the money to supply Amy Foster with drugs. She'd been withdrawing funds from her father's account. Karen would have loved to have been a fly on the wall when Nigel Palmer was told that he was almost broke.

'And the case against Phil Carver looks strong,' DI Morgan said, keeping his voice low so no locals would overhear him.

Karen nodded. She wanted Phil Carver to go away for a long time. In the end, he'd had nothing to do with the girls' disappearance, but Karen believed he'd been in the early stages of grooming Emily Dean when she went missing. The images on his computer were a good basis for prosecution, and another team at Lincoln Central were focusing on the forums and groups Phil Carver had visited online. With a bit of luck, that investigation would track down a few more visitors to those sites and bring them to justice.

'It was our first big case working as a team,' DI Morgan said. 'Do you see ways we can improve? Perhaps at a communication level? I've been reading up about a new tiered system for reports. It's very interesting. We might be able to incorporate it into our current workflow.'

Karen rolled her eyes. She didn't think it sounded interesting at all. 'I don't know about all that technical reporting stuff but I thought we all worked together pretty well. Of course, I still have to persuade you to listen to my hunches . . .'

DI Morgan laughed. 'Maybe one day, but for now I think I'll rely on good old-fashioned police work, thanks.'

A couple came up and said hello to Karen, and when she introduced DI Morgan and mentioned he had only moved to Lincolnshire a few months ago, they warmly welcomed him to the area.

When the couple went to find a table, DI Morgan said, 'Friendly locals around here. I'm glad I moved. I can see myself settling in quite well.'

Karen leaned forward, resting an elbow on the dark wood table. 'And why did you move here? You know you're the talk of the station.'

DI Morgan looked down at his pint. 'I know you think there's some big secret behind my transfer, but there isn't. I'm really very boring.'

Karen narrowed her eyes and decided to let him off for tonight. She should have known better than to expect he'd open up just like that.

'We'll have to make up an interesting backstory for you. One that'll really get tongues wagging.'

'I'm not sure I like that idea.'

One of the girls from the kitchen brought out their plates then ducked back to get them some gravy.

DI Morgan looked down at the huge slice of steak pie and his eyes widened. 'Well, it certainly looks good.'

'Wait until you taste it,' Karen said, reaching for her knife and fork.

They made short work of the pie, chips and fresh vegetables, pausing only briefly to comment on how delicious it was.

Stuffed to the point of bursting, Karen leaned back in her chair and sipped her drink. She looked around the pub full of happy locals, feeling content. DI Morgan was a good boss and despite their differences, they'd worked well together.

Karen raised her glass. 'Here's to a good result.'

'And many more to follow,' DI Morgan said, clinking his glass against hers.

◆ ◆ ◆

Karen walked home from the pub hoping to burn off some calories. The bitter westerly wind whipped at her short hair and made her eyes water so she walked with her hands buried deep in her pockets, her chin tucked into her chest and her scarf covering the bottom half of her face. It was only when she was level with Christine's house that she noticed the security light above her garage was on. As she approached the drive, she scanned the front garden and saw Mary pacing back and forth. A small suitcase sat beside the garage door. This was getting to be a habit.

She called out as she walked towards Mary, scanning the woman's face for new injuries. But something made her pause. Mary seemed different. Her head was raised, and her movements were quick, almost frantic. Although Mary's old bruises were still dark and looked painful, Karen couldn't spot any fresh ones.

Mary rushed up to her, full of nervous energy. Her eyes were wide as she clutched Karen's arm. 'I've done it. I've left him.'

Mary wasn't wearing gloves and her cheeks were flushed pink with the cold. She was trembling.

Karen put her arm through Mary's, drawing her towards the house. 'That's brilliant news. Come inside and we can plan the next step. We should be able to get you a place in the shelter tonight, but if not, you're welcome to stay here until a place is available.'

'No,' Mary said, surprising Karen by shaking her head firmly. 'Thanks, but I won't be needing a place at the shelter. I'm going to stay with my sister in Norfolk.'

Karen opened the front door. 'You reached out to your family?'

'Yes, and you were right. They were pleased to hear from me. I thought they'd given up on me but they haven't. They still want to help.' Mary blinked. 'I don't deserve it. I put them through hell.'

'How are you getting to your sister's?'

She waited for Mary to step inside before closing the door behind them. It was a relief to be out of the biting wind. Mary propped her suitcase against the wall. It wasn't a large case, but Karen imagined it contained all of Mary's possessions.

'My sister's coming to pick me up,' Mary said, sounding breathless. 'I hope you don't mind but I gave her your address. I didn't want to wait for her in the flat. She should be here any minute. I'm glad you got home before she arrived. I wanted to say thank you.' She pulled a stubby pencil and a folded sheet of paper from her pocket. 'I was going to leave you a note if you weren't home.'

'I'm so pleased for you, Mary,' Karen said as she removed her coat. 'I'm proud of you.'

'You shouldn't be. I'm a nervous wreck. I can't believe I let it get this far. It's my fault that—'

'Don't say that. None of this was your fault. Have you got time for a cup of tea or coffee?'

'Better not. It's a long drive.' The smile slipped from her face and excitement was replaced with apprehension. 'I'm doing the right thing, aren't I?'

Karen unwound her scarf. 'Of course. This is your fresh start. Your new life.'

Mary took a deep breath and nodded. 'Yes, my fresh start. I like the sound of that. I've already got a job lined up. Well, it's only part-time bar work at the pub in the village where my sister lives, but it's a start. She's a single mum with two boys, so I'll be able to help her out with childcare as well to earn my keep.'

'I bet your sister was thrilled to hear from you.' Karen held out her hand for Mary's coat and hung it beside her own on the coat stand.

They went into the kitchen and Karen switched on the kettle.

Mary was too nervous to sit down, pacing back and forth. 'I thought I'd burned my bridges with my family. I wouldn't have blamed them for cutting me off. I should have accepted their help a long time ago, but I just kept thinking he'd change . . . that if I could just make him happy, things would be different.'

Karen poured hot water into her mug and stirred her coffee. It was sad the way society blamed victims. Karen was just as guilty of judging Mary as her family. She'd been impatient with the woman, unable to understand why she'd stay with a man who beat her black and blue. Sometimes in cases like this, frustration and anger could be misplaced.

The only person in this situation deserving of anyone's anger was Mary's ex-partner. 'There was nothing you could have done differently, Mary. He was responsible for his behaviour, not you.'

Mary nodded. 'You're right. I know you're right. He made me doubt everything about myself. You wouldn't believe how different I used to be. I was strong once. I had plans and dreams. I was going to travel but I lost that part of myself. I couldn't stand up to him. My family were furious. They couldn't understand why I let him walk over me, and to be honest, I don't really understand it either.'

A car pulled into the drive and Mary smiled again. 'That must be her.'

Karen put her coffee down on the kitchen table and followed Mary into the hall.

Mary couldn't get her coat on fast enough. It was good to see her so eager to embark on the next stage of her life.

She helped Mary with her suitcase and waved to Mary's sister, who was attempting a three-point turn in the driveway.

'Thank you for not giving up on me and for listening even though I probably bored you to tears.' Mary reached out and surprised Karen by pulling her in for a hug.

'Be happy,' Karen said and then waved at the two little boys sitting in the back seat. 'Your nephews?'

Mary smiled proudly. 'Yes, aren't they gorgeous?'

Karen helped Mary put her case in the boot and then waved them off, hoping this really would be the turning point and the fresh start Mary needed. No one had a guarantee of happiness, but Mary had a fighting chance now. She'd let go of the unhealthy, damaging relationship that had been holding her back.

She took a deep breath and walked back inside. Like Mary, Karen needed to face something unhealthy and damaging in her own life.

It had been a long time coming but she was finally ready. She walked into the small room off the kitchen that had once been Tilly's playroom. From the bottom drawer of the desk, she pulled out the blue folder and noticed that for once her hands weren't shaking.

Tucking the folder under her arm, she walked back into the kitchen and grabbed some matches. She left the house by the conservatory doors and strode down to the bottom of the garden, towards the old steel bin that had been used for bonfires in the past.

It was a damp, misty night but the paper would burn easily.

She tore the first printed page, a copy of the accident report, from the folder and watched as the flame took hold, spreading across the paper. Slowly and methodically, Karen burned every page in the folder. It was time to let go of her obsession with the accident. She didn't want to remember Josh and Tilly in that way. She didn't need to hold on to the memory of that awful period in her life. She needed to remember all the happy times.

Just like Mary, Karen needed a new start. She waited until the last of the smoke died away and only charred fragments remained, then she turned and walked back to the house.

It was time to move on.

ACKNOWLEDGMENTS

I am very grateful to all the people who have worked hard to produce the first book in the DS Karen Hart series. Many thanks to Jack Butler and the team at Thomas & Mercer. It's been a pleasure to work with you.

A huge thanks to my family and friends. I'm very lucky to have such a fabulous group of people around me who are my biggest supporters. They encourage me to follow my dreams, cheer me on and make life fun.

And a special thanks to all the amazing readers who have shown me so much support over the past few years. The messages and emails I get from people who have enjoyed the stories mean the world to me – thank you all so very much.

ABOUT THE AUTHOR

Born in Kent, D. S. Butler grew up as an avid reader with a love for crime fiction and mysteries. She has worked as a scientific officer in a hospital pathology laboratory and as a research scientist.

After obtaining a PhD in biochemistry, she worked at the University of Oxford for four years before moving to the Middle East. While living in Bahrain, she wrote her first novel and hasn't stopped writing since.

She now lives in Lincolnshire with her husband.

South Dublin Libraries

www.southdublinlibraries.ie